THE
CASE
FOR
Jamie

A Charlotte Holmes novel

THE CASE FOR

Jamie

A Charlotte Holmes novel

BRITTANY CAVALLARO

KATHERINE TEGEN BOOKS
An Imprint of HarperCollins Publishers

Katherine Tegen Books is an imprint of HarperCollins Publishers.

ISBN 978-0-06-239897-0

18 19 20 21 22   CG/LSCH   10 9 8 7 6 5 4 3 2 1
❖
First Edition

For Annalise, Lena, Rachel,
and every other girl genius
I've had the privilege of working with

HOLMES

(for Jamie, because he insisted)

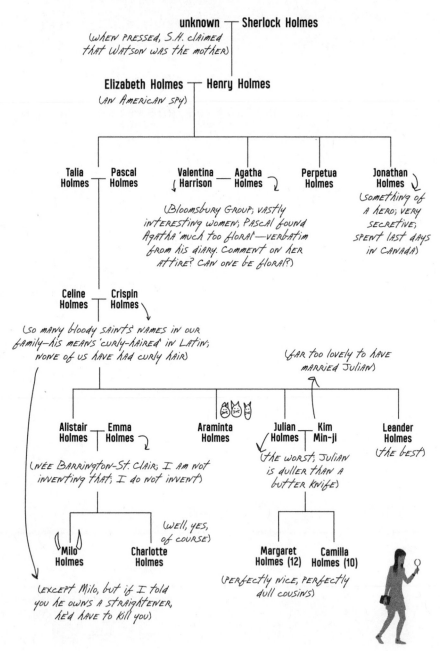

unknown ── **Sherlock Holmes**

(when pressed, S.H. claimed that Watson was the mother)

Elizabeth Holmes ── **Henry Holmes**

(an American spy)

Talia Holmes ── **Pascal Holmes**

Valentina Harrison ── **Agatha Holmes**

Perpetua Holmes

Jonathan Holmes

(something of a hero; very secretive; spent last days in Canada)

(Bloomsbury Group; vastly interesting women; Pascal found Agatha 'much too floral'—verbatim from his diary. Comment on her attire? Can one be floral(?)

Celine Holmes ── **Crispin Holmes**

(so many bloody saints' names in our family—his means 'curly-haired' in Latin; none of us have had curly hair)

(far too lovely to have married Julian)

Alistair Holmes ── **Emma Holmes**

Araminta Holmes

Julian Holmes ── **Kim Min-ji**

Leander Holmes

(the best)

(the worst; Julian is duller than a butter knife)

(née Barrington-St. Clair; I am not inventing that; I do not invent)

Milo Holmes

Charlotte Holmes

(well, yes, of course)

Margaret Holmes (12)   **Camilla Holmes (10)**

(perfectly nice, perfectly dull cousins)

(except Milo, but if I told you he owns a straightener, he'd have to kill you)

MORIARTY

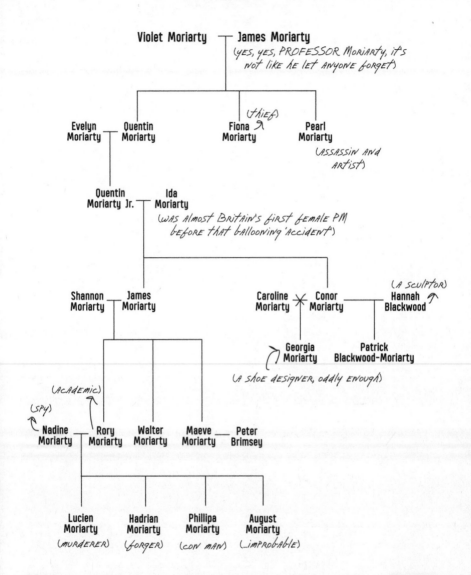

Violet Moriarty — James Moriarty
(yes, yes, PROFESSOR Moriarty, it's not like he let anyone forget)

Evelyn Moriarty — Quentin Moriarty

Fiona Moriarty *(thief)*

Pearl Moriarty
(ASSASSIN and ARTIST)

Quentin Moriarty Jr. — Ida Moriarty
(WAS almost Britain's first female PM before that ballooning 'accident')

Shannon Moriarty — James Moriarty

Caroline Moriarty ✗ Conor Moriarty — Hannah Blackwood *(A SCULPTOR)*

Georgia Moriarty *(A shoe designer, oddly enough)*

Patrick Blackwood-Moriarty

Nadine Moriarty *(SPY)* — Rory Moriarty *(ACADEMIC)*

Walter Moriarty

Maeve Moriarty — Peter Brimsey

Lucien Moriarty *(MURDERER)*

Hadrian Moriarty *(forger)*

Phillipa Moriarty *(CON MAN)*

August Moriarty *(...improbable)*

There you have them. PLEASE tell me you don't have any plans to frame these.
—C.H.

You are the one fixed point in a changing age.
SIR ARTHUR CONAN DOYLE, "HIS LAST BOW"

one
jamie

IT WAS JANUARY IN CONNECTICUT, AND THE SNOW HADN'T stopped falling in what felt like forever. It gathered in the window wells, in the hollows between the bricks of the rebuilt sciences building. It hung from the boughs of trees, tucked itself up in the root systems below. I shook it from my wool cap before every class, ruffled it out of my hair, pulled it from my socks. Underneath, my feet were rubbed red. I found it everywhere, snow that never seemed to fully melt, that lingered on my backpack and my blazer and, on the worst days, my eyebrows, melting down my face in the warmth of first period like it was sweat, like I was guilty of something.

When I got back to my room, I took to laying out my parka like a body on the spare bed, so that the snow could drip somewhere other than into the carpet. I was tired of having wet feet. A wet spare mattress seemed less important. But as the winter stretched on, it was hard not to see a metaphor in that pathetic almost-man, especially on those nights that I couldn't sleep.

But I was done finding metaphors everywhere.

MAYBE I SHOULD START HERE: THERE AREN'T A LOT OF benefits to being framed for murder. Once I would've told you that meeting Charlotte Holmes was the only good thing that came out of that mess. But that was my former self speaking, the one who mythologized that girl until I couldn't see the person beneath the story I'd made up.

If I couldn't see her for what she was, what she'd been all along, then I'd had trouble seeing myself clearly as well. It's not an uncommon delusion, the one I had. The Great Big Destiny delusion. That your life is a story that twists and turns its way up to a narrative precipice, a climax, the moment where you'll make the hard decision, defeat the villain, finally prove yourself worthy. Leave some kind of mark on the world.

Maybe it started when I read my great-great-great-grandfather's story about Sherlock Holmes going over the Reichenbach Falls, after finally vanquishing the evil Professor Moriarty. A great sacrifice made by a great man—to defeat great evil, Holmes had to give himself. I studied "The Final Problem" like I'd studied all the others, using those tales to cobble together an instruction manual for adventure and duty and friendship, the way any kid looks for models, and then I'd clung to those ideas for years longer than I should have.

Because there aren't any textbook villains out there. There aren't any heroes. There was Sherlock Holmes, who faked his own death and reappeared three years later like nothing had happened, expecting to be welcomed with open arms. There were selfish people, and there were those of us who yoked ourselves to them out of a misplaced sense of loyalty.

I knew now that it was stupid, the way I'd obsessed so much over the past—not just my own ancestry, but over the recent past, the months I'd spent with my own Holmes. I'd lost too much time over it. Over her. I was done. I was changing. Butterflies, chrysalises—whatever. I was building one. I was going to emerge from it a more realistic Jamie Watson.

At first, it was hard to stick to the plan. When I'd gotten back to Sherringford from the Holmeses' estate, I'd found myself more than once on the fourth floor of the sciences building without any real memory of taking myself there. In the end, it didn't matter. I could have knocked on the door of 442 as long as I wanted. I wouldn't have gotten an answer.

It didn't take long for me to decide that moping wasn't doing me any good. I had to take stock. On paper. Instead of making a story out of it, the way I'd done in the past, I'd be objective. What had happened to me since the day Lee Dobson turned up dead in his room? What were the facts?

The bad: dead friends; dead enemies; utter betrayal; widespread suspicion; heartbreak; concussions; kidnappings; my nose broken so many times that I was beginning to look

3

like a two-bit boxer. (Or like a librarian who'd been violently mugged.)

The good?

My father and I were on speaking terms, now. I was beating him at cell phone Scrabble.

As for my mother—well, not a lot of good there, either. She'd called the other night to tell me she was dating someone new. *It's nothing serious, Jamie,* she'd said, but the hesitancy in her voice suggested that, in fact, it was. That she was afraid I'd bite back with the same resentment I had for my father, way back when I was a child, when he'd met and married Abigail, my stepmother.

"Even if it is serious," I'd said to my mom, "especially if it is. I'm happy for you."

"Okay." A pause, then: "He's Welsh. Very kind. I told him you were a writer, and he said he'd like to read some of your stories. He doesn't know how dark they are, but I imagine he'd like them anyway."

Those stories that I wrote, the ones that were all about my own life. They weren't stories at all, and my mother knew it. She just couldn't bring herself to say it aloud.

Weirdly enough, that was the last straw—not the list of pros and cons, but the realization that the months I'd been friends with Charlotte Holmes were so depressing my mother was handing out content warnings.

Ten minutes in the headmistress's office, pleading my case, and I was packing my things to move down a floor in Michener Hall. I'd used the whole wrongfully-accused-of-murder thing to wrangle myself a single room. That excuse was a year old, but it still held water. It got me what I wanted. No more roommate to stare at me while I cried. No more anyone at all. Just me, alone, so I could rebuild my life into one I actually wanted to be living.

So time passed, as time tends to do.

It was January again in Connecticut, and it wouldn't stop snowing. I didn't care. I had a literary magazine to edit, drills for the spring rugby season, hours of homework every night. I had friends, new ones, who didn't demand all my time and patience and unearned trust.

It was my final semester at Sherringford. I hadn't seen Charlotte Holmes in a year.

No one had.

"I SAVED YOUR SPOT," ELIZABETH SAID, PULLING HER BAG off the chair beside her. "Did you bring—"

"Here," I said, pulling a can of Diet Coke out of my backpack. The dining hall had done away with soft drinks last year (and the all-day cereal bar, a loss we were all publicly mourning), but my girlfriend neatly sidestepped the rules by keeping a six-pack of soda in my room's mini-fridge at all times.

"Thanks." She popped the top and poured it into a waiting glass of ice.

"Where is everyone?" I asked, because our lunch table was empty.

"Lena is still microwaving her tofu. She's trying this soy sauce—honey thing this time, it smelled awful. Tom's therapist had to reschedule his session, so he's there, but he should be almost done. Mariella's still in line with her friend Anna, she might sit with us today, and I don't know where your rugby bros are."

I grimaced. "I saw them over by the bread. I think they're carbo-loading."

"Gettin' *huge*," Elizabeth said, in a credible imitation of Randall.

This was an old joke; I knew my line. *"Huge."*

"Huuuuge."

"Yuuuuge."

We snickered. It was part of the routine. She got back to her burger; I got back to my burger. Our friends showed up, one by one, and when Tom finally arrived, he patted me on the back and stole a fistful of my fries. I raised an eyebrow at him, the *how was therapy* eyebrow, and he shrugged back that it was fine.

"Are you okay?" Elizabeth asked. In my darker moments, I thought it was her favorite question.

"I'm fine."

She nodded, looking back down at her book. Then looked back up. "Are you sure? Because you sound a little—"

"No," I said, too quickly, then forced a smile. "No. I'm fine."

It was like a dance I knew all the steps to, one I could perform upside down, backward, on a sinking cruise ship that was also on fire. In the fall we ate on the quad; in the spring, the steps outside the cafeteria. It was winter, so we'd claimed our usual table inside by the hot bar, and I listened to the low hum of the lights keeping the food warm. Mariella and Tom went over their odds of getting into their choice of college early decision. They were supposed to hear this week (Tom, University of Michigan; Mariella, Yale), and they couldn't talk about anything else. Lena was texting someone under the table, eating her tofu with her free hand, while Randall and Kittredge compared bruises from practice. Kittredge was sure someone was digging holes into the rugby field at night. Randall was sure that Kittredge was just a clumsy asshole. Elizabeth, as always, was reading a novel next to her tray, deaf to everyone else as she turned the pages in her own Elizabeth-world. I never knew what went on in there. I didn't think there was enough time before graduation for me to find out.

More than anyone else I knew, Elizabeth was competent. Frighteningly competent. If her uniform pants came back from the tailor a half-inch too long, she'd learn how to hem them herself. If she wanted to take both Shakespeare and Dance II, and they were scheduled for the same time, she'd have an independent study in *Romeo and Juliet* Through Irish Step Dancing approved by the end of the day.

If the boy she'd had a crush on came back to school heartsick and bitter, she'd wait a semester for him to get over himself before she asked him out. *Go with me to homecoming?* the note slipped in my mailbox had said, this past fall. *I promise not to choke on a diamond this time.*

I'd accepted. I really wasn't all that sure why, at the time—though I wasn't still mourning my and Holmes's not-relationship, I hadn't been looking at girls. Mostly, I'd been studying. It was as boring as it sounded, but if I didn't bring up my grades, there wasn't any possibility of me getting into college anywhere, much less where I wanted to go.

Dobson's murder won't excuse your grades forever, you know, the guidance counselor had said. *Though it'll make for a really compelling college essay!*

So I studied. I played rugby, both seasons, in hopes that if my grades still weren't good enough, some dream college somewhere was looking for a wiry English halfback. I took Elizabeth to homecoming out of a sense of duty—that plastic diamond down her throat was more or less my fault, even if I hadn't put it there myself—and to my surprise, I'd had a better time with her than I'd had with anyone in months.

It hadn't surprised Elizabeth. "You have a type, you know," she'd said, laughing under the dance floor lights. Her blond hair was in long, ribbonlike curls, and she had this bright necklace that swung as we danced, and when she laughed, she did it with her whole body, and I liked her. I really liked her.

I had the strange sense that I was taking an old chapter of my life and writing over it until the text beneath was gone.

"What's that?" I asked. I wasn't really sure I wanted to hear the answer. Already, with the music, the smoke machine—I had one foot in this year and one foot in the last.

But she'd grinned at me, wickedly. It was a different kind of wicked than what I was used to. Wicked without secrets. Wicked without danger. It was the smile of a smart girl who was coming into her own, who knew she was about to get the thing she wanted.

"You like girls who don't take any of your shit," she'd said, and kissed me.

She was right. I liked girls who pushed back; I liked girls with thoughtful eyes. Elizabeth had both, and even if sometimes I got the sense that I was an item on her checklist that she had successfully crossed off (*Date boy you crushed on freshman year*), well—

Well, it was more my own bullshit than anything I got from her. Because, as usual, I was staring out the bright-lit window, thinking about my essay for AP Euro, my problem set for calculus, about the million other balls I had up in the air— and more than that, convincing myself that I *did* need to think about them, that I needed to make myself care.

Then someone dropped a tray behind me with a sharp pop and a clatter, and I was back there again.

Me on a lawn in Sussex, August Moriarty at my feet, blood on all that snow. Police sirens edging closer. Charlotte Holmes's white, chapped lips. Those last few seconds. That other life.

"I'll be right back," I said, but no one was listening, not even Elizabeth, lost in her book. At least I made it to the bathroom before I started to dry heave.

One of the lacrosse starters was in there washing his hands. "Brutal," I heard him say over my retching. By the time I came out of the stall, I was alone.

I braced myself against the sink, staring at the drain, the fissured ceramic around it. The last time this had happened to me, it'd been a slammed car door, and that time the nausea had been followed hard by rage. Horrible, mind-bending rage, at Charlotte for making assumptions, at her brother, Milo, for gunning a man down and getting away with it, at August Moriarty, who'd told me, two weeks too late, to run—

My phone pinged. *Elizabeth,* I thought, as I fished it out. *Checking on me.* It wasn't a bad thought.

But it wasn't Elizabeth. It wasn't any number I knew.

You're not safe here.

That feeling, like someone hit Play on a movie I'd forgotten I was watching. A horror movie. About my life.

Who is this? I wrote back, and then, horrified, *Is that you? Holmes?,* and then I called the number once, twice, a third time, and by then they'd shut the phone off.

Leave a message, it said. I stood there, stunned, until I realized I'd let it record a few seconds of my breathing. Hurriedly, I ended the call.

I made it back to our lunch table somehow, my head crackling with dehydration and fear. Elizabeth was still reading. Randall was eating his third chicken sandwich. Mariella and Kittredge and that Anna girl were bitching again about the cereal bar, and there was a whole ecosystem here, a landscape that functioned fine without me.

Why would I put any of this on them? What did I want to do, go back to being some kind of victim? Even Elizabeth, the person I'd usually turn to, couldn't help me here. She'd dealt with enough because of me.

No. I squared my shoulders. I finished my burger.

I kept one hand on my phone, just in case.

"Jamie," Lena was saying.

I shook my head.

"Jamie," Lena repeated, frowning a little, "your father's here." I was dully surprised to see him hovering over our table, his wool cap dusted with snow.

"Jamie," he said. "A bit in your own head?"

Elizabeth smiled up at him. "He's been like this all day," she said. "Off in dream land." I didn't point out that she'd been ignoring all of us in favor of *Jane Eyre*.

I put on a smile as best I could. "Ha, yeah, you know. Lots of, uh, school things. Schoolwork."

Across the table, Lena and Tom exchanged a significant glance.

"It's true," I said, and my voice wobbled a little. "Uh, Dad. What's up?"

"Family emergency," he said, sticking his hands in his pockets. "I've already signed you off campus. Go on, grab your bag."

Oh God, I thought. *This again.* Plus, I wasn't sure if my legs would hold me if I stood. "Can't. French class. We have a quiz."

Tom frowned. "But that was yester—"

I kicked him, weakly, under the table.

"Family emergency," my father said again. "Up! Come along!"

I ticked it off on my fingers. "AP English. Physics. I have a presentation. Stop *looking* at me like that."

"Jamie. Leander's waiting in the car."

A surge of relief. Leander Holmes was one of the only people I could be around when I was like this, all shaky and strange. I knew as well as my father did that he'd played his trump card, and that I'd lost this round. I packed up my things, ignoring Lena's stage-wink across the table.

"See you tonight," Elizabeth said, already back in her book. But then, she was used to this by now.

"I actually do have a presentation in physics tomorrow, you know," I told my father as we left the cafeteria.

He clapped a hand on my shoulder. "Of course you do. But that's hardly important, is it?"

two
charlotte

WHEN I WAS FIVE YEARS OLD, I CONVINCED MYSELF I WAS psychic.

It wasn't a wild conjecture. My father had always said to *build only on fact*, and the facts were there. For a solid week, I'd been having dreams about going to London. These dreams were based on fact. My aunt Araminta had to go to settle some financial affairs, and she'd offered to take my brother and me along and after, to a national history museum to see an exhibit on dinosaurs. Milo was mad for the stegosaurus.

In the dream I'd been having, we stepped off the train into a smoky station. My aunt bought us both a pretzel. We had to wait a very long time in a marble lobby, and Milo pulled my hair, which was in curls. My hair was never in curls; it was impractical to take that much time on one's grooming. At his teasing, I cried—this was an oddity, I did not ever cry—and we did not go to the museum.

When the day finally came, everything went off as I'd dreamt. My mother had wound my wet hair up into a bun before we'd left, and in our compartment, when I pulled the hair elastic out, my hair had dried into a mess of ringlets. We were bought pretzels at the stand in the station. At the bank, my aunt conducted her affairs in an office with frosted-glass windows, while we were made to wait in the marble lobby. For a very long time. I could not stop fidgeting, and since we were not allowed to fidget, Milo reached out and yanked one of my curls. It hurt, but I did not yell. We were not allowed to make noise. We were not allowed to do much of anything at all, except notice everything about where we were and remember it for later, and we had been four hours in that lobby, and I had to use the toilet very badly. I had a horror of wetting my pants. I could not imagine what would happen to me if I did.

At that thought, I started to cry. I had never done so in public before, not since I was old enough to remember, and Milo reached out to pull my hair again, a warning—Milo was twelve, old enough to want to keep me from experiencing the consequences of these things, but not old enough to express himself in a rational manner—just as Aunt Araminta came out of the office to find that tableau. Me weeping. Milo prodding me. "*Children,*" she said, in a voice like cold water, and at that, I couldn't hold it anymore.

We didn't go to the museum. We took the next train home.

Hours later, before bed, I rapped on my father's study door. I intended to apologize briefly for my actions before telling him what I had deduced about my being psychic. He would be proud, I thought.

My father listened while I laid out my case. He did not smile. But then, he rarely did.

"Your logic is flawed," he said, when I had finished. "Correlation isn't causation, Lottie. Your mother bathes you in the morning at seven o'clock. Araminta was fetching you at half past. It makes absolute sense your mother wouldn't have time to do your hair, and that she would put it up, as she always does on such occasions. You knew about the pretzel stand at the station, that Araminta could be persuaded to buy you a treat. As for the bank, you knew you would have to wait, perhaps long enough that you wouldn't have time to make your special trip to the museum. You ensured that possibility with your behavior."

"But the dreams—"

"—cannot predict the future, and you know that." He frowned at me, hands folded. "The only thing that can is the reasoning of the waking human mind. As for the situation with the toilet, I trust that won't happen again."

I kept my hands behind my back so he couldn't see me fidget. "Aunt asked me to wait."

"Yes." A muscle above his eye jumped. "You are only to

follow rules that are reasonable. It is reasonable to stand up, inquire about the nearest bathroom, and use it before returning to your seat. It is not reasonable to create a mess for others to clean up."

This made sense to me. "Yes, Father."

"It's time for bed," he said, his frown loosening a bit. "Professor Demarchelier arrives at eight tomorrow to go over your equations. I can see from your fingernails that you haven't finished your homework yet. Now, tell me how I knew."

I stood up slightly straighter, and did.

ONLY FOLLOW RULES THAT ARE REASONABLE.

The issue with this axiom is that very few rules are reasonable when examined closely.

Case in point: there are laws that forbid locking someone in a closet against their will. On the whole, this seems sound—violation of someone's personal autonomy, potential damage to the closet itself—and yet I had at least seven reasonable reasons for keeping this particular bullyboy locked away until I acquired the information I was looking for.

Not that he was much of a bully or a boy. He was a passport office worker, and we were in his building after hours. There is nothing efficient about that description: passport office worker. It said nothing about his ruddy face, or his New Jersey accent, or how easily I'd been able to corner him here, on this Sunday night, to make my demands.

Sometimes language ultimately fails us. It would be most

accurate to refer to him as my mark.

"I'll tell the police," he threatened. He was rather hoarse at this point from all the threatening.

"That's an interesting decision," I told him, because it was. I was sitting with my back to the closet door, examining an unfortunate scuff on the toe of my boot. To clean them, I would have to purchase mink oil again, and though minks are vicious, they are also small and fragile-seeming. (I realize I am a hypocrite here—my shoes are made of leather; leather comes from cows; cows should not be thusly punished for being less adorable, but regrettably, here we are. The world is cold and bitter, and I continue to wear my wing-tip boots.)

He was talking again. "Interesting?"

"Interesting because you'd have to explain to NSY all the falsified documents I found in your office." From my pocket I pulled a photocopy example (EU passport, expiration 2018, name TRACEY POLNITZ) and slid it, folded, under the closet door.

A rustling as he opened it. "That's not a fake, you stupid little girl—"

"The original didn't have an RFID chip. It failed a UV test. The watermarks and microembossing didn't hold up to basic flashlight analysis—"

"Who *are* you?" I couldn't hear him run a hand over his sweaty face, but I knew he did it just the same.

Irrelevant question. "I want any documentation you've forged for Lucien Moriarty."

"I don't have anything by that name—"

"Of course it wouldn't be under his name. I understand that you're familiar with his aliases; when he flies to America, and he does so frequently, he always touches down at Dulles here in D.C., no matter the expense. I've tracked his flights for the last six months. Do you think that there's a reason that he only arrives on Wednesday?"

Silence.

"Let's try this. How long has your mistress been working Wednesday nights? Convenient that she's a customs officer, isn't it. Convenient that her RFID reader always reads positive, even when the passport's chip isn't there."

Silence, and then the sound of a fist striking the door.

At that point I'd finished examining my boot. That scuff was a simple fix, really, and once I was no longer dressed as this near-version of myself (black clothes, blond wig) and instead as someone so far afield from me as to be a kind of personal moon (Hailey, a confection made entirely for the male gaze), I would go have them shined. I was only mostly-myself tonight because the man in the closet had seen me in every other disguise I had at my disposal, and I wanted my appearance at his work this evening to be a stealthy one.

I digress. My shoes, as I said, would be fine, so I instead picked up my hammer.

"This is how the next five minutes will happen," I said, lofting it. The dull metal looked black in the late-evening light. That was a detail that Watson would notice, and at that realization I heard my voice grow harder. "Either you give me every last one of Lucien Moriarty's aliases and their corresponding passports, or I'll return to your house and let myself into your son's bedroom. I'll make sure he's sleeping. Then I'll smash this directly into his throat."

My father had taught me to always wait a second for emphasis, so I did. Then I drove the point home—in this case, I swung the hammer into the closet door at speed.

The man inside yelped.

"I can be there and gone in the time it takes you to crawl out of your miserable little hole. Or we can bypass that whole tedious process, and you can provide me with the information I've requested. Out of respect for your emotional turmoil, I'll give you thirty seconds to consider my offer."

"You're Genna," he said wonderingly. "You were Danny's girlfriend. The one that he met at the dog park—"

It was out before I could stop myself, in Genna's *please-please-like-me* voice. "Oh wow, Mr. B, your terrier is adorable. What's her name? I always wanted one, but my parents never let me. She is *so* lucky to have a family that loves her this much! Look at her little tail!"

He didn't respond for long enough that I had the fleeting fear that I may have given him a stroke. Then I recognized the scrap of sound coming underneath the door for what it was—he was crying.

I looked down at the hammer in my hands.

I HAD, LATELY, BEEN COMING TO TERMS WITH THE KNOWL-
edge that I could be cruel.

Given the facts at hand about these past few years (thanks,
again, to Watson), this might sound like a facetious revelation.
I wasn't a prize on the best of days, but I hadn't ever parsed
out why.

I simply was what I was—a girl who had forged herself into
a statue. I'd believed it best to look for the cracks and flaws in
others, to chart them, to exploit them, to smooth my own flaws
over until I gleamed like marble. I needed to be impervious. I
told myself I was until I believed it. Unfortunately, what followed was a series of explosions. It's a fine thing to be a stately
marble column in a city. It's something else entirely to find
yourself in pieces while that city burns.

It felt like that city had been burning for a very long time.

Every night before I slept, I shut my eyes and remembered
what had happened the last time I'd properly lost my head. I
thought about August. August, who believed in fighting your
worst instincts, in hope and in the police and probably in puppies and Christmas, who had loved me like I had been his
own impossible shadow. August, who had only been in Sussex
because I'd wanted to watch him suffer.

It was too much for me to think of it as a story. I had to
pull it apart into disparate facts, hold them up one by one in
the light.

1. Lucien, after his failure to string me up on false murder
    charges in Sherringford, had come up with a new plan.

2. Blackmail, aimed at Alistair and Emma Holmes, my parents, and my favorite uncle, Leander.

3. The terms: either they keep Leander out of the picture, and away from the forgery ring supporting his siblings, Hadrian and Phillipa, or

4. Lucien would alert the government to the existence of my father's only assets, a series of offshore bank accounts lined with Russian money.

5. When they initially refused, Lucien ordered my mother's home care nurse—a woman under his employ—to poison her.

6. My parents told me none of this.

7. Instead they ordered me away to my brother Milo's offices in Germany, where August Moriarty was working in his employ. There, they imagined, I would be safe.

8. In the meantime, my mother gained the upper hand on her home care nurse while our house's security system was off, dressed the nurse as herself, then drugged her. Then staged the scene to appear as though their positions hadn't been flipped.

9. This involved wigs and costumes, and in that way (and only that way), it was after my own heart.

10. Leander hid in their basement while my parents debated their next move.

11. To reiterate: I knew none of this.

12. For a long time I used that fact to absolve myself of guilt.

13. *Nota bene*: Lucien Moriarty was orchestrating these schemes from abroad, untouchable, unreachable, and soon

enough he disappeared from even my brother's surveilling eye.

14. In a sick sort of way I admired him for that.

15. All I had figured, all I had learned, was that Lucien was poisoning my mother, that my family's finances were in trouble, and that my parents were holding my uncle in their basement. I assumed they had been keeping him captive to demand he hand over his share of the inheritance, thus smoothing over their financial issues.

16. You see, I'd been given few reasons over the years to believe that my parents could have good intentions.

17. And still I felt the need to protect them from the consequences of my own mistakes. With the additional bonus of locking up Lucien Moriarty and throwing away the key.

18. My plan was simple: I would take apart the Moriartys' forgery ring, then bring back the perpetrators, Hadrian and Phillipa, to our family's house in England. There, I would frame them for my uncle's disappearance, freeing my parents from blame. This action would flush Lucien out of hiding, as he would never let his family take the fall for a Holmes's actions.

19. My mother's plan was simple: my uncle Leander would agree to take a nonlethal dose of the same poison Lucien had given to her, then go to the hospital and claim that Hadrian and Phillipa Moriarty had poisoned him. Which would flush Lucien out of hiding. As he would never let his family take the fall for a Holmes's actions.

20. You would think, perhaps, from this information, that these two plans would dovetail beautifully.

21. You would be wrong.

22. With everything in motion, I dragged Watson back to England with me, and when we all gathered on the lawn outside my house, every two-bit player in this drama— Hadrian and Phillipa loose, having shaken their guard; my father furious at my interference, at my presumption of his and my mother's guilt; Leander horrified and beaten-down and ill, so ill; and August. His hands up. Pleading for a cease-fire.

23. When my brother, Milo, arrived rather later than he expected, mistook August Moriarty from a distance for his brother, and from a distance, with a sniper rifle, shot him dead.

24. Those are the facts.

25. As far as I understood them. If I understood anything at all.

You see, I had become so used to trusting no one. Being the only one with any kind of plan.

Where did that leave me? It left me left. Leander gone. Milo a murderer. August dead on the snowy lawn, and Watson there, knowing it was my fault, and that was as far as I could go with it, that was as much as I could take.

It was a forced remembering. A penance. It wasn't meant to dull the ache, but instead to keep the ache alive. It had been so easy for me to isolate that part of myself that *felt* that I had begun to believe it was natural. I had been wrong. I was unlearning.

You need to feel the blood underneath all that reason, Detective Inspector Green had said. *You need to* feel *it, and not apologize for feeling. Or else, every now and then, it'll happen anyway, and you'll be so overwhelmed that you'll act only on that instinct, and you'll continue to do very stupid things.*

I had disliked the implication that I was stupid, but even if I hadn't, I knew for myself that my methods had stopped working. Also I was nothing if not a good student. So I set myself to "feeling things" as often as I could. To let my control go, to let whatever small nasty thing that lived in the space behind my heart go free.

I imagine DI Green thought I would begin to make amends with my family, with Watson, with myself, that I would take "advantage" of this opportunity she had granted me. That I would perhaps break down in tears on her sofa picturesquely while she made me a picturesque cup of chamomile tea. How could one blame her for that?

I didn't blame her. I didn't cry. I took my fury with me, and fled. I had, as they say, bigger fish to fry.

HENCE, THIS BIT OF CASUAL CRUELTY ON MY SIDE OF THE closet door. The petty kind, the *girl you let into your house for two straight weeks was building a case against you for the government* kind, unnecessary to the case I was solving, a string of words specifically engineered to pour salt into an open wound. And yet it was human to feel it, to know that this awful man had been aiding and abetting an even more awful man for money, and to want to make him understand the full weight of his stupidity.

He had looked at a girl, his teenage son's girlfriend, and seen a Shirley Temple where he should have seen poison.

"My God," he was saying. "You're disgusting. How *old* are you? What have you been doing with my boy?"

"Ten seconds." I slammed the hammer again into the closet door. The wood was beginning to divot. "Nine. Eight."

I felt badly about his son in an abstract way that was, still, an improvement on not feeling at all. Danny had been an easy mark—lost-looking, sweaty even in the cold, a boy whose tiny dog made him look comically large. He had been too scared to try anything physical with me, which suited me just fine. Mostly we played with Button, his terrier, in the family's backyard. Button was a runner, and when she escaped through the board in a fence (a board I had of course pried loose myself), I let Danny tear after her while I took myself to his father's office to find the documentation I needed. The photos on the fireplace were nearly enough: Danny and his father on a catamaran; Danny and his father beneath the Sagrada Familia in Spain; Danny and his father on safari, the vague blur of Danny's mother behind them in the Jeep. I knew then how Lucien Moriarty's blood money was being spent. All I'd needed was the proof.

Button escaped every day for a week. Enterprising dog.

I had no actual plan to hurt Danny. His father didn't need to know that. "Three," I said, "two, one," and on cue, the man in the closet drew in a shaky breath.

By the time the sun had finished setting, I had everything I needed.

"What do I tell my son?" he asked as I packed up my kit.

I didn't answer. It wasn't any of my business, after all.

IT TOOK ME THE USUAL FORTY-FIVE MINUTES TO WALK THE five blocks to my lodgings. Twice I thought I was being followed, and once, I knew I was—no one carries a copy of the local paper under their arm in such a manner, much less puts it up to hide their face when you pass the shop window they're spying from. I doubled back, ducked into a Starbucks toilet to change my disguise (wig, yoga pants, trainers), then waited until a group of girls in athletic wear jogged by and, keeping a safe distance, joined them.

By the time I arrived, I was exhausted. Still, I had work to do—the removal and safekeeping of my wig, laid gently in silk and stored in the wooden box below the bed; a thorough cleaning of my face and the soles of my boots; blocking the door, three windows, and the too-large air vent whose existence had nearly kept me from renting these rooms in the first place. Sublet ads on Craigslist were rarely so detailed. One had to know the right questions to ask.

This process took time, but I have never found routine

tedious so long as it directly contributed to keeping me alive. Once I was sure I was secure, I put on a Chopin etude at a level loud enough to drown out any noise I might make, and then I methodically took apart my room, looking for cameras, listening devices, or finely drilled holes. There were none.

This only brought me to nine o'clock. After some consideration, I decided I had the following options for the rest of my night:

1. Take the remainder of the oxycodone in the lining of my coat.

2. Find a television show to stream that did not mention murder and/or bodily harm, opiates, romantic relationships, the United Kingdom, or, oddly enough, Sherlock Holmes. I say oddly because my great-great-great-grandfather was referenced in the oddest places. I'd taken to watching select episodes of *Star Trek*, as it both fit my criteria and featured an android character I was fond of. Then came a spate of episodes where he dressed up in a deerstalker and solved crimes with some *Star Trek* Watson. I was now in need of a new show.

3. Take the remainder of the oxy in the lining of my coat—a coat which my uncle Leander, in his infinite good taste, had given me for Christmas two years ago and which still fit because that was the year I'd decided to stop eating to starve the bad thing out of me, a coat whose pockets I had ripped the lining of for this exact purpose; after, perhaps, I could go out into the dark and let some Moriarty

thug trace my steps down to that particular bridge over the Potomac where, over the past few days, I'd seen four if not five opportunities to score properly; I would have my stash, and then I could take the high of that feeling (not the high itself, but the high of knowing that I was steps away from a night into which I could finally, irrevocably escape) and use it—really, if it were going to be over, finally over, I'd take the knife out of my boot and drive its point through that Moriarty thug's throat to know, once and for all, that one less man would be chasing Watson, that Watson would be that one small bit safer. Back in my room, waiting for the inevitable heavy fall (police interference or violent retribution), I'd write out my confession. Perhaps, as a finishing touch, I'd pull out the photograph from that Sunday in March when my mother gave me my first chemistry set. She had a hand on my shoulder. I was smiling, a child. I could put it now in my pockets to be found. Play the lost little girl card one last time. That wordless admission of guilt would certainly appeal to certain members of my family, though I imagine Watson would find it tasteless. (Every evening I acknowledged the possibility of engineering that ending, and every night I reminded myself what a waste it was, what a waste of *myself*, my skills, my strength, and I wasn't a waste. I wasn't. I wasn't. I would not do it.)

4. Photograph the remainder of my pills, text that photograph to DI Green as proof I hadn't taken them (an honor system, obviously; I was, among other things, attempting

to be honorable), put the pills back into my coat, and then clean out my goddamn makeup bag.

I took the photo and sent it. Then, gritting my teeth, I dumped my cosmetics out onto the floor. I wet a paper towel and started scrubbing.

My train left in eight hours. I would be in New York by noon.

three
jamie

MY FATHER PLAYED MADONNA ALL THE WAY TO NEW YORK City.

Not the hits, the stuff you'd generally hear on the radio, but deep cuts. *Weird* stuff. My father was more of a Bob Dylan guy, so I'd already raised an eyebrow at his choices, but this was weirdness squared. Especially since he apparently knew all the words to "This Used To Be My Playground."

I didn't usually give much thought to my father's weirdnesses (there weren't enough hours in the day), but it was either wonder about that or why Leander had been so distant when I'd gotten into the car. He hadn't said a real hello, just nodded, miles away from the front seat of my father's Camry.

Leander never greeted me, or anyone, like that. He was my

honorary uncle, Holmes's actual one, and from what I'd seen, by far and away the most humane member of her extended family. He called his friends on Christmas, smiled at you when you came into a room, threw parties for my father's birthday. You know. Human things.

But it was more than that. Last year, in the weeks after my father had fetched us home from Britain, when Leander was still wasted from sickness and I was so battered and heart-broken that no one, especially not my family, wanted me to be alone . . . well. After days hovering over us, my father had finally left to make a trip to the grocery store. My stepmother was at work, my half brothers at school.

Which left me in the guest room, staring up at the ceiling fan, as I had been whenever I wasn't sleeping. I was sleeping most of the time—mornings, the hours before dinner or just after the sun went down. Anytime but at night, when I lay still and quiet, counting my breaths, watching the hours shed themselves until, finally, I got up to wander the halls, unable to shake the thought of August sprawled out in the snow.

We hadn't been good friends, August and I, but he was decent, thoroughly decent, and he'd paid a price for that decency. Once I'd thought that I could live in this world of Holmes's. That I could grab knives by their blades, punch my hands through glass, could survive the violence that followed her around like a shadow. But I knew now that I couldn't, that there was nothing there for someone like me.

That day my father finally left us alone, I realized I hadn't spoken in what felt like forever. My broken nose had healed, but it still hurt when I opened my mouth, and anyway I wasn't sure what I could say. *I've just realized that I'm a coward. I fold under pressure. I make house fires into conflagrations.* It didn't matter. I'd go back to sleep. There was still another week until classes began; I didn't have to be a human just yet.

Leander had other plans. From downstairs, he called me down into the kitchen—to persuade me to eat, I imagined, though I'd forced down some broth that morning. I took the stairs slowly and stood there in front of him, light-headed from lying down so long.

He stared at me. For a long time. Then he leaned across the table, cleared his throat, and said, hoarsely, "Jamie, did you know your new haircut makes you look like Donkey Kong?"

I'd laughed. I'd laughed until I couldn't breathe, until I had to sit down, until I was crying, Leander's hand on my shoulder, until I finally, stammeringly, began to talk about what had happened.

All of that was to say that Leander didn't usually indulge in the same black moods his family did. But now he seemed like he was going through something, and though my instinct was to try to help, I reminded myself that was the old Jamie's tactics. The one who fought other people's battles for them, who made things worse. I was trying to be normal, now. Normal meant letting adults deal with their own problems. (Besides, I was too busy checking my phone. So far, no more texts from Weird Threatening Number.)

My father, the adult, was dealing with his adult best friend's melancholy by singing "Material Girl" at the top of his lungs.

He had, at least, switched to the singles.

"Dad," I said. *"Dad."* We were still forty minutes from Manhattan.

He had one hand on the steering wheel and the other in the cup holder, rooting around for change. "We're liv-*ing* in a material *world*, and I am a material—"

"Please stop." I watched as a muscle in Leander's jaw began to jump. "Dad."

"I need *quart-ers* for the very next *toll*—"

"Dad—"

"James," Leander said, without turning to look. "Do you mind turning that down?"

"We used to play this back in Edinburgh," my father said. "When we threw our summer solstice parties. Don't you remember?"

"Yes. Please turn it down."

My father didn't touch the radio. "We don't need to talk about this, you know."

"You've taken your son out of school," he said. The music played tinnily under his words. "We're driving into the city. I imagine we have to talk about it."

We approached the toll plaza. My father rolled down the window, and with a viciousness I didn't expect, hurled the coins into the basket.

If I'd learned anything over the last few years with Charlotte, it was to let a scene like this play out without interruption. One wrong word, and your Holmes would change the subject, leave it behind you in the road.

33

Finally my father spoke again. "He's graduating this spring. He's doing well in his classes. He has that little girlfriend—"

"I don't understand how any of that matters," Leander said, soft but insistent. Sometimes I could hear it when he spoke, an echo of Charlotte in his inflection. She would have used fewer words. *Irrelevant,* she would have said, or *Watson, stop,* but the impatience would have been the same.

My father glanced up to the rearview mirror. "Jamie," he said, meeting my eyes. "For the past year—well, you know that Leander has been keeping tabs on Charlotte. Her whereabouts. What she's gotten into. That sort of thing. However wise that decision is—"

"It doesn't matter," Leander snapped. "I'm not there to *approve*, I'm there to keep tabs. Someone had to make sure she's alive. Her brother certainly isn't."

Milo Holmes had taken a leave of absence from leading Greystone to deal with the small matter of his murder charge. I say "his" murder charge as he was the one who pulled the trigger, but as far as the world (and the court system) knew, he was innocent. One of Milo's mercenaries had been set up to take the fall instead, I'm sure for a handsome payout after he was on the other side of a prison cell.

Still, a Holmes employee shooting a Moriarty? Milo had always had the kind of power that could scrub a media story clean, but this one was beyond his control to suppress. It was sensational. It was everywhere. I was doing everything I could to ignore it.

As far as we could tell, Milo had kept his promise: he'd

washed his hands clean of his sister and her problems. He wasn't the only one.

What had happened on that lawn in Sussex? I'd realized how little I'd known.

I had been watching Holmes so closely, trying to understand her behavior, that I hadn't taken the two steps back I'd needed to see the whole picture. She had decided from the beginning that her father was keeping Leander captive. That he had been blackmailed to do so by Lucien Moriarty, that it had something to do with her family's finances. And instead of confronting any of this head on, instead of accepting that the parents who treated her so terribly could in fact be terrible people, she had dragged me along on some wish-fulfillment mission to pin the blame on someone else.

It didn't end well. To put it mildly.

In the wake of Leander's kidnapping and the murder on their front lawn, Emma and Alistair Holmes separated. Who knows how much romance had been left between them, anyway. None that I could see. As far as the press knew, Emma had taken their daughter to a retreat in Switzerland to ride out the media storm circling her son. Alistair stayed, stoic and alone, in their Sussex house by the sea. It was up for sale. He couldn't afford it anymore.

That was the official story,

Last July, while I was staying with my mother over summer break, Leander took me out to lunch. He was in London to "settle some affairs," he'd said, and then it became clear those affairs had to do with his niece. *I know you don't like talking about this, Jamie, but—*

Charlotte Holmes wasn't in Switzerland. She wasn't in Sussex, either. She had turned seventeen, and petitioned early access to the trust fund she was meant to receive when she was twenty-one. She'd been denied. That was the last official record of her.

That's what Leander had discovered in Lucerne, when he'd gone to check in with Charlotte's mother, and when he couldn't find his niece—when Emma had refused to tell him where she was (*For her own safety, Leander, don't you know that Lucien Moriarty is still in the wind*)—he had spent weeks tracing her through France, to Paris, to the Eurostar train to London. There, the trail ended. He was hoping to pick it up through his contacts at Heathrow Airport.

Leander took me out for burgers, waited until I had my mouth full, then dumped this out on the table like an upended salt shaker.

I don't want to know, I'd told him, furiously chewing. *I'm done, Milo's done—we're all finished with this. I thought you were too.*

I'm not bailing her out of her mess, he'd said.

I'd swallowed. *So why are you telling me this? Actually* why? Before he'd been able to answer, I'd said, *Don't,* and that was that.

But here we were again. New York City's skyline was bearing down on us like a bullet train. "Dad. I thought you were just dragging me to another weird lunch with the Sherlock Holmes club. What is this about Charlotte—"

"Wait." Leander roused himself slightly. "You took him to Sherlock's birthday weekend celebration? The one in January? I've been refusing to go to that for years."

"Oh, come now. Buffet lunch, limericks about the year in Holmesiana—"

"You might feel differently," Leander said, "if the subject in question was Watsoniana, and all anyone wanted to do was put you in a top hat and have you say things like 'Brilliant, Holmes!'"

"I have to say it often enough in my normal life," my father muttered.

"You never do. I've never once heard you say it."

"I can hear the moments where you want me to say it. It's unnecessary. You're supplying it yourself."

"Just once I'd like to hear you—"

"The Sherlockians were very nice to us," my father said, clearing his throat. "The food is very good. Yorkshire pudding. And every year, I win at trivia—they call me the Sherlockian Shark. Anyway, Abbie won't go with me to these things, ever, she says I behave like a Civil War reenactor, so can you blame me for bringing my son—"

The sound from the front seat was like a car starting up after a long cold winter in the garage. It was Leander, laughing. Without taking his eyes off the road, my father reached out and gripped his shoulder.

I don't know why watching the two of them made me so incredibly sad.

"Neither of you," I pointed out, "have actually told me

what we're doing here. So this isn't Sherlock club, or whatever. This isn't you springing me from last period to go see *Les Miserables*, or to go get bacon donuts, or listen to your police scanner in the Walmart parking lot. What was the rest of that? A rehearsal? Tell me what's going on."

"I thought you didn't care," my father said to me, mildly. "That when it came to Charlotte, you didn't want to know."

We might have had years now to work on our relationship, weekend lunches and dinners at home and the occasional bizarre trip to Broadway on a Wednesday night, but one word from my father in that smug, self-satisfied voice, and everything inside of me rebelled. I was this close to saying, *Fine, I'll just wait in the car. Maybe I'll call Mom to talk about her new boyfriend* just to see the look on his face.

Thankfully, I wasn't a child anymore.

"You're right," I settled for saying, as carelessly as I could. "I don't."

"Wait in the car, then," Leander snapped, and though I wasn't a child, I felt like one then.

So I waited in the car.

We were in SoHo, I thought. I liked New York, the bits I'd seen of it, but it was hard for me to tell where exactly I was. I knew that the stately avenues of Upper Manhattan turned into the winding, almost-lovely streets of the Lower East Side, but from what I'd heard, I couldn't afford to live in this borough at all. I'd decided against applying to college in Manhattan, though I'd looked at Brooklyn College. Reading through the application, I kept picturing artisanal rice pudding, hipster bowling alleys, people who wore hats with brims and actually pulled them off. I doubted I'd fit in there, and so I'd scratched it off my list.

Of course, I'd never been to Brooklyn, so any sense of it I had was artificial.

That was one of the things that I'd realized, running around with Charlotte Holmes—all my ideas about the greater world weren't actually *my* ideas. It's difficult to solve a series of copycat crimes without taking a long, hard look at the source material, and Holmes and I had been childish enough to play at being Sherlock and his doctor. (My father and Leander never seemed to have grown out of it at all.) Behaving like you were someone you only knew from literature was one thing, but my tendency to romanticize didn't stop there. When I looked around my boarding school, the place itself warred with what I remembered from films like *Dead Poets Society*, books like *A Separate Peace*. Fiction layered over reality. I was somebody who only wanted to see the world through paintings, never a photograph.

It seeped into everything, my tendency to assume, imagine, judge. Last fall, Elizabeth had told me off-handedly that she liked that I wasn't a "romantic" boyfriend. *It makes me uncomfortable, romance. Flowers and stuff, I hate that,* she'd said, but with a wistfulness that made me think that she wanted me to disagree. I'd never been a bad boyfriend before, not really, anyway, and so I decided to clean up my act. I took her on a picnic in the woods. *Pretend it isn't romantic, if you have to,* I'd told her, and she'd laughed, and we drank the wine we'd stolen from one of Lena's sister's booze packages, and it all would have been terribly romantic had I not realized halfway through that I'd jacked the idea wholesale from an L.A.D. music video.

And now I was realizing that how I felt about New York came from movies that weren't even set there. Today, while the snow fell halfheartedly around my father's car, I kept thinking of a film I'd seen late at night, years ago, where a boy and girl wandered a city all night long, talking and falling a little bit in love. They'd been in Europe. They'd agreed to meet again the next year if they still felt the same about each other. People came to cities for things like that, I thought—possibility, chance. A girl putting her face into the cloth of your coat, breathing you in like you were something that mattered.

That was the other ghost that was drifting through SoHo today. I'd be lying if I didn't acknowledge it. These girls, dozens of them, in black coats with the collars turned up, in smart black boots with their hats pulled down over their ears. Girls with determined walks and straight dark hair. Charlotte Holmeses, all of them.

Pale imitations.

Wait here, my father had said, and before the door swung shut, I'd heard Leander say something about "Morgan's son." Morganson? They'd gone into the flat above the pàtisserie. 191 Spring Street, Apartment 5. If nothing else, I'd learned how to pay attention. While he and Leander did something interesting upstairs, something that probably didn't even have to do with my ex-best friend, I was watching her walk by the car over and over again.

I kept waiting for one of them to pause. Cock her head. Slowly turn to peer into the window, eyes shrouded by the steamed-up glass like some horror movie villain made especially for me. Maybe they were just dark-haired girls on their way to work or school, dressed for the weather. It didn't matter. I was falling back into my old habits, dreaming myself up a different world, seeing things that weren't there.

I wasn't pining for Holmes. I wasn't looking for her. I wasn't hoping she'd come back to deduce my stalker from my phone, to solve my small mystery, to ruin me all over again.

I'm not, I told myself, and got out of the car. Locked it. Went up to ring the buzzer.

four
charlotte

Tracey Polnitz. Michael Hartwell. Peter Morgan-Vilk.

Under normal circumstances I wouldn't be carrying a list of anyone's aliases around with me, much less Lucien Moriarty's. I would have memorized them and disposed of the evidence. But I had the corresponding passport numbers to contend with as well, which I hadn't yet stuffed into my brain.

That description, if clumsy, was accurate. It was as though I were packing Styrofoam into a too-small box whenever I tried to commit long strings of numbers to memory. Words had always been manageable. Proper nouns especially, places and people and their vehicles, any identifying detritus of a life lived out in the world. Numbers I managed if I could manipulate them. Equations, fine. Number theory, fine. But memorizing pi to the twentieth digit was an exercise I found both useless and impossible.

"The two aren't always conjoined," Professor Demarchelier had said. I was eleven, and lonely. That was my main realization for the year: that I did in fact want to be around other people, and that there were no other people to be had, and so I had to disguise what was turning out to be a very inconvenient failing. Demarchelier believed I had many failings. In that, we disagreed. I liked myself quite well.

That morning, in fact, was one of the last times that I remember liking myself. I was daydreaming about the tumbling practice I had that afternoon. My instructor had promised that today, I would learn to walk across a rafter in a darkened room.

In heels.

I was not thinking about numbers.

Demarchelier snapped his bony fingers in my face. "Charlotte. Just because you're terrible at something doesn't make it useless. The only common denominator in everything you attempt—"

"Is yourself," I repeated. Perhaps my tumbling instructor would also blindfold me, if I asked.

"Indeed." He frowned at me across the table. "Take some responsibility."

Perhaps she would even remove the net. If I were polite enough.

Demarchelier tapped the list of national insurance

numbers. It stretched down the page. "You have five minutes to learn these. Go."

Normally I would have needed twenty. On a tumbling day, I needed twenty-five. That day I was distracted enough that when time was called, I didn't have a single one of the numbers memorized.

"You realize that, if I let you loose into the real world with the skills you have now, you'd be dead." It conveyed something about my relationship with my tutor that making this statement gave him obvious pleasure. I knew because his eyes were crinkling at the corners, as though he'd just told a joke.

"Because I couldn't memorize a list of numbers, I would die," I said. "May I please be excused." I dropped the question marks on purpose.

"Yes," he said. "Of course."

That afternoon, I made it across the rafter blindfolded in twenty-two seconds. The next week, at Demarchelier's suggestion, I was put on Adderall to fix my "attention problem."

After that things progressed rather quickly.

On the Acela train to New York, I memorized the list of Moriarty's forged passport numbers, then shredded the sheet into slivers. I was in the real world and, as I was coming to realize, I had no desire to be dead.

I spent the afternoon in a restaurant in Chelsea, drinking sparkling water at the bar. Across the room, in a beautifully upholstered booth, my quarry was having the sort of marathon business lunch that made me glad that, for whatever kind of person I was, I was at least not a twentysomething banker.

The olives I'd ordered were seventeen dollars. There were twelve of them. I was trying to make the wretched things last.

When will you get there, the text said on my phone. *Can't plan my day around you.*

Soon, I replied, and tucked my phone away. With a casual expression, the bartender removed both my drink and my olives. "Unless you're still working?"

I was, but not in the way she thought. "I'll have—"

My quarry stood, a bit unsteadily. A result, perhaps, of the two gin martinis I'd watched the bartender make him.

"The check," I said, and even given time to have it printed, presented, and paid, I still beat my quarry to the front door.

Following him was child's play. It was insulting. He wasn't even very drunk; perhaps he was just very stupid. Or unaware. When I first met Watson, I was fairly sure that, if I tried, I could unhook and remove his belt from his pants without him noticing. I informed him of that, once, and it seemed to shock him. He fussed with his belt for a full hour after that.

My mark walked south for so many blocks that I wondered why on earth he hadn't gotten a cab. Certainly his calfskin gloves suggested that he had the money. It was frigid, the kind of winter in New York that I remembered from a trip I'd once taken to see my uncle. Leander had hosted me in his pied-à-terre when my parents hadn't wanted me back after a stint at rehab—if memory serves, at Paragon Girls San Marcos. My uncle had taken me to the very nicest restaurants in Chelsea and then insisted that I ate the food he ordered for me, and it all went well enough until I met a girl in a bathroom at 9 p.m. on a Thursday who asked me if I "partied" before pulling a baggie out of her bra, which of course led to three months at Paragon Girls San Marcos's sister location, This Generation Now! Petaluma.

It was what I was doing now, thinking *This Generation Now!, This Generation Now!* to the beat of my footsteps as we wandered down Seventh Avenue. At the end of every block, like a tic, he pulled out his phone to check the time, then stuffed it back into the pocket of his overcoat. We went like that, long trudging blocks in the melting snow, our progress punctuated only by Don't Walk signs and the recurring image of Saturn on his phone's lock screen. Finally he turned off onto a smart little street in SoHo that I was surprised, calfskin gloves and all, he could afford.

He was going home. He was meeting someone. I could tell from his walk, and from his blithe unconcern for his surroundings, and because I am who I was raised to be.

Still. Something was not right. I had a scratching at the back of my eyes that meant I had seen something I should have noticed, but didn't.

As we approached a patisserie, he began to dig in his pockets for his keys. I lingered, pretending to look at the brioche in the shop window. The door beside me opened, and he disappeared into it; before it shut, I had my hand on the handle.

There was an art to this. I counted ten seconds, long enough that passersby wouldn't mark me as a loiterer but long enough that he'd be well up the stairs, and then I slipped inside behind him. I made sure my footfalls rang, rummaged in my bag for coins. Girl sounds. That particular nonthreatening rustle that puts men at ease.

It was a tenement building in the old style, with a hollow under the first-floor landing where the lodgers had left their bicycles. A faded Christmas wreath was tacked up above the line of mailboxes. I could have looked to confirm his apartment number, but I didn't need to. He was on the third floor. I could tell from the sound his keys made in the lock.

Tracey Polnitz, I said to myself. *Michael Hartwell. Peter—*

"Peter Morgan-Vilk." The voice curled down the stairs. "It's been a long time."

The feeling.

The feeling I'd had on the street that I hadn't had time to catalog and identify.

I couldn't pull up the street outside in my head, freeze it, turn it from every angle, examine for discrepancies, then file it back away. I didn't have an eidetic memory. I wasn't an unprecedented genius.

I was still smart enough to know that James Watson's car had been parked at that curb, and that I was only realizing it now.

"How much did you sell your name for, Pete?" my uncle Leander was asking, but by then, I'd already hidden myself behind the bicycles and the mopeds and the empty recycling bins below the first-floor landing and far out of sight.

"Leander Holmes," Peter Morgan-Vilk said, every young,

moneyed syllable dripping with scorn. If he was drunk, I couldn't hear it in his voice. "Is that your way of saying hello? It's been a long time. Who's your friend?"

"My colleague, James."

"A pleasure." Jamie's father, speaking.

"The Watson." Peter sounded bored. "Of course. How can I help you?"

"We're looking for your father," James said. "Thought you'd know where we could find him."

"Listen, if this is about Lucien, I—"

"Lucien? Moriarty?" Leander laughed. "No. This is about your father owing me money."

Peter whistled. It echoed in the stairwell. "Didn't realize Dad was still doing that shit."

"He needs to keep less expensive mistresses."

"I'm aware. Look, I'm not in touch with him. Last I heard, after his political campaign fell apart and Mum left, he took off to Majorca with his heiress to live off her wealth. Broke my kid sister's heart. That was three years ago." A pause. "Are you sure this isn't about Lucien? Because my dad still blames him for it. All of it."

"Makes sense." That was James—warm, inviting tone, drawing Peter in.

"They had a contract, right? Was he consulting on his campaign, or managing, or—"

"Consulting. When Lucien bailed on him, it was at the worst possible time. Hard to make a mistress disappear when your *fixer* disappears the week before that." Peter coughed delicately. "Anything else? Or can I go shower before I get back to the office?"

"One more thing," James said, still friendly. "How much is Lucien giving your dad to rent out his son's identity?"

So.

Leander was tracking down Lucien too. He knew at least as much as I did. It could be a matter of days before I was found, by him, and before everything would be ruined. I attempted a steadying breath through my nose and nearly gagged on the garbage smell.

Before Peter could answer, the buzzer inside his apartment rang.

"Of all the—" Peter swore. "Hold on." A pause, and the door unlocked, and swung open.

A teenage boy walked in.

Jamie Watson pulled off his knit cap, ruffling the snow out of his hair. His hair was longer. Different. His coat was different. His shoes were the same, but the treads were further worn down, and there was a dusting of snow on his right trouser knee that wasn't there on his left, and a scar on the back of his right hand that was too precise to be from rugby. (Glass? A razor? It had a straight edge.) But he *was* playing rugby, and his team was still losing, and he was up late the night before, studying, and then I couldn't stop. I was greedy with it, the looking. He hadn't finished his lunch, he had that peaky look that meant that he'd be grumpy until someone made him eat a protein bar. He had grown a full inch and put on seven and a half pounds. No. Seven. No, he . . . he had a girlfriend, one he'd had for a long time, now, at least several months, and she'd knit him the brown-and-white scarf he was wearing. The fringe was ragged. No one in his family crocheted. No one else would give such a haphazardly done gift that the recipient would then in fact choose to wear. As I watched, the tail of the scarf brushed against the floor.

Watson.

It had been a solid year since I'd seen him last.

Once I had learned his habits. Had them catalogued. Had known him down to the ground. The boy standing in front of me was a stranger, a house rebuilt exactly but from parts that were strange to me.

"Dad?" he called. "Are you ready?"

"Coming down," James said. Footsteps on stairs.

I had missed the end of their interrogation.

Watson looked down at the floor. His eyes traveled over the mailbox, the dingy wreath, the bicycles, the bins—all the evidence that Peter Morgan-Vilk was a man who would pay the money to rent a bad apartment in an expensive part of town. It would be easy to theorize, from there, that he himself had negotiated the loan of his identity to Lucien for a substantial payout, that his father had nothing to do with it. If Lucien's fake IDs were confiscated, this then would be his backup: entry into America without any repercussions, for three months at a time, as a man who actually existed.

And Peter taking money from the man whose misbehavior brought down the father he despised? That was a fair motive on its own.

50

I had arrived here with those theories, but I had, as I'd said before, learned my lesson. I was done beginning at conclusions; this time I would begin at the beginning, and I had planned to interrogate Peter myself. And still, despite this planning, I had missed obtaining the information I needed, and barely, and all because the only friend I'd ever had was standing so close I could see the crease in the corner of his mouth.

Perhaps I made some sort of sound. A whisper of disappointment.

Watson's gaze sharpened; he was staring at the bins in front of me. Slowly, he took a step forward. Another.

I couldn't breathe. I wouldn't have been able to, even if I dared.

"Come on." James thundered down the last of the stairs, Leander at his heels. "We'll get dinner, get you home." Watson looked again up the landing, at Peter Morgan-Vilk's shut door. Then he shrugged, and followed James and Leander out.

I stayed in that stairwell a very long time.

five

jamie

"I STILL MAINTAIN THAT WE COULD HAVE JUST PHONED him, and saved ourselves the trip," Leander said as we pulled through Sherringford's main gates. "Especially since Jamie won't even let us stay in Manhattan for dinner."

I sighed. "I told you, I have—"

"A presentation," the two of them said together.

"Well, I wasn't sure you were listening. I'm sorry if I didn't want to get designer grilled cheese—"

My father sighed. "It looked lovely, didn't it? Through the window?"

I tried not to snap at him. We were approaching my dorm, and I had missed the dining hall's dinner hours because of the traffic back into Connecticut, and I was starving. I was always a jerk when I was starving. Holmes used to—no. No matter what I thought I'd seen, I wasn't allowing myself to go down that road.

"I don't know why you took me with you," I said patiently. "I thought I'd made it really clear. I like spending time with you guys, and I know you're headed back to England soon, Leander, but next time, can't we just, like . . . go to the movies? In town? I don't want to do this . . . this playacting anymore. I think I've grown out of it. And anyway, if I need to study, that should take priority."

It felt good to say that. Final. Adult.

"Priority," my father echoed. He and Leander exchanged a look, and then Leander turned back to me.

"Jamie," he said. "You will get into school somewhere lovely, I assure you. You can study literature, and read on the weekends, and go punting or whatever they do at Oxford—"

"Hush, you went punting," my father said, pulling up to the curb. "Don't pretend you don't know what punting is."

"Well, then, your son can punt too, the rivers there are lovely for boating."

"Punting?" I asked. "Also, who just, like, gets into Oxford?"

Leander cleared his throat. "Listen, Jamie—you can behave yourself. You can play by the rules. And I'm sure after that you'll get a job working for some newspaper, or writing your novel in a little turret room somewhere, just like you've always talked about. Of course, in those lives, you wouldn't possibly need any of the investigative skills we're offering to teach you now. None of the learning to *read* people, or to *understand* them, or *sort through their motives—*"

"Oh, come on—"

My father nodded. "No, it's not at all useful to learn to catalog the world and then winnow it down to the most important details. Especially for a writer. Can't have that."

"You're not *asking* me to do that, though," I said, a bit desperately. "This isn't solving puzzles or logic problems, this isn't a second stain under the carpet or some ginger encyclopedia league, this is *Moriarty* shit, and Leander, I was there on that lawn, too, in Sussex. I heard what you said. I *heard* it. You said you were done. So why are you out here, looking for Charlotte?"

His eyes darkened. "We're looking for Lucien."

"Dad," I said. "Please."

Silence, heavy like the shadows in the late-January light.

"Because"—Leander's voice went rough—"because after that awful mess, I thought her parents would finally step in. I thought that Emma and Alistair, bless their black little hearts, would stop farming out their daughter's emotional upbringing to rehab facilities and tutors and finally pay some attention to what was going on with her. Do you know, in that week I spent with Emma, in that basement, I found out that she didn't know her own daughter had been raped? And her reaction was to be—disappointed. She told me that she thought Charlotte could take care of herself. In the meantime, her daughter is happily cultivating an honest-to-God *blood war* because she thought her father had kidnapped me, and she wanted to blame it on a Moriarty instead." He went quiet for a long minute, staring out the window at the students streaming by. "I should have stepped in earlier. I should have taken her in. I don't—I don't know how hard I would have had to fight her father for custody. Probably not very."

"She's almost eighteen," I said, after a moment. "She's nearly an adult." *She made her own decisions. I made mine.*

"*You're* seventeen," my father said, "and I'm not giving up my claim to you anytime soon."

"Why do you really want me to come along?"

"Because you should want to," Leander said. "Because it appalls me that you don't."

"To track down Lucien Moriarty. That appalls you."

"Charlotte's looking for him—because yes, this is the best way to find her." He looked out the window. "She is your *best friend.* I don't see anyone else taking her place. I see you lonely, and lost, and she never dragged you into anything you didn't go into willingly. Jamie—"

My father frowned. "Leander—"

"Are you two even talking about me?"

"No. Both of you. We'll talk about this later." My father pulled his wallet out and handed me a twenty. "Order some delivery. Say hello to Elizabeth. Write your presentation, and think about it. Leander's only in town for another few days."

I was hardly listening. *She could have told me what she was planning,* I thought, *what she thought was true, and she didn't tell me, and then when it was over, she*—I tried to take a breath. I couldn't—*I know it isn't all her fault but I can't get myself hurt like that again.*

55

I told them I'd think about it. What else could I say?

I waited until the car had pulled away, for my heart to stop battering against my ribs. A line of trucks were making their deliveries; food came in on those giant blank trucks to the cafeteria at all hours. The last one in the line had a man hanging off the back like he was on garbage collection. He was built up like a weightlifter under his jumpsuit. Under his watch cap was a thatch of blond hair.

He looked like Hadrian Moriarty.

My face felt hot, my neck, hot, and as I bent over my knees, I unwound my scarf from my neck. Reacting like this to the mere mention of a Moriarty, thinking I was seeing ghosts—

No. I knew why. I knew exactly why I felt like I was trapped in a small, dark box, and I was even more of a coward if I couldn't admit it to myself.

The man on the truck hopped off; they were delivering to my dorm. His hair was dark, not light, and he gave me a worried look as he trotted up to the door with a clipboard.

"All right there, Watson?" Kittredge asked, jogging by in a pack of my teammates.

An extra practice, one I'd skipped. They were wearing shorts, the heat steaming off them like they were kettles.

I nodded, held up a hand. The universal symbol for fine. All around me, campus was pale and bright in the snow. I could see all the exits. Everywhere was an exit. And still somehow it was like the paths away were disappearing, one by one.

When I finally made it into Michener Hall, Mrs. Dunham was at the front desk, doing a crossword puzzle over a cup of tea. "Jamie," she said. "Have fun with—oh, dear. Are you all right?"

I smiled. It was automatic. I loved Mrs. Dunham with a strange sort of fierce pride, as though she belonged to me alone. She didn't, of course. Our house mother knew all of our names and our birthdays, brought us soup when we were sick, and oversaw the small interchangeable army of hall assistants who were constantly getting fired for drinking with their students or sleeping through their shifts. Mrs. Dunham was the only real constant in our dorm, in my day-to-day life, and though I could've applied to live in the fancy senior residence hall this year, I hadn't. I wasn't ready to give her up.

"I'm fine," I said. "Just starving. I missed dinner. I'm about to order in."

"Well, Elizabeth was just here to pick you up for your lit mag meeting," she told me, "and if you run, you might be able to catch her down the lane. Here. Do you have money? Chicken pad thai? Cherry Coke? Of course I know your order. Just pick it up here when you get back."

I felt an obligation to tell Elizabeth what was going on, the text message and the throwing up and the details of the trip to New York. And at the same time, I didn't want to at all. Maybe it was a habit I'd developed with Holmes, my choosing one person to confide everything in; maybe it wasn't a healthy one. Though I thought Elizabeth could probably help me sort it out, I also didn't want to dump it into her lap.

Especially after what happened to her last year.

"Let me just drop my bag," I said, leaving the money with

Mrs. Dunham and heading up the stairs. The whiteboard on my door was blank, the hall quiet but for the buzzing overhead lights. People were lingering in the dining hall, making their way to the library, studying with their doors shut.

I dug around in my backpack for my keys. No one at Sherringford locked their doors, except for me and Elizabeth.

No one except us had any reason to.

And despite my decision not to drag Elizabeth into this, I realized I had my phone in my hands. *I had an Incident at lunch today,* I wrote her. *That's why I disappeared.*

It was the code we'd developed the first time she'd seen me have a panic attack, after I realized it was impossible to hide them from her.

Her response was immediate. *Do you want me to come over? Maybe we can blow off lit mag and watch Incident-curing puppies?*

We'd been watching a show called *Puppy Surprise.* It was, unsurprisingly, about people being surprised with puppies, and at her suggestion, we only let ourselves watch it when one of us was having a really, really awful day.

I don't know if today qualifies, I wrote her, flopping into my desk chair.

Was it a puking Incident? she asked. *Did anyone see? Do you feel okay now? Did your dad help? Or oh God did he make you go bowling again??*

Her questions were stressing me out—she had a tendency to interrogate me in a way that wasn't exactly soothing—but I laughed anyway. Bowling, at least, wasn't on my father's list.

It was; no; sort of; he made me go sleuth something; I have to write a presentation or else I would puppy show so hard. After a moment, I said, *That sounds really wrong but I'm not sure why?*

But it had worked; I was smiling.

See you at lit mag, babe, she wrote, and I put my phone down.

For a long minute, I twirled in my chair, then opened my laptop on reflex. I had an email from my sister (*Can hear Mum and Ted having sex I think?? What does sex sound like? Jamie this is the LITERAL WORST,* line of vomiting emojis) and a whole bunch of spam. I sent Shelby back a vomiting emoji and two knives and told her to call me. I opened my physics presentation. Looked over my homework for tomorrow. The King's College London banner I'd tacked above my desk. A goal. I'd be on to the next part of my life soon. I had a nice girlfriend. A nice group of friends.

I was fine.

Sure, I was late for lit mag, but I felt calm, finally, and grateful for the quiet, and though I hurried down the stairs, I didn't run. The night stretched out before me, calm and quiet too, and if I was five minutes late, nothing would change. Slowly, I wrapped my scarf back around my neck and picked my way through the snow.

As I approached the student union, I could see her through the glass door. Elizabeth, lingering by the stairwell. The harsh lighting made her blond hair fluorescent, and as I watched, she checked her phone. I stood there for a second, just looking at her. I knew that she had a poem in her backpack that she had written about the willow tree in her backyard at home. I'd been writing about last year, stories about art thefts and explosions and kidnappings that the rest of our club found "unrealistic." Despite what they—and everyone at Sherringford—knew about the details of Dobson's murder, the facts of my European misadventure were still too wild to believe.

And while I wrote compulsively about my life, trying to make heads or tails of it, Elizabeth refused to write about any of it at all. Her attacker. Her hospital stay. In the world of her poems, none of it had ever happened. I admired that, weirdly enough. Her determination to rewrite her life with the worst parts excised.

Standing there in the hallway, she looked a little like a stranger. I never looked at her from across a room anymore; she was always under my arm. In a lot of ways, boarding school made it difficult to date without feeling married. Every morning, I passed the three redbrick buildings between my front door and hers. I met her in the lobby of her dorm, which always smelled like microwave popcorn and too-sweet perfume. Because I usually slept through breakfast, she had a to-go cup of tea for me, and we walked to class together, talking about homework, warming our hands with our hot drinks. Four times a week, we'd walk together to lunch; three times a week, to dinner. We worked in the library most nights in the table by the café. After lights out, we didn't send each other selfies, or even really text—what else did we have to say?

Now that it was winter, we'd stopped wandering the grounds, looking for places to make out; instead, we laid together in my bed, me on the outside, her on the inside, and instead of talking, we listened for a hall assistant to come by so that I could drop my right foot down onto the carpet. (*During guest hours, keep one foot on the floor!* said the signs in the stairwells. Below, someone had drawn an anatomically correct picture of something you could do with all four feet firmly on the ground.) Mostly, we were talking. About New York City versus London; about her sister, who wrote and recorded these strange, aching songs we played off YouTube; about where we'd go if we had a car and I could take her on a proper date. Sometimes she'd just sleep on my chest while I read for AP English, and I listened to her breathe while I dog-eared my text. It made me feel sort of guilty, but I had enough to do that finding time to work was a relief. My American applications were in, but the English ones weren't due for another few months, including King's College London, my top choice. Unlike Tom and Lena, who were set to coast through senior spring, I was still on hard burn.

Most of the time, I felt like I was being sensible with her, this girl who was willing to trust me with her heart, even after everything that had happened to her because of me. I was treating her carefully. She was treating me carefully. Elizabeth had brought up the idea of us sleeping together a few weeks ago, and we tabled it—maturely. But maybe we only felt comfortable doing that because if we weren't making out, why would we be having sex?

In other moments, I felt like I was dating the foreign exchange student who lived in my house. She was familiar, almost too much so, and still she was strange to me. And safe. She was safe.

Together, we were safe.

And still, for whatever reason, I couldn't make myself go inside to meet her.

I watched her, now. Her worried eyes, her mouth. Her making the decision to go upstairs without me. When she was out of sight, I sent her a text—*sorry, just got back, go on without me.*

It's okay, babe, she wrote back. *I'll call you after.* I didn't think I could sit and listen to a group of people critique a piece of my thinly veiled autobiography tonight. If you were on the lit mag staff, you'd have to sit through them critiquing the work you'd submitted for each issue. Last fall, someone had said, *Your narrator should make some better decisions.* It was like therapy, except the therapists had been given bludgeons.

I wandered back to the dorm, slowly, trying not to live in my head. My presentation. I had to think about my presentation. A wind picked up, enough to drive the cold up my sleeves and down my shoes, and I strayed off the path to cut through the sciences building.

The first floor of the sciences building. Not the fourth. (Why was I thinking about the fourth floor? *Stop thinking about the fourth floor,* I told myself.) A straight path through.

Physics. I needed to get my head on straight. I was giving a presentation on astrophysics tomorrow, a five-minute introduction to basic theories that involved no math and still had taken me hours to wrap my brain around, and though I'd done all the heavy lifting, I still needed to organize it into something resembling a speech. I wandered through the physics wing, looking at the displays that the teachers had made on matter and force and energy, and by the time I made it back to my dorm, I'd managed to regain some semblance of focus. Why did I feel like I was going to fly apart?

At the front desk, no Mrs. Dunham. Just her MAKING ROUNDS sign, the letters faded. The bag of Thai food was hanging from my doorknob. I took it and unlocked the door.

Two steps in, I stopped. A warning in the back of my chest, some kind of panicked pull that surprised me. No. Nothing was wrong. It was just an aftershock from earlier, from my Incident, or that text, or maybe my panic over my father's offer, and I forced myself to shut my eyes and breathe. I was safe. I was fine. To emphasize the point, I shut the door behind me and locked it.

I could see all the exits. I could see the whole of my room. No one else was there.

Still.

Grimly, I made myself check. In the closet. Under the desks. My papers were where I'd left them, the physics syllabus and my notes and the essay I'd written on *Beloved*. My sheets were a mess at the end of the mattress. I'd left the window cracked to counteract the overeager radiator, but I was three floors up, and no one could have climbed up the front of our building to break in here, not since the school installed all those spotlights after Dobson's murder.

A breath. Another. I set my dinner up next to my laptop and went to click over to my physics presentation. With luck, I could be done and in bed by midnight.

It wasn't there.

I had left with my presentation open on my laptop, and it wasn't there.

I checked the cloud. My email. I searched my files. I opened up a different word processing app, just in case I'd used it by accident. Nothing.

Five hours of work. I had been gone for fifteen minutes. And it was gone.

How could I be so stupid? I rifled through the papers on my desk, knowing there wasn't a hard copy but looking anyway, like an idiot, a panicking idiot. I would have had to shut the application. Drag the file to the trash. When I'd come in, was I really that distracted? That upset? How could I have—

A feeling, like a finger skimming the back of my neck. I whirled around in my chair, but I was alone.

That was, of course, when my phone buzzed.

six
charlotte

I HAD HAD ONE FINAL CONVERSATION WITH MY BROTHER, Milo, in the weeks after the incident at Sussex.

He'd come to Switzerland, to Lucerne, where I was living with our mother. She had let him in. She made a small fuss over him—brushing invisible lint off his shoulders, adjusting his collar—and then, those gestures completed to her satisfaction, returned to her desk to complete her onboarding materials for her new employer. She'd found a lab in Switzerland to take her on. A place to disappear into, to forget.

She and I were more alike than most people noticed, initially.

I was left with Milo. I could hardly bear to look at him.

"Get out," I said to him, and locked myself in my room,

where there was, at least, an opaque door between me and the man who had shot August dead.

"Lottie," he said through the keyhole. "Lottie, you know it isn't safe, for either you or for Mum. You know you can't be here. I can take you to Berlin, where you'll be safe. Wouldn't you like that?"

"Stop talking to me like I'm a cocker spaniel," I told him. I was a bit out of breath, as I was moving an end table in front of the door. "You're disgusting."

"Be reasonable. You know he'll be coming for you."

"Let him," I said, and meant it.

"He can't travel," Milo insisted. "Not without my knowing. My hands are tied as to any direct action, but he can't travel anywhere as himself without my knowing. I have fail-safes in place. Ones that can't tracked back to me. I'll make sure he's taken out. Lucien knows this, of course—"

I had been hauling my bedframe over to the door to reinforce my barricade. I stopped. "Your hands are tied because you're confessing?" I said. "You'll be turning yourself in to the police?"

"Lottie," he said, and his voice was loving, paternal. It was the way our father spoke before he'd hit me. "Don't be silly. Someone needs to keep an eye on things. We need to talk contingencies. I can't do anything if Lucien isn't traveling as himself, the police are watching any new moves I make—"

I jerked at the bedpost again, and this time I put my back into it. With a bang, it slammed the end table into the door. The legs splintered. The door buckled. It wasn't satisfying at all.

"You're a *murderer*," I said, panting.

To his credit, Milo hadn't backed away from the door. I could see his eye through the keyhole. "You know full well you're the one who's responsible for his death."

It was true. It was also true that he had pulled the trigger. "Get out of this house," I said, "you murderous piece of shit."

The eye blinked. Then it retreated. "It's your funeral," he said, and I didn't see any more of him after that.

When I finally emerged from behind those rubbish bins, I was furious with myself.

I hadn't done any of the work I'd intended to do, and now the only option I had left was attempting to pick a lock in an apartment stairwell to find documentation that I really didn't need.

Ultimately, what I wanted—what I *needed*, I would allow myself that urgency—was a comprehensive list of Lucien Moriarty's access points in and out of this country. Perhaps I was up my own ass, to steal an expression from Watson, but I had a working hypothesis. I was finished assuming that my suppositions were correct; this time, I intended to test them. Thoroughly.

I knew what would happen if I didn't. Had my feelings for August been responsible for the actions I took to ruin his life? Yes. Had the steps I took to find my uncle resulted directly in August's death? Yes. Yes, a thousand times, yes.

The only question, then, was how I could devise myself a punishment while bringing Lucien down in the bargain.

In the months after August's death, I painted a very deliberate target on my back. I opened social media accounts and tagged my posts with my location. I walked along the river in Lucerne every day for hours, slowly, in bright colors, talking loudly on my mobile. (I told my mother these walks were "constitutionals," meant to bring me back to full health. Her response was a shrug and a reminder to bring my mace.) I photographed myself walking along the river, and posted it to said public social media accounts.

Lucien hadn't even feinted in my direction. The last I heard, that bastard was in America. In New York.

I took several months to craft myself a snare, and then I came here myself.

But Watson? I never wanted Watson to be here. And it looked as though he might be again, if he was in fact following my uncle and James Watson on this frankly idiotic search for Lucien Moriarty. Why on earth did they want to find him?

This was my mess, and I would be the one to clean it up.

I waited until I was on the subway to write down the details I'd heard in the stairwell. It was enough to confirm, at least, that Peter Morgan-Vilk was an identity I should keep in mind when I took my next step. I would confirm at least one more, then move on.

We passed through a station with Wi-Fi. My phone buzzed. *Tell me you're there.*

There in ten, I texted back, and then I was.

Six bloody flights of stairs again. New York was taxing, though not in any interesting way. *The key is in the frog,* the text read, as if I wouldn't immediately know to fish it from the small ceramic animal next to the doormat.

My choice in lodgings this trip was giving me some pause. In the past year, I had undertaken most major travel (trains, planes, et cetera) in the guise of a girl named Rose from Brighton who was traveling on her gap year, filming videos for the YouTube channel she hoped to launch upon her return. Her accent was similar enough to mine to be unchallenging, her interest in film allowed me to carry around recording equipment, and her attention to fashion was easy enough to affect, as far as these things went. I'd built her persona around the nicest wig I owned, an ashy-blond one I'd had made in London. Rose wore a lot of black, as I did, in tailored styles, as I did—but with her hair and cat-eye sunglasses, her clothes took on a purpose. Even though she made me look like a fashion vlogger, I appreciated her.

I thought of her this way, like a person I kept propped up in the corner until I climbed inside. She'd taken short-term sublets in London for the duration of last fall, but this winter in America had proved more expensive. Rose's finances were limited. *My* finances were limited, and it was unclear as to when I could replenish them without exposing myself to more attention than necessary in the process.

This is why when DI Green offered me the use of her sister's apartment while she, the sister, was on holiday, I accepted, though with some hesitation.

You do know you're funding vigilante work, I told her via text.

She was saved in my phone as "Steve." *I brought you in on a case when you were ten. I don't think this is the craziest decision I've ever made.*

The apartment was unremarkable. Before I dropped either character or bags, I swept the room for surveillance. An hour later I had my laptop set up at the kitchen counter, and though I'd had the Wi-Fi base station removed, I still checked to make sure I hadn't connected to any network. I'd even filled in the Ethernet port myself with glue so that no one could force a connection. This computer had to stay off-grid; here I kept my files, organized in the method my father had taught me.

They held the facts of my investigation thus far.

Lucien Moriarty was entering America often, "on business," and not under his real name. He flew directly in, oftentimes from London, and once he reached the States he disappeared. He was in effect a ghost, one whose movements I could only really track when he was belted into a plane over the Atlantic.

I had determined this by staking out the most likely airport for three weeks straight. I hadn't even had to buy a ticket. Heathrow Terminal 5 is rather large, but when you've determined that someone is flying out and back every week and then made a color-coded list of direct flights to four major American cities on the Eastern Seaboard, you can be assured of some measure of success. Especially if you set your mind to nothing else.

Besides, no one looks too closely at the girl holding the WELCOME HOME DADDY sign in Arrivals, amongst a half-dozen other girls doing the same.

I had never been interested in where Lucien Moriarty was going to. I wasn't even interested in where he was coming from. That would come later. I wanted to know on which days he chose to return, and why.

From there things grew very technical, and I spent some time lurking in customs officials' neighborhood Starbucks, taking temp jobs at their offices, interviewing them for my "high school newspaper." I learned who he had bribed in England, and from there I made a plan to learn who he was bribing in America.

Why on earth wasn't he traveling under his own name?

Why he was in America was never a question, not to me. Lucien Moriarty was a British political consultant. He was a fixer, a man who made scandals disappear. And yet for the last year, his client list had grown unwieldy and unpredictable. A Manhattan prep school. A large posh hospital in D.C.

And perhaps most disturbingly, a wilderness rehabilitation facility for teenagers in Connecticut.

He handled their public crises. He helped them build a brand. He kept a base in England, and he flew back and forth weekly, and still he made no move on me, none at all. But Lucien Moriarty had an idée fixe, and I wished it was something as simple as conceit to know that it was me.

Enough. My navel wasn't growing any more interesting for all my gazing. Besides, the more I allowed myself abstract thought about this case, the more I found myself wandering to thoughts of what life could be like after. Seafood, perhaps, in a nice restaurant, in my own clothes, with my own face on.

Uninterrupted sleep, and making a real go at getting myself off of cigarettes. And after . . . I had a storefront in mind, something in Cheapside, and I had hopes it would still be available once I had finished with the prison sentence I would likely serve when all this was over.

In the meantime, I had a plan.

1. Contact Scotland Yard, provide report.
2. Contact source at Sherringford, receive report.
3. Purchase new bulletproof vest. One with moisture wicking, this time. (I was tired of emerging from Kevlar a sweaty mess.)
4. In bulletproof vest, shake loose information from a certain shop in Greenpoint.
5. Begin running down remaining specs on Michael Hartwell identity.
6. Confirm interview with Starway Airlines.
7. Arrange CPR certification for candy-striping credential.
8. Text DI Green a photograph of my untaken pills.
9. Go ten minutes without thinking about Jamie Watson unwinding his girlfriend's scarf.
10. Five minutes. Three. Any time at all.

seven
jamie

I DON'T KNOW HOW LONG I SAT THERE IN MY DESK CHAIR, making myself breathe in and out.

Finally, I stopped to look at my phone. The text was from my father: *Leander wants to know if you've made up your mind.*

The worst thing about my life so far? I wasn't stupid. It would be so much easier if I was. But we'd been in New York City today, chasing after Moriartys, and I'd come back to an instance of casual sabotage. Even now, I saw the big red circle I'd made on my physics syllabus—*individual presentations, 40% of your grade.* It wasn't murder. It wasn't a kidnapping. It was small, and insidious, and I knew the way things would work now. I could recognize a pattern.

It would only get worse. But I was tired of giving in.

Someone was punishing Charlotte by punishing me.

It was either that, or my girlfriend was really mad at me for skipping writing club.

"Fine," I said out loud. "Fine," and I stayed up until dawn to get the damn thing redone.

THE NEXT DAY I HAD FRENCH CLASS FIRST THING. ELIZA-beth walked me there, her hand in the crook of my arm. She was telling a story about her roommate leaving piles of orange peels underneath their bunk beds, how they smelled amazing until they began to rot. They'd argued last night about what point they'd need to sweep them out from underneath the bed—four days? Five? Should they leave them there at all? Despite my exhaustion, I was interested by the story's strange poetry, Elizabeth's gestures, her laugh. The normalcy of it all.

"So the oranges feels like a metaphor for something," she concluded, outside the steps up to the languages building. "I don't know what."

"I have that feeling a lot," I said.

"I missed you last night. Writing club was stupid, as usual. More poems about people's dead grandmothers. You know, you don't look like you slept at all." She hadn't touched her own tea, though I'd drained mine, and she pressed her paper cup into my hands. "Were you thinking about . . ." She trailed off, but I could hear the end of the sentence: *about last year,* or *about Charlotte Holmes.*

"No, I had some work to do still for today. I left it until the last minute." I hadn't told her about my ruined physics presentation; saying it out loud made it feel real. Besides, just hearing the anxiety in those four words—*were you thinking about*—made me hesitate to tell her. I had to keep things positive so that I could keep going. "More evidence that I shouldn't ever run off with my father in the middle of a school day."

"He's a bad influence." She kissed my cheek. "But you should go with him more often, it makes you happy. Try to stay awake. Monsieur Cann already has it in for you."

He did, but only because I'd skipped French III so many times last fall in favor of Sciences 442. How could I blame him for hating me? Today, I fumbled through his class so badly that Tom texted me under the table, *are you okay?* and I had to wave him off. Through AP Euro, I kept pinching my own arm until I gave myself bruises, and in Physics I read as carefully as I could from my presentation on the screen, trying not to sway on my feet, and the second it was over I made the executive decision to bail on the only class I knew I had an unshakeable A in—AP English—to get some sleep. On the way back to my dorm I passed Lena, bright like a robin in her red uniform blazer. She looked so awake it made me want to cry.

"Jamie," she said, grabbing my arm. "What's going on? You like . . . you look like hell."

"Didn't sleep," I said, and forced a smile. I was so exhausted I could barely get back to my dorm.

In the hall outside my room, I made myself listen. Just in case someone was inside, waiting for me behind the door with a club. But I guess that was never the Moriartys' way of doing things.

That was more Charlotte Holmes's style.

I gritted my teeth and let myself in.

Inside, I pushed back against the urge to catalog my things, just in case my presentation-ruining fairy had paid another visit. What was the point? It was the sort of thing that would make you feel crazy—was I the one who left my planner on the chair, when I'd always put it instead on my bookshelf? Had I been the one to leave the window open? The window was open now, I noticed, and who knew if I'd been the one to prop it open—

A wave of panic. Despite my sharp, sleepless nausea and the scraped-out feeling in my head, I wasn't at all tired anymore. But it was too late now to trek it to English.

I sat on the bed with my phone in my hands. What I wanted was to speak to someone who knew me. A conversation that would tie me back down to the knowable ground. It was dinnertime in England, I realized. My sister would be home from school, and if last night's email was any indication, she was in desperate need of someone to complain to. I rang her on videochat, and she answered almost instantly.

"Hi," she said, harried. "Shouldn't you be in class?"

"Probably," I said.

She shook her head. "Here, let me shut my door. Not like Mum is paying any attention to what I do anyway."

"Still wrapped up in Dreamy Ted?"

Shelby shrugged. "I don't know how dreamy he is. He's bald, but not in that hot-guy way. His only hot-guy selling point is that he's a little younger than she is. Rawr."

"But Mum's happy?"

"She's happy, I suppose," my sister said. "I don't know. I think maybe I'm, like, an awful person, but I've decided I hate sharing her attention with someone else. You've been gone for so long, it's become very Gilmore Girls around here. But Mum and I haven't gone out for frappucinos in ages. We used to go almost every day."

There was a note of apology in her voice. Shelby had been too young to really remember what it'd been like when my father left us for his new family in America. My years-long refusal to talk to him had struck her as a ploy for attention. (Looking back, I can say that it definitely was.) She didn't have the same memory of him that I did; it mattered a lot less to her either way how often he called or if he remembered to send us cards on our birthdays. Weren't all dads just a voice on the phone? Weren't optional once-yearly visits across the ocean just the way things went?

I wasn't enjoying the tables being turned on her. She and Mum had always been close, and if I could spare my sister anything, it would be taking a starring role in my own teen drama—*My Parents Are Dating Other People Burn It Down.*

"Tell her," I said. "Tell her you miss her. Ask for Shelby-time. She adores you, she wants you to be happy. It won't be an issue."

Shelby flopped down backward on her bed. The camera wobbled, then steadied. "It doesn't matter anyway, because— no. Hold on. I meant to tell you this. I—he like, scolded me last night. He told me to go back to my room and change."

I raised an eyebrow. "Ted did? Seriously?"

"Yeah. I was wearing these shorts—kind of high-waisted, with tights, nothing that I hadn't worn loads of times before, and he asked if I was going out to see a *boy* in those, and maybe I shouldn't wear it if so, and he was 'kidding' but he wasn't. Mum shut him down quickly." She pursed her lips. "I want to give him the benefit of the doubt, you know? Like, he doesn't have any kids. Maybe he's trying it out, the dad thing."

"He's doing a gross job of it, then," I said, making a mental note to follow up with Mum. "I hate that shit. It makes it sound like *he's* looking at you, and finding you—"

"Attractive. Or whatever. I know. It's horrid. And he's not even that old." Her voice went steely. "He better not try it again."

I had that feeling I got every now and then, that I was missing out on something pretty significant, not seeing my sister grow up. "Or else?"

"Or else," she said firmly. "Anyway, it might not matter, I'm not going to be around. I'm going to school in America."

I sat up so quickly I hit my head on the bookshelf above my bed. "What? No. Absolutely not. Not Sherringford."

At that, she laughed. "Not Sherringford. I refuse to go to your weirdo murder school, no matter how much money they offer me. No, there's this, like, other boarding school in Connecticut that Mum dug up. It's close to yours. But this one has a one-to-one student-to-horse ratio." She waited for that to sink in. "Jamie, I know you're awful at maths, but seriously. One-to-one. Everyone gets her own *horse*. And it's an all-girls' school, which is great."

It wasn't really all that surprising, when she put it that way. Shelby had **spent** our childhood begging for riding lessons, but Mum could never afford them. Instead, she'd given Shelby a Shetland-sized stuffed pony that my sister dragged around behind her on a lead. "I knew you were shopping around for a school, but I always sort of thought you'd stay in England. Isn't this place expensive? How can she afford it?"

"I think they offer, like, gold-plated financial aid. Or maybe her new boyfriend is feeling generous. I don't know."

"And you're okay with all this?"

"I—" She chewed her lip, thinking. "Mum has her own life here now. And I sort of feel like I'm in the way. This place sounds better than staying in London, slowly making myself invisible."

I sighed. "I'm sorry."

"Yeah." Shelby blinked quickly, rubbed her eyes. "Anyway, I'm not going without looking at it first, I'm not stupid. That's what I wanted to tell you, that Mum booked tickets to come out so I could see the campus, and if I like it, I can start right away. She was talking about wanting to see Dad. I guess she hasn't seen him since—since—"

"Since last winter. Since he came to pick me up after Sussex."

Past the phone in my hands, I could see the snow falling thickly out the window. Just this morning the weather was clear.

"Are you okay, Jamie?"

Shelby had sat up on her own bed. I didn't like the pitying look in her eyes. "Fine," I said, too sharply. "I'm fine."

"Don't be a jerk," she sang, the way she'd do when we were kids. "You're being a jerk, such a jerk, such a jerk—"

"Don't you 'Jerk Song' me—"

She went up an octave. "You're the biggest jerk in Jerk-fordshire—"

"Shel, oh my God," I said, trying hard not to laugh. It'd been a good instinct, to call my sister. "I hope you like that horse school. It sounds perfect. We'll talk more about it when you're here."

"I miss you too." She wrinkled her nose at me. "Bye, Jamie. See you soon."

I stood and pulled the curtains closed. Enough light still snuck through to speckle my bedspread, like I was living underwater. I watched it for a while, lying down on my bed, the shimmer of it against my wall. Thought bleary thoughts about the ocean in winter. I wanted to see it again, I decided. Maybe the North Sea up in Scotland, instead of the southern coast. I'd go once I was in uni. I'd take the train up alone. Watch the sheep out the window, the rolling hills. Stop a night in Edinburgh to tour my father's old stomping grounds. I wanted to relearn what it was like to be me, in places that I loved, to remember what it was like to be enough. Pretend there wasn't anyone out to get me.

Maybe there wasn't. Maybe I had made some kind of mistake, had saved over the file for my presentation, named it something stupid and lost it in a folder. Maybe, after the last two years, my instincts were just shot to hell. None of this had ever been about me, after all.

The exhaustion rolled up and over me like a blanket.

In the dream I had, I'd been an orphan living in Holmes's house. Her father had been chasing me, had the two of us terrified, hiding together in a basement. We were alone down there in the dark, but I could hear a crowd murmuring around us, someone stutter-coughing, the beginnings of applause. When I turned to tell Holmes we were being watched, a spotlight drew down over her face. Her eyes went fluorescent.

Just say your lines, she said.

The basement's dark edges bled out beyond us. Footsteps, above, on the ceiling. We would be found. They were an audience in search of a play.

I don't know them, I whispered back. *Do you?*

I watched her mouth, the site of every bad decision. She'd light a cigarette and put it between her lips. She'd take a fistful of pills. She'd kiss me. She'd say something unforgiveable, she'd do any of the wretched things she did, this girl who existed only to be in opposition to the world, and she'd wait for me to tell her to stop and I never would, ever, I would have myself shot in the snow before I told her to stand down.

You wanted it both ways, she said, *so you get nothing. No. You get to spend the rest of your life waiting for permission.* The spotlight flickered. It did that when she told the truth. When it steadied, it was so everyone could watch us. The audience had arrived, but it only made her that much more intimate. Her hand stole up to my cheek. She whispered, *Even now, you want permission to be a victim. It's all you've ever wanted. Someone to come and save you.*

She said it like she was reading a love letter.

Charlotte, I said.

That isn't my name. The light flickered. *Jamie. Jamie. Jamie—*

"—WAKE UP." SOMEONE WAS FLICKING THE LIGHT ON AND off, on and off. Were we still in the basement? Where were the windows? The exits? I'd been taught to look for the exits. I'd had it drilled into me.

No. I was in my room. I sat up so quickly I saw spots. "Who's there?"

"Wow, you're really out of it." Elizabeth was leaning against my closet door. Her red blazer was startling in the dim light. Was it nighttime? Was it even still the same day?

"Sorry," I said, rubbing my face. "Sorry, I was— I'm awake now. Um. Is it dinner?"

"You slept through dinner." She crossed her arms. "I came to check on you. Mrs. Dunham said she hadn't seen you since this morning."

I swallowed. "I missed the rest of my classes," I said.

"You missed the rest of your classes."

I'd never heard her use this voice with me. Ever. The last time she spoke to someone this flat, it was when she eviscerated Randall for making a sexist joke.

And then what she was saying sank in. "Shit. Oh, shit. I can't—" AP calc. I'd missed AP calc. Did I have anything due?

Would Miss Meyers notice? She never even looked up from her notes, and I never raised my hand anyway, did I—

"Jamie," Elizabeth said, low. "Seriously."

I couldn't account for the murderous look on her face. "Did I do something?" I snapped. "Why are you pissed? Last I checked, you weren't the one who blew an entire class day because of a nap."

She stalked toward me with a sudden intensity. "You emailed me," she said. "You emailed me, which is already super weird, and you told me that you needed to talk to me, but not until after dinner, and I'm supposed to come in at this specific time, so I show up—I blew off my English study group, by the way—I come in to find you, what, *pretending* to be asleep, whispering your ex-girlfriend's name? *Charlotte, Charlotte, Charlotte.* You're covered in sweat, and your room is disgusting—why are your walls sticky? What the hell is going on? Is this some kind of horrible joke? Why would you do this to me?"

She was inches from me now, her finger up like she wanted to stab it into my eye, or my throat, and she seemed seconds away from crying—I had never seen Elizabeth cry, I didn't know that anything could push her this far out of control—and I should have been horrified, stumbling to deny it, to explain.

I didn't. Because, as my eyes adjusted, I could see the wall behind her, sprayed down with brown liquid that ran in winding lines to the desk below. To my laptop, open, my email inbox visible on my screen. The top half of my screen, anyway. The bottom half was flickering between black and static. The keyboard was dripping wet, the desk chair, the corkboard, the end of my bed. The King's College London pennant above my desk.

Beside it, a crumpled can of the Diet Coke I kept in my fridge for her. I brought it to her every day at lunch like an apology. For liking her, liking her so much, and for still loving someone else instead.

Someone had shaken it and sprayed it all over the laptop my mother had bought with the money she'd been saving to buy herself pottery classes. My mother, who never did anything for herself.

Guilt on guilt on guilt. It closed its hand around me, tightened.

"Jesus, Jamie," Elizabeth was saying. Louder now. Loud enough to be heard in the hall. "What is going on? I know you're having panic attacks, I know you're feeling like shit about *something*. Is it something else, other than what you've told me? What's happening?"

All I could think about was how, earlier, I'd been so certain that a Moriarty was after me, that this was their new ploy. Punishing me until Charlotte reappeared to save me.

Either that, or my girlfriend *was* punishing me for something. It had been funny when I thought it last night. Not today, with her standing in the middle of the wreckage of my room.

"Did you do this?" It slipped out of my mouth like a curse. I hadn't meant to say it, to think it—I hadn't ever wanted to feel this scared again.

"Are you serious?"

"You heard me. Did you do it." It was like I couldn't stop. "Did you wreck my laptop to get me back for something?"

Elizabeth's eyes welled. "What did that girl do to make you like this?"

With that, it was like our fight jerked into a higher gear.

"What she did? Or hey, how about if I was just this way all along?" There were certain things I didn't want Elizabeth to touch. Not ever. This was one of them.

Nobody knew the whole of it. Nobody except me and Holmes and Scotland Yard, and I wanted to keep it that way. How else could I possibly move on, if everyone looked at me and knew how much of a fool I'd been?

"So what, you've just been an asshole from the start?" Elizabeth was crying. "Why are you talking to me like this?"

I opened my mouth, then shut it. Did I mean my accusation? Had she really gone into our club meeting last night, or had she beaten me back to my dorm to delete my project? No. It was impossible. She wasn't any part of this. I wasn't so selfish to drag her back into this mirror world where Moriartys had gemstones shoved down girls' throats.

I was selfish in other ways.

"I'm sorry," I said. It was all I had.

"Fine. Say nothing. Fine," she said again, and she turned on her heel and marched out into the hall.

Noise out there. Doors opening, closing.

"No, Randall," I heard her say. "Leave me alone. Leave me *alone*. Don't talk to him. I'll do it myself, when I'm ready."

He stuck his meaty head into my room. Before he could

say a word, I slammed the door in his face.

Then I picked up my phone, pulled up my father's message. *Leander wants to know if you've made up your mind.*

The whole bloody world wanted me to go find Holmes? Fine. I'd go find Holmes. I'd find her and show her exactly how much damage she'd done.

I have, I wrote back. *Pick me up in ten.*

eight
charlotte

THE SUMMER AFTER THE INCIDENT WITH MY TUMBLING
teacher and the Adderall and Professor Demarchelier, my family took our yearly retreat to Lucerne.

We spent a fair amount of time in Switzerland in those
years. Milo was attending boarding school there, at a place
that, even at twelve, I knew our family could hardly afford. The
winter instruction took place at a ski lodge in Austria, in Innsbruck (hence the name of the place, the Innsbruck School),
and during the spring and fall, Milo took his classes with the
sons of prime ministers and kings in Lucerne.

"I don't want to go back," he'd said at the end of spring
break, in a rare moment of dissent. My brother took his orders
from our father unflinchingly, as though our family unit were

a military operation. "I know enough already to start my own business. That's all we've—I've—ever wanted to do, anyway. Plenty of people finish school at eighteen."

We were at the dinner table. It was the only guaranteed time during the day for the four of us to be together. Consequently, it was my own personal hell. I pushed my plate away, watching my father closely.

He tilted his head to the side. "Why do you think that you attend your school?" I studied his hands on the table. They were still.

Milo considered the question, chewing. He never seemed to feel the reflexive dread I did when our father considered us like that, like prey. "For the connections?"

"Not for the skiing?" I asked under my breath. In those days, I had less control over myself.

Luckily, my father didn't hear. My mother reached out one viselike hand under the table and captured my knee. She wanted me to shut my mouth. This was because she loved me.

"The connections," my father said. "A bit baldly stated, but yes, good. Now, as you noted, you are eighteen. How useful is it for you to know the Belgian prime minister?"

"For me to know the prime minister?" Milo said, slowly. "But I go to school with the prime minister's son."

"And?" my father asked. On the table, he curled and uncurled his hands. This was a warning. If one lay flat on the table, it meant a punishment was forthcoming, and whether it would be directed at Milo or me was a coin toss.

In the silence, our housekeeper came around and refilled

our water glasses. The sound was soothing, and—and I couldn't focus. I kept staring at my father's hands, thinking, *I will not throw up*. It would make too much noise. My father would hear and there would be consequences, perhaps he would comfort me or perhaps he would be mad, I never did know and there was no way I could control it then so I would control it now, my panic, and I would not throw up.

I was twelve. I wanted to make him proud. I swallowed.

Milo was watching our father's hands as well. "It isn't important for me to know the Belgian prime minister. Except that I could introduce you to him. Through his son."

My father's fingers were curling around his fork. They were spearing a piece of meat and bringing it to his lips.

"Then you understand why you'll stay at Innsbruck," my father said, and "Charlotte, eat your veal," and that was that, and I did not throw up. Not that night.

Our trip to Lucerne coincided with Milo's return to school. We took a guesthouse outside the town, small and "sweetly Scandinavian" and full of tatty, comfortable furniture. We would be there for his orientation week.

It was not economical for both of us to attend boarding school, my father had told me, and unlike me, Milo had already learned everything that Alistair Holmes had to teach him. He needed an advanced education. But I was taken along on these trips because I still had my uses. I knew how to listen. I knew how to remember, and how to report back the important parts to my father in digest. I was left to play with the children, to glean what I could about their parents.

That year, the year I was twelve, the children I played with weren't precisely children. I spent the first week thrown together with the table-tennis prodigy Quentin Wilde. He was fifteen. His family had gotten him access to the school's facility before classes had even started so that he would not miss a single day of his training regimen.

Quentin needed an audience, apparently, and I was to be said audience. I was told to watch him play. I was told to be suitably impressed. His mother was an American energy secretary of some sort and his father stayed at home to care for their children. I wasn't sure what care he was providing, as Quentin and his siblings all attended boarding school, but it didn't seem to extend to his son's physical well-being. It was hard to focus on the table tennis, as I hated it, and as Quentin's hair was, as his name suggested, wild. I couldn't help thinking how badly it needed to be cut.

(Late the night before, so late that it was nearly morning, my parents had had an argument, and I'd been awake to hear it.

This is absurd and you know it, my mother had said. Even through the wall I could tell she was seething. I was good at listening through walls. I'd been trained, after all. *You realize that it costs nearly my entire yearly salary to send Milo here. You don't apply for aid—*

Which would make our financial situation publicly known. Which would defeat the purpose of all of this. A slammed drawer, the same sound that had woken me. Another soft, hollow thud. *Be rational, Emma.*

I am being rational, she said, lower. *Being a woman with a contrary opinion does not render me hysterical. The very least you could do would be to pretend, at least to your children, that they're something more than stepping-stones for your career. That you love them.*

For God's sake, I believe in being honest *with them—they know I love them—*

Do you, now? Take some responsibility, Al! You've lied so much that you're beginning to believe yourself. You were *sacked from the ministry! You* were *caught selling information! It's like you're beginning to think that you're the wronged party, and now you're putting our children through the—the gauntlet of your expectations so that you can use them like some ladder to climb back to the top—*

You're mixing your metaphors, my father said coldly. His tone meant, *You're drunk,* and perhaps she was. I didn't know if that negated her argument.

You should want better for them. I do. I'll take them and leave, I will—I'll take Lottie, at least—don't you see she's skin and bones? Don't you care?

I had never supposed my mother liked me this much. I allowed myself to feel pleasure for a few moments before my critical brain resurfaced. My father had taught me: *People have motives, Lottie. People aren't blindly altruistic. Even if all they're getting is the thrill of self-righteousness, they're seeking some reward.*

But if my mother said he was wrong about my education, perhaps the things he'd told me during lessons were wrong as well. Still, I'd never heard her contradict him in person. Not ever. And now she was saying that he, too, had motives, and they were even less altruistic than most people's, though I was also old enough to know that perhaps she was just emptying her arsenal at him as an offensive. (Arsenal. That was the football team my father had been discussing yesterday. I played with the idea for a moment. *Arsenal, games, arsenals, losing*—)

It wasn't clear who was telling the truth, if anyone was at all.

You're coddling her, my father was saying. *She shows so little promise anyway. The Jameson diamonds? That was a sad accident, and you know it. You'd take her and in the name of her protection, you'll spoil whatever potential she actually has. I won't allow it.*

Your expectations—

This time, the sound was glass, and shattering, and loud enough to wake my brother in the twin bed next to mine. *Go to bed, Emma,* my father said, and this time he said it, *You're drunk,* and Milo reached out to touch my shoulder before he shut his eyes again.)

It's important to know that I had this in mind.

Quentin needed a haircut. I knew how to cut mine; I did quite a nice job at it. I offered to cut his, and he accepted, and back at our empty guesthouse, taking my shears out from my kit, I stood in the bathroom alone. I knew I was a few steps away from breaking.

But I could fix it. Myself. I had a method: I let myself feel it, my crackling, sleepless brain, the boredom of watching some idiot boy hit a ball for hours and hours, the unfairness of spending my days in late July, in Switzerland, in a stuffy gymnasium when I could be reading the encyclopedia or blowing things up in the backyard, and the sad fact that even if my mother wanted me as a bargaining chip it was preferable to not being wanted at all, and then I scooped up those feelings the way I'd been taught and buried them in the ground below my feet.

For the first time, my method didn't work.

I tried again. I stood there for some time, shivering with the force of it, and it rose up from my stomach this time, a clutching, sad sort of panic, and my thoughts moved faster. I felt it. Felt everything. I knew I wanted to erase myself from the top down, like a drawing, and that still I wanted someone to touch my edges and tell me that they loved me despite them. I tried again. I failed. I was crying, and marveling at the idea of myself crying (crying!), when Quentin found me.

Unexpectedly, he pulled me into a hug.

"Home stuff?" he asked when he let me go. I nodded. "Fuck them."

There wasn't much to say to that, so I didn't.

His eyes roved over the bathroom counter, over my cosmetics kit. With one snakelike hand, he pulled out the bottle of Adderall. "You a fan?"

I considered. "Not particularly."

"You're a weird kid," he said, and emptied a few of my pills into his palm. "Listen. I'll trade you. We're having a party later—me and Basil and Thom. You're a little young, maybe, but if you want you can come along. Want a sampler?" He dug a bottle out of his backpack and shook out two little white pills. "Here," he said, giving one to me, "cheers," and tossed his back. I hesitated.

"It makes all that shit you're feeling go away," he said, and I swallowed it down so quickly that he started laughing.

When I returned to the guesthouse at midnight, my father asked me where I'd been. He trusted me to provide details. I provided them: Quentin and I had eaten pizza in the gymnasium together while he talked about his girlfriend, Tasha. I'd always liked the name Tasha. It was the first time I'd successfully lied to my father.

In actuality, once I arrived at the "party," I was ignored. Basil and Thom had drunk a bottle of tequila between them, then spent the night retching in the restroom. After I cut Quentin's hair, Quentin had practiced table tennis for hours with a laserlike focus I hadn't seen on him before. As for me, I wandered down to the school swimming pool and read my encyclopedia Q–R with my feet in the water. It was de rigueur, except for the part where I'd swapped my bottle of pills for Quentin's.

His I actually liked.

TWO YEARS LATER I TOLD MILO, IN A FIT OF HONESTY, THE real events of the night. The handwritten apology I received from Quentin was done in such a shaky hand that I could only assume that Milo had been holding a knife to his neck.

This was love. This is what love looked like.

AT 4 A.M., I PUT THE KETTLE ON. I RAN THE NECESSARY information back through my favorite American business database (subscriber-only) and took down the results, then filtered them, then filtered them again. I spent some time looking at Brooklyn's Greenpoint neighborhood on Google Maps. Then, at four thirty, I phoned the Yard.

There was a certain pleasure in calling Scotland Yard and asking to speak to the detective inspector on duty. I was an official source. I was listed in the records as such. That knowledge was pleasurable too, though I didn't put too much stock in such institutions.

"Stevie," DI Green said today. "Good to hear from you."

"Hello," I said. Stevie was my code name, as in Nicks. It was why Green was saved in my phone as "Steve." The detective inspector had a fondness for seventies folk rock and a certain cheesy sense of humor. "I'm settled in."

"Excellent. You have a report to make?"

I suppose I had a soft spot for Lea Green.

I'd known her for some time. She was the detective from the famous Jameson incident, the one where, if the papers were to be believed, I'd drawn a crayon map to lead the police to the stolen emeralds. I often wished I could go back and take a pair of scissors to that day, like I was removing scenes from a play. So what if the play was my life.

Really the worst-case scenario I could imagine, had I never gotten involved with the Jameson case, would be that my father had overlooked me entirely. That I turned out to be an ordinary girl, studying for my A levels somewhere in London, on hard burn to get into Oxbridge for chemistry. Instead, I'd been a child with a famous detective's last name, hiding behind a sofa while her father talked case notes with New Scotland Yard. All because *his* famous last name had given him such delusions of grandeur that he styled himself a tiny crime-solving king.

Green had been studying detective fiction at Cambridge before joining the force. Hence, her coming to my father. (I often thought she and Watson would get on quite well. He always liked formidable women.) I'd been informing for her ever since, though the operation she and I were running right now was only half legal, at best. She trusted me. Whether or not that was wise was her own business.

"I confirmed the Peter Morgan-Vilk identity," I told her. "If you have any sway with customs, I'd pull that passport. Morgan-Vilk won't miss it, but Lucien Moriarty will."

"Good." She was typing. "Your uncle came up with this information, then?"

For months I'd been telling her I was shadowing Leander as he'd been investigating Lucien Moriarty. I hadn't been speaking with DI Green every day; I had reached out sparingly, at odd hours, to provide her with intel I had "gleaned" from my uncle's "case notes."

"We've split up," I told her. "It was my birthday present. I'm striking off on my own."

"Right," she said. "Congratulations, girl. What will you do now?"

"Look into certain insinuations Morgan-Vilk made about

Lucien's political career," I said. "I have some thoughts about Michael Hartwell's daughter—"

"Stevie." Green huffed a laugh. "The answer is, 'I'm going to Disneyland.'"

"What?"

"Nothing—look, I'll pull the Polnitz and Hartwell passports too."

"I'm going to look into their provenance anyway. I imagine Moriarty didn't choose them out of a hat. He's been careful to avoid assuming identities of the deceased, for whatever reason—except for this Polnitz identity. But the others I don't understand."

"Leave me to figure it out. I need you to go to Greenpoint today."

"Greenpoint," I said. It had been in my plan, and still I disliked being ordered there.

"You could hide a little of your disdain for me, you know. Might take you further."

I opened my mouth to apologize, and instead said, "I saw Watson yesterday. He didn't see me."

DI Green exhaled. If she didn't know the full extent of my and Watson's history, she did see firsthand how everything went to shit. "How are you feeling about it?"

It was a simple question. Why did it always make me want to bite the person asking it? "I didn't sleep well. Is something in particular happening in Greenpoint today?"

"There's a shipment due for Connecticut from the gallery. It leaves at close."

Whatever mawkish emotion I was feeling was gone, erased as though with a damp cloth. "Where? Where in Connecticut?"

"Stevie—"

"Where?" I loathed asking questions to which I already knew the answer.

"You aren't to be on the truck. You aren't to be anywhere near the truck, do you understand? No. Lorries. You're on intel only. I don't want you to be seen by them. I don't want you to be—"

"Saying something five different ways doesn't make it more effective—"

"—or any of your Lara Croft bullshit, I mean it, Stevie—"

"Fine," I said.

A pause. "I should go," she said with a huff. I could hear someone—her supervisor?—in the background. "You didn't send me that photo last night."

Of my pills. I'd fallen asleep. "Sorry."

"Doesn't cut it. Send it now." Green put the phone down.

I supposed I was going to Greenpoint, then. The ease with which I had taken her advice surprised me. Certainly, the DI had given me a good reason, but in the past, that hadn't had been enough.

I knew, at this point, that I should have a handler. The briefest of glances at my last operation would tell you that.

If you'd said anything *at all,* Watson had said to me that day on the lawn. *Anything. I could have changed your mind! But you maneuvered me here just to—*

This is love, I'd told him. *This is what love looks like,* and then I'd left him to the wolves.

Yes, I needed a handler. If DI Green wasn't the exact right fit, she was a beginning.

I took my stash out of my coat lining. I photographed it. I made another cup of tea, put on my Rose-from-Brighton kit, topped it off with flat-black, cat-eye sunglasses, and went off to buy myself some Kevlar.

The man in the body armor shop was incredulous. "What—"

"It's for my Fashion Institute admissions portfolio," I said impatiently. "I'm putting together work that's a commentary on personal security. It has a lot of tulle."

"Tool?"

"*Tulle.* T-u-l-l-e. Like a tutu? Attached to a vest." I shrugged my bag from one shoulder to the other. "Here are my measurements. I'm going to model it myself." When he continued staring at me, I stomped my foot. "Honestly. How hard is this to understand?"

Thankfully the shop was empty; I was having to make a scene. At least I was providing this clerk with exactly the sort of girl he expected to be buying his wares, and so he'd forget me soon enough. Had I arrived as myself and quietly made my purchase, I would be the sort of oddity he would remember.

"It's your money." Shrugging, he turned to pull the least expensive model from the wall.

"No. I want the Byzantium Express Level 3X-A. With the moisture wicking if you have it."

"You've done your research," he said, obnoxiously surprised.

I blinked at him. "With the wicking," I repeated.

"Wicking?"

"It's a high-stress interview."

The man hesitated. "That one's seven hundred dollars, kid."

Which would bring me down to two hundred total. Still—
"I like the color," I told him. "It goes with the skirt. Can you
wrap it for me, please?"

On an empty subway platform, I did up the vest over my
chemise and under my oversized blouse. I tucked my blond
hair into the bag and, with quick fingers, undid the curls I'd
made this morning to stick the wig's pins into. I was myself
again. Other than the ringlets.

As the train came, I found myself checking the fasten-
ings on my vest. Was I nervous? Perhaps I was. This wasn't an
errand I'd been looking forward to. It had been number four
on the list, after all.

But then, I had to see Hadrian Moriarty at some point. No
better time than now.

nine
jamie

TEN MINUTES TURNED OUT TO BE . . . A LITTLE LONGER than ten minutes. My father replied, *I appreciate the dramatics, but I have to finish my monthly sales report. We can fetch you after school tomorrow.*

It was fine. I needed time to gather my thoughts, anyway. I begged uncooked rice and a garbage bag from the cafeteria, then settled my turned-off and upside-down laptop inside. The internet had told me the rice would soak up the liquid. I was dubious. The inside of the bag smelled like weird tapioca pudding.

With my laptop marinating beside me, I sat down to make a timeline. It wasn't a complicated one. Whoever was doing this didn't think they needed to *make* it complicated.

Their loss.

Deleting my physics presentation? It happened in the thirty minutes between my leaving the dorm and coming back. My father had dropped me in front of my building, so it's possible that someone clocked my arrival—but they would have had to then watch for me to leave again, and to know I wasn't going to creative writing club as usual. Mrs. Dunham had seen me enter and leave, but she hadn't known when I'd return. Sure, maybe she'd immediately broken into my room and deleted my files, but—

My stomach curdled. Mrs. Dunham. I refused to believe it.

And anyway, it was beyond belief to imagine that she would have emailed Elizabeth and told her to come to my room, much less sneak in herself and sabotage my laptop while I was sleeping. It took someone with brass balls to do something like that, and while I didn't doubt Mrs. Dunham had courage—she was the house mother to a hundred teenage boys; I was sure she'd seen some of the grossest scenes imaginable—I couldn't imagine her being so stonehearted or so cruel. Not even for Lucien Moriarty's money.

Because that's what it came down to, wasn't it? Who could be bribed. Unless we had another fanatic on our hands like Bryony Downs, made from Holmes's bad behavior, the culprit had to be someone being paid off by the Moriartys. It made it impersonal. Gross. It maybe made it easier to solve.

Notes, then. A plan.

I would start by apologizing to Elizabeth. She deserved it. It was just dumb luck that she'd shown up while I was having that nightmare; no one could have counted on that. More likely they had snuck in to ruin my laptop, found me sleeping, and then sent Elizabeth that email, urging her over to take the blame. Muddy my understanding of the situation.

I had no illusions about my own importance. In the end, this was a person who was after Charlotte Holmes, and I was the means to that end. That had to be my working assumption, right? Me being the collateral damage.

Either that, or I'd made some brand-new enemies at Sherringford without even knowing.

I rubbed at my eyes for a minute.

Right. I had to toss my room for bugs. It only took ten minutes; the room was small, and last year I'd learned the most effective way to dismantle my dorm furniture. I slit the mattress, felt down the closet, checked the shelves, looked behind the mirror. I didn't find anything.

Why on earth had they called in Elizabeth? Had they known I would flip out and blame her? It was more likely that they'd just hidden the bug well. I put a pin in that for now.

The next question was how they got in, and when. I could check the keycard records for the dorms. We each had one, a heightened security measure after Dobson's death that allowed the school to track who entered every building and when. You beeped in. The problem was, you didn't need to beep out. Someone could have been waiting in the dorm all day, waiting. There were security cameras, though. Holmes would know how to tell if the footage had been tampered with. And would someone go through all the trouble to do that? Wasn't there an easier way to strike at Holmes? What was their motive, bringing me into this? *You don't need to know the motive,* Holmes would say. *You need the method. You need a pair of eyes. What you need is to get out of your head, Watson—*

I shut my notebook.

I was thinking about it—her—like we were in this together. We weren't. This was just blowback from last year. From my former life. I'd solve this, and be done. Still, it wouldn't happen tonight. I had homework to do, and I didn't even know what it was, thanks to my ill-advised, relationship-ending nap.

Lena was in my AP English class. It was a place to start.

Homework? I texted her. *Slept through class.*

Her response was instantaneous. *Not talking to you you made a butt of yourself to Elizabeth and you didn't apologize?? Jesus Jamie.*

Elizabeth. Who I'd blamed for all of this. Who I was too ashamed to think about right now.

I'll talk to her tomorrow. Giving her time to cool down.

It was a lie, and Lena knew it. *You're a coward. I'm not doing you any favors,* she texted back.

It was fair. Still, I rolled my eyes. Elizabeth was the only sophomore in upperclassman housing, and she lived in Lena's dorm. Carter Hall housed the school-wide security team on the ground floor. Elizabeth's room shared a wall with them. Living there was the only way her parents would let her come back to school after last year, and who could blame them?

I knew that if I went to Lena's, I wouldn't be leaving until she (and probably a squad of security guards) personally supervised my apology to my girlfriend. Ex-girlfriend?

Oh, God. I'd fucked up.

Experimentally, I pulled the laptop out of its rice bath. It made a sloshing sound. I stuck it back in.

My phone buzzed. *I'm throwing a party tonight and if you bartend and apologize to Elizabeth and suck generally less I will give you the assignment.* There was a pause. Then she sent a knife emoji.

Today was not going as planned. I'd might as well just roll with it.

THAT WAS HOW I FOUND MYSELF AT AN UTTERLY DEBAUCHED party in the access tunnels on a Tuesday night.

The tunnels that ran below Sherringford were built back when the school was a convent, and nuns needed a way to walk to prayers in the freezing months without freezing themselves. When the school purchased the property back in the early nineteenth century, they'd walled the tunnels off. It was only in the last fifty years or so that they'd put them back into use. Now they were used by the maintenance staff.

Also by the school drug dealers, couples looking for places to hook up, the deputy head of school looking for a safe place to stash his thousand-dollar reclining bike, the rugby team during Spirit Week to lock freshmen overnight in the boiler room, and Charlotte Holmes, back when she was looking for a place to practice her fencing.

Tonight, the party was in a cavernous room midway between Carter and Michener Halls, far enough away from either to be heard. That was the idea, anyway. Lena had apparently weaseled the access code from a janitor ("Weaseled how, exactly?" Tom had asked) and sent out the invitations.

Mine hadn't exactly been an invitation, I guess. Usually I wouldn't be cradling eight designer shampoo bottles filled with vodka in a dark room somewhere underneath the quad at ten o'clock. On a Tuesday.

It was the Tuesday part that was really getting to me.

"Would it be better if it was on a Friday?" Mariella was asking. She seemed genuinely curious, but it was hard to gauge sarcasm over the thumping EDM.

The room Lena had picked was for Winter Wheel storage. Students paid forty bucks to keep their bikes underground through the snowy months; come March, they'd be hauled back out again. The brick walls were hung thick with them. They deadened the sound. Right now, the room was only half-full of people, but knowing Lena like I did, we'd be at capacity by midnight. Already there was a game of poker happening in the corner, a kind of bastardized five-card stud. Holmes would have been horrified.

"Are we celebrating something?" I asked Mariella. She was setting up a strobe light. I had no idea how or why she had a strobe light.

"Tom got into Michigan," she said. "Which is shocking to everyone, including Tom."

"Thanks for the vote of confidence," he said, coming up

behind us. I didn't know how he could eavesdrop over the bass.

"Congratulations, man." I freed a hand to shake his. "When were you going to tell me?"

Tom looked a little uncomfortable. "Tomorrow, maybe? I heard you had a . . . well, a bad day. Here, let me get you a table. I think Kittredge said he was bringing mixers for the shampoo vodka."

"So it'll be Bright and Shiny Volumizing Vodka Diet Coke," I said. "Great."

Tom stuck his hands in his sweater-vest pockets. "Can I talk to you for a second?"

"Yeah," I said, surprised. "Mariella, could you—"

"I'm on it," she said, and took over laying out the bar.

He and I wove our way out into the hall. Lena had been right; when we shut the door behind us, almost no noise escaped.

"I meant what I said," I told him, my voice too loud in the silent hall. "Congratulations. Michigan's a hard school to get into."

"My parents wanted Yale," he said, then winced. "No. Sorry. I'm working on that. They want Yale, but I don't, and it's not, like, unreasonable to not want to go there. I want a good education and no student loans, because God knows they want the Ivy League but won't pay for it. And anyway, only one Sherringford student a year gets into Yale, and it's not going to be me."

I nodded.

"Therapy," he said, as explanation. "I'm working on things."

"Therapy. Do you like it?" It'd been one of the conditions of Tom coming back to Sherringford, after he'd worked with Mr. Wheatley to spy on me last fall. Therapy, and biweekly check-ins with the dean, and no grades lower than a B. The Tom Bradford I knew this year was more subdued, but also much more grounded.

Sometimes I was shocked that he and I were still on speaking terms. But then, he and I hadn't really been great friends to begin with. If betrayals were measured by how close you were before they happened, then Tom hadn't betrayed me all that much.

"Do I like therapy? I mean, I don't know. I think it's working. I feel like I understand my decisions more. Sometimes I make better ones." He scuffed a foot on the ground. "Look, Watson—"

"Jamie," I said, pained.

"Jamie." Tom looked at me. "I didn't invite you tonight on purpose, and it's not because of this thing with Elizabeth."

I didn't know what to say. We weren't that close, sure, but we were friends. We ate lunch together most days. We studied together in the library at night. I knew his business, and he knew mine.

At least I'd thought I did.

"I don't really know what to say to that," I said.

Somehow that pissed him off. "See? Look at you! I say something totally fucked up to you and you're not even mad. It's like it doesn't even make a dent."

"You're like, five steps ahead of me right now. What are you even talking about?"

"This! All this!" Tom kicked at the dirty linoleum. The sound echoed down the empty hallway. "You don't care. We're not friends, not really. You're not really friends with Lena. You're not even really with Elizabeth—oh sure, you think you are, and maybe she does too. But it's a total lie."

He was hurt, and it was his party, and even if I wanted to push back against what he was saying, I still felt like shit about it. "I guess I didn't realize it," I said. "I'm really sorry."

"It's not— Jesus, Watson. Nothing. I get nothing from you. You don't tell us anything. It's clear there's something going on—"

"Jamie," I said.

"What?"

"Jamie. Don't call me Watson."

A group of girls rounding the corner paused, not sure if they should interrupt. The one in front had blond hair and a party dress and a baggie full of bright pills in her hand. She looked like the girl Mariella had brought to our lunch table yesterday. A freshman. They all looked like freshmen, too young to be here.

"Why?" Tom demanded. "Because I'm not on the rugby team with you, I can't use last names? Are you still punishing me for last year? I don't care if you are, just tell me so we can work it out! I—"

Whatever defense I'd been marshaling came apart. Because while I wasn't punishing him, I was doing something worse. I didn't think about him at all. Him or Lena or even Elizabeth, not in the way she deserved, not even now when I knew I had hurt her.

Once I had been good at friendship, or I thought I'd been. I'd followed friendship abroad, to art squats and police stations and cavernous parties, to my father's house when he and I weren't speaking, to Holmes's room to hold vigil at night. And now I didn't even know what to say to someone who was telling you, clumsily, that they missed you. Maybe Tom and I had been closer than I thought.

What would I have said, back when I was still myself? How did you slip back on a skin you'd shed?

What was wrong with me?

"It's fine," I said, turning to open the door. The girls took that as their cue to sweep by us; the one in front knocked into me, dropping her purse and her baggie of pills. I stooped to pick up her bag, then kicked the drugs behind me. She didn't seem to notice.

I turned back to Tom. "Hey, how about you call me whatever you want, and I'll stop being a shitty friend. Let's get you a shot, yeah?"

I sounded like a buffoon.

He gave me a disgusted look. "Talk to your girlfriend," he said, pushing past me into the party.

When I looked up, I saw, to my horror, that Elizabeth was trailing along the hall ghostlike, a scarf wrapped around her shoulders like a shawl.

The music swelled. Someone cheered, and then the heavy

door clicked shut and closed us off from the sound.

"Hi," Elizabeth said, standing there under the horrible industrial lights. It was obvious that she'd been crying. Her eyes had a glassy, faraway quality, and with the shawl around her arms she looked like a seer, or a sea-witch. "Listen—"

"I'm sorry," I said straightaway.

"You are." It wasn't a question.

"Yeah. That whole thing—it was crazy, and awful, and I shouldn't have blamed you. Of course you had nothing to do with it. But I didn't send that email. All this weird shit's been happening, it's like it's last year all over again, and I didn't want to tell you because I didn't want you to have to deal with it—"

"I know," she said.

"You know?" This hallway, apparently, was the place where I knew nothing. "How?"

She lifted her chin. "Because you sent me another email asking me to meet you at this party. But Tom told me he wasn't inviting you. He thought it'd make me want to come out, if I knew you wouldn't be here."

"Oh," I said stupidly. My email. Like an idiot I still hadn't changed my password. I'd been too busy pretending to be a detective. Pretending, and totally failing.

"It's the Moriartys, right?" Elizabeth stumbled over the words, like they cost her something.

"I don't know," I said. "I think—I think so."

"And Charlotte?"

"Yeah."

She pulled the scarf more tightly around herself, her gaze drawn inward. "Okay."

"Okay," I said, and waited. I found myself waiting for her to unveil, layer by layer, her intricate, ridiculous plan. We'd charge back in. We'd be the heroes. We'd end it, finally, once and for all.

But that was a different girl. That was a different me beside her.

"All I know," Elizabeth was saying slowly, "is if they want us at this party, then we need to get the hell out of here, now."

We made it all the way to the door to Carter Hall before the panic started.

ten
charlotte

THE FIRST TIME I MET JAMIE WATSON, I DIDN'T PAY HIM much attention at all. I'd spent months underwater. My summer in Sussex after my first Sherringford year had been unbearably quiet. I'd been reading about anglerfish because I was certain that I had hung some terrible inadvertent lantern over my head that had drawn Lee Dobson in. Like the anglerfish, I had sizable teeth, but I was coming to learn I used them poorly in a crisis.

Reading took me away from myself, so I tried to be reading all the time. When I wasn't, I found myself doing small things I'd never done before. Imagining some noise when there was none. Scratching my right knee, only the right knee, until I finally broke the skin. Standing up at dinner while my father was speaking because I was certain I was about to start screaming. My father was starting to look old. My father had stopped looking at me at all.

I spent that summer getting myself clean. As clean as I could. This had, as you'd imagine, suboptimal results, but I was working with what I had. I was realizing I had hardly enough of myself to keep for myself, and then at Sherringford in the fall when Watson came up to me on the quad, all I thought was, *Here is someone else who wants something from me that I am unable to give.*

Watson followed up on his rather ridiculous overture of friendship by punching Lee Dobson in the face. If anyone was going to punch Dobson in the face, it was going to be me. Not some moony half-American boy who thought, like my father, that our names meant we should be something other than we are.

I've never been a good detective. I am far too impatient for that. What I actually am is another matter.

In the past few months, I've had enough time to consider the question. Here is my working theory: I am a girl who came to the world rather late. I didn't know how to care about someone else because I had no one to care for (save my cat Mouse, who did not need all that much from me, considering) and no real training on the subject. I learned quickly, if somewhat painfully. I never wanted someone like Watson to be my test subject.

Good intentions, road to hell, et cetera.

FROM THE LOOSE LEAVES ON THE SIDEWALK AND THE wreath on the door, I thought at first that perhaps I'd taken down the wrong address. It was clearly a floral shop, though the sign above just said JUST SO OCCASIONS, obnoxiously vague. If I were to name a shop I'd name it for the proprietor and the purpose. MORIARTY SABOTEURS, for example. It was good to be clear for your customers' sake.

Just So Occasions "did" flowers, though they'd taken them in against the cold. They did framing, too, of family snaps like the sort they had hanging in their window and the paintings spotlit on the back wall. And they were hedging their bets against both of those things, because they were hosting some kind of Art and Wine afternoon patronized by kind-looking forty-something women who had two or three children in school and a husband who wouldn't help with the wash.

The woman in the window had just been laid off from her secretarial job. You could tell from the short nails on her right hand, by her smart but well-worn shoes, and, most obviously, from the cardboard box under her table holding three picture frames, a lamp, and a jar full of pens. She was looking for an escape before she had to face her new reality, and this place, with its comforts and warmth and the nice blond man wandering the room refilling glasses, provided that.

I felt rather badly for her.

Part of me had thought perhaps I'd arrive and plow through the front door, guns blazing. It was what I would have done last year. That fact alone meant it was a terrible idea, and anyway I rather wanted to see what her finished painting would look like. Right now it looked a bit like a gold-plated skeleton.

There was an alley to the right of the shop. I'd known this already, from studying the satellite map. As I'd surmised, this was where the delivery truck waited, hazard lights on, until it was ready to go off on its run.

I set off down the alley purposefully, as though I were taking a familiar shortcut home. Once I made it to the driver's side door, I cast a quick look toward the street and then let myself in. It was unlocked. The fact that it was unlocked gave me momentary pause, but whether or not this was a trap didn't ultimately matter. I had three minutes at most. I would make good use of them.

I pulled on my gloves and got to work.

At first glance the cab was empty except for a half-full bottle of soda. There would be prints on that; I quickly emptied it out the side and stuffed it into my bag. Then I flipped down the sun visors; clipped to the passenger side was a manifest. I assumed the list of goods being delivered was incorrect. It would hardly say *hazardous materials* or *items that would subtly but irrevocably injure James Watson Jr.* I didn't bother scanning it now; instead, I confirmed the address at the top—yes, there it was, Sherringford School—photographed it, and put it back precisely where I found it. With my phone, I took a quick shot of the odometer and the radio preset stations. I searched the seat for hair that I could take away with me, found a stray on the seat, and put it into a jar with a pair of tweezers.

Watson used to watch me do this with bated breath, imagining that every last action I made had a specific end. It didn't. Not always. Much like when I solved a math problem, I had an order of operations that I followed, a series of things I searched for ranked by importance. This way if I were interrupted, I had accomplished the most essential tasks first. This strand of hair, for instance, was likely useless, but on the off chance it wasn't—

Three minutes had passed. I cocked my head to listen (nothing), and then I stepped lightly out of the cab and circled to the back of the truck.

DI Green had told me not to look, and it had been a relief to hear it at the time. *Intel only, Charlotte,* she'd said.

But the truck was going to Watson's school, and so I was looking now.

The lock keeping the rolling door shut had a standard-order padlock. The street was empty, but I didn't doubt that Just So Occasions had a number of security cameras pointed at this exact spot. And I had thought to come as myself, to prove a point. Even this deciding moment was long enough for the security cameras to get a good shot of my face.

Professor Demarchelier's voice in my head: *Idiot girl.*

I snarled. Then I pulled out my phone to check the weather, rifling in my knapsack with my free hand for the pack of chewing gum I kept for this precise occasion. I pulled out the gum, then dropped my bag. Then dropped the gum as well. There was no one around to see or to offer help; that was necessary. Grumbling out loud, I sat on the edge of the truck, inches from the padlock, and began putting my spilled belongings away. When I was halfway finished, I patted down my pockets, ostensibly for my phone—I looked behind me, then under the truck, then in my pockets, and then I put my bag on top of the padlock, hunched over its open mouth, and, with the cover it provided, quickly put my pins into the lock and took it apart.

That was my cue to triumphantly pull out my phone, stuff everything back into my knapsack, shake my head, and take off down the street at speed.

A good fifty percent of my work was mimicry. Twenty percent, as Watson would say, was magician's tricks, and the rest was forensics and dumb, dumb luck. Except for the one percent that was entirely reliant on the ubiquity of Starbucks locations and their public restrooms.

I didn't even have to wonder; there was one at the end of the street. I ducked into the women's. Changed into a dress, but kept the Kevlar; put my coat and shirt and pants into neat rolls at the bottom of my knapsack. The store was empty and the barista might notice if I changed something as obvious as my hair, so I moved my wig to the top of my bag. I would put it on at the next blind corner. Bless America and its lack of CCTV cameras; there would be no footage of my transformation.

Within ten minutes I was back at the truck as a different girl altogether.

In another century, Holmes, Watson had said, *you would have been burned as a witch.*

"Let them try," I said aloud, and rolled the delivery door up and open.

It wasn't the right look to be unloading a truck—fashion vloggers rarely made deliveries—but one had to make do with what one had. I hopped in, then pulled the door back down far enough to hide all but my feet.

With the flashlight on my mobile, I scanned my surroundings. Boxes, yes, but the kind you'd put around a painting or at the very least a frame. Experimentally I prodded the center of the one beside me, then the edges. Frames and canvases, then, for sure. There were professional handling services that moved valuable art, but this had been deemed unimportant enough to flop around in the sort of truck you used to deliver to grocery stores.

I needed my box-cutter. It was at the bottom of my increasingly full bag; I pushed aside coat, lockpicks, pipette case, soda bottle, silencer, vlogging camera—there.

The rolling door flung up and open.

The nice blond man wasn't holding a wine bottle anymore. He was holding a bowie knife instead. The Kevlar, then, had been a miscalculation.

"Hello. I'm here to make a delivery," I said, because at heart, I was a bit of an asshole.

"Charlotte Holmes," Hadrian Moriarty said. His eyes raked over me in a vicious sweep. "What is it that you want?"

"I like your shop," I said, because I did. It was confused and a bit crowded, but even through the half-open front door I could tell it smelled like roses. I was fond of roses.

It was often in my best interest in these situations to think abstractly instead of whether or not my quarry was about to kill me.

"No costume?" he snarled. "No stupid little glasses?"

"Doesn't the wig count?"

"No sidekick?"

"No," I said. "You took care of that."

We regarded each other. His eyes narrowed. He put one heavy foot on the lip of the truck, then the other, and then he was muscling me to the back, up by the cab, past the boxes and out of sight.

"Where's Phillipa?" I asked. "Or was she not given her very own passport and allowed to skip along out of the country, too? Are only the boys allowed to hopscotch the pond?"

"There it is," he said. "That cheeky mouth. I was wondering where that girl had gone to."

"I'm not here about your sister. I'm here about Connecticut."

I was, I realized, on guard for more than just straightforward assault. Hadrian had that sort of low, hungry stare I associated with men like Lee Dobson. Sex, it seemed, was never about sex. It was about power and about subjugation, and Hadrian had been on the losing side of both those dynamics for quite some time.

That said, I was currently sober, and I had stopped scratching my right knee months ago, and even if everything inside of me was screaming, I was still holding my box-cutter and would not hesitate to carve out both his eyes if he laid a single finger on me.

Distantly, I remembered that this man had made out with my uncle. I would have to have a word with Leander about that, if we ever spoke again.

"Connecticut," Hadrian was saying. "Forget Connecticut. Let's talk about Sussex for a second, shall we? How about, your mother drugged Leander and sent him off to hospital to blame it on me and my sister? Tidy, wasn't it. Brother-sister forgers with a cursed last name poisoning one of your sainted Holmeses. You must have *loved* that."

"Lucien had been blackmailing my parents. He sent a 'home nurse' to poison my mother. Turnabout is fair play."

"Is it, now? Is that why Milo killed August? Fair play?"

I had been waiting for this question. "No," I said, as coldly as I could. "He thought August was you. He thought you were trying to hurt me."

We regarded each other.

"Kid," Hadrian said, and there was the smallest touch of humor in his eyes, "you've opened quite the can of worms, haven't you."

"You could say that." Someone was walking quickly by the truck; he and I both fell silent. "You don't seem to have a bad setup here," I said finally.

"No. It could be worse." His sister, Phillipa, was languishing under house arrest for poisoning my uncle—one of the few crimes she hadn't in fact committed. His brother August was dead. His brother Lucien was still by all accounts pursuing a vendetta that would bring the rest of us to our knees.

Working in a floral-stroke-frame shop in Brooklyn was not a bad deal, all considered.

Hadrian saw my mood soften. He smiled, toothily.

"Connecticut," I said, squaring my shoulders. "It isn't worth it. I don't care what it is you're actually delivering. Stop while you're ahead."

"I have my orders," he said.

"From your brother. Your brother orders you around," I said, and watched that one land. "Do you actually want to get back into this game after you've escaped it? What, your brother gave you a passport, so now he owns you? Please. You're better than that. Get out from under his thumb."

Hadrian set his jaw. "Don't tell me who I'm beholden to."

"I'm telling you what's in your best interest."

"And what's that?"

I stared at him, gauging the size of the bluff I was about to make. Despite our shared history I didn't know him well enough to read a change in his tells or his behavior from the last time I'd seen him. All I knew was that once, he had been a talk show guest all over Britain, discussing art and antiquities with a sort of smart charisma that I saw no sign of now.

The forged paintings that he and Phillipa had sold, the ones that fetched the highest prices, were ones that he had painted himself. He still was painting now. Any child could have told you that from the pigment beneath his fingernails. Through the shop window I'd seen the canvases hung against the back wall—darkly romantic portraits, done as though in a series. *The Last of August,* I thought. *The Thought of a Pocketwatch.* August had said that art was his brother's only passion.

I reached out a hand for Hadrian to shake. He took it. My fingers were dwarfed in his.

"Don't make the delivery," I said. He stared at me. "Don't

make it. I don't care if they're going to exhibit your paintings. It isn't worth it."

Hadrian jerked his hand away, and I knew then for sure what was in the boxes at my feet.

"They're not worth it, the students there," I said. I believed what I was saying; it would be pearls before swine. These particular pearls were also made by swine, though that wasn't the issue at hand.

"I thought you'd be here to get some revenge for that Watson boy." Hadrian cleared his throat. "You don't seem here for that."

I looked at him.

I had brought a small revolver. I had worn a Kevlar vest in case it came to a scuffle over the gun. I had come as myself so he could know, without a shadow of a doubt, that it was my doing, if I had in fact decided to kill him.

I had thought about it for months. Hadrian, Phillipa, Lucien. Remove them as though they were rats that had gotten into the walls of my home. Remove the threat, and then I would let the matter rest. Let my former friend get on with his life, as he so obviously—and wisely—wanted nothing to do with me. I would perhaps go to prison. Prison didn't scare me; I understood how to handle monotony interspersed with the occasional deadly interlude, and anyway I'd always thought I'd end up there eventually. Perhaps I wouldn't. I was tidy in my methods, and I might walk away from it all. Perhaps I would finish my formal schooling and take a position in a lab somewhere. Do graduate work in chemistry. I'd have to find a specific topic to pursue, instead of dabbling, but there could be pleasure in specialization. I'd certainly interacted enough with poisons to want to know more about antidotes, and perhaps . . . perhaps I could change my name—a symbolic gesture, but one that might allow for appropriate mental gymnastics. No one had expectations for Charlotte Something. No one directed her Saturdays but her. I thought about it: an apartment over-looking something appropriately scenic, some rain or fog or smog. I could compose again on my violin. I hadn't written a melody since I was a child. I could, after refining it, of course, perhaps play it for—

For myself. I would play it for myself. It was what I'd always done, after all, and if I was lonely, I could cry myself to bloody sleep.

You need to feel the blood underneath all that reason, DI Green had said. Looking at Hadrian Moriarty, I didn't feel angry. I felt very, very tired.

I knew, then, that I didn't want to kill the three of them after all.

"Leave Watson alone," I said, "and I'll leave you alone."

To his credit, he considered it. "If I don't?"

"Then I'll see you again soon." With that, I jumped down from the truck.

I wasn't a sentimental fool. I didn't plan on forgiving him, but neither would I gun him down. I had the manifest, the delivery confirmation, the bottle and the hair and the radio presets and my seven-hundred-dollar Kevlar vest, intact. I had seen a moment of doubt in Hadrian Moriarty. It had been a productive afternoon.

As I passed the women in the shop, I saw that they were all painting the Eiffel Tower. The woman I'd been watching had turned her skeleton into a tall, elegant structure. She'd depicted it at night, lit up and twinkling.

Perhaps she hadn't been fired. Perhaps she'd quit her job, instead, to take a trip to Paris. The evidence didn't quite suggest it, but perhaps, this time, I'd give her the benefit of the doubt.

I had been to Paris before. I had been to Berlin and Copenhagen and Prague and Lucerne and most of Western Europe, in the name of an education or in pursuit of a crime, and I had seen nothing of what made the world worth looking at.

That was a pity, now that I thought about it.

At the subway stop, I checked the weather again. Then my email. Then my bank account balance, and when I saw the number, I swore out loud. I had to refill my coffers.

I made three calls and got on the train, my nerves already shot. My day had taken a turn.

I would have to spend the next few hours reading celebrity gossip blogs.

eleven

jamie

THE YELLING WASN'T THE KIND FROM A FIRE OR AN EXPLO-
sion. It was panic, for sure—how else could I hear it through
the heavy door?—but from what, I didn't know. All I knew was
that there wasn't any screaming.

At least not yet.

Elizabeth looked at me, her face white, her hand on the
push-bar of the door. We were seconds from making it out of
this unscathed.

"Go," I told her. "No one's seen you."

Elizabeth had always been smarter than me. She didn't
protest or ask what I'd do. She didn't take my hand and refuse
to go. Without another word, she bolted into the open air.

I pounded down the tunnel toward the party. The overhead

lights cast shadows down the hall, catching in the doorways, making monsters, policemen, Moriartys.

By the time I reached the door, the noise had stopped.

Somehow that was worse.

There were twenty people at the party, and they were all clustered around something on the floor. Someone had turned the music down instead of cutting it completely, and the sound skittered crazily above us, a voice howling *get it get it get it get it* while the strobe light flickered in time. The power strip was by the door. I jerked the cord out of the wall.

Everyone looked up at me.

"That's him," someone said.

"Watson?" Kittredge said, incredulous.

"Tom said his laptop got all fucked up—"

The girl on the floor, curled up with her arms around her knees, crying and crying.

"What happened?" I asked. "What did she take?"

Murmuring. Exchanged glances. Randall clambered to his feet, his eyes hard. "What do you mean, what did she take? What did you give her?"

The feeling like I'd done this all before, that I knew how it would end.

"That's the girl who brought pills with her. Right? I saw she had a baggie with her. She dropped them in the hall. I didn't pick them up because clearly I didn't want her to take them— what is *going on*. Is she sick? Does she need a doctor?"

Randall did that rugby-player thing I'd never been good at, where he squared his shoulders to make himself look bigger.

"Someone stole her poker money. She had a grand with her."

"A *grand*?" Usually the buy-in for a game was two hundred, which was already too rich for my blood. With a grand, you could buy an entire car. A crappy one, but still. "Are those the new stakes? You guys are out of your mind."

"Of course they aren't," Randall said. "Anna was staking her friends. Because she's nice like that. And someone took it right out of her bag. Which you picked up in the hall."

Whatever the saying was about good intentions and the road to hell . . . "I hope you've all turned out your pockets already," I said.

"We all did," Kittredge said, still on his heels. He had a hand on the girl's—Anna's—back. "You haven't. Do it."

I reached into my pants and pulled my pockets inside out, then the pockets of my jacket. I kicked off my shoes and shook them out. I tossed everything I had onto the floor—which was nothing except an almost-empty wallet and my mobile phone.

"He was out in the hall after Tom came back in," Anna said. She lifted her chin. "He could have stashed it somewhere."

"Tom, you were there. Did you see me take any money?"

He was staring at the ground, unresponsive. *Right,* I thought, *I'm the bad friend.* The reversal didn't bring me any satisfaction. "Is this thousand dollars for real?" I asked. "Did your friends see it?"

Her friends looked at each other. "I saw it," the brunette girl said, but there was a note of doubt in her voice.

"I'm calling the police," Anna said. "This is so messed up, I can't even *believe* you guys."

Kittredge rocked back. "Whoa. No. We'll settle this here. No one is calling the police."

"No one is getting expelled, more like," Randall said. "Because we all would if they caught us here."

"Where did you put the money, Jamie?" Kittredge snarled. "Just tell us and we can pretend it didn't happen. There are like a million rooms down here—"

"The mythical money. The money no one's seen." I stared at him. "The money you've arbitrarily decided that I've taken. Don't condescend to me, Kittredge."

"You're the one who sounds condescending," Tom said into the sullen silence.

"Hello?" Anna was saying into her phone. "I'm calling to report a theft—"

Randall looked at Kittredge, who looked at Tom, who looked at the girls who'd come in with the girl on the floor. Everyone waiting for permission to do the shitty thing, and leave.

"Just go," Lena said from the corner. I hadn't seen her; she was sitting silently on a folding chair in the corner, flanked by the rows of bikes on the wall. She had her top hat on, the one she always wore to parties, but tonight it made her look like a sort of sad clown. "I'll stay. If you're so sure Jamie's done it, then he can wait here for the cops too."

"Sherringford School?" The girl was saying to the 911 operator. Everyone else filtered out, whispering. "Carter Hall. We're underground. Yes, the access tunnels, how did you know—" She followed them out into the hall, presumably so she didn't have to keep looking at my face.

Lena leaned back in her chair. "Fun party, huh."

"They decided it was me pretty quickly."

"You've been, like, so much fun recently and so awesome to hang out with, I think it's obvious why."

"Thanks," I said, sourly.

"Anytime."

It was a good space for a party, I thought, industrial and strange, made entirely of metal and bike wheels. Someone had set up a poker game in the corner by a broken-down ATV, but now the little piles of cards were kicked out, scattered on the ground. Beside me, Lena's shampoo-booze bar had been organized according to what looked like bottle color. I started pulling them off the table, intending to toss them out.

"Stop," Lena said. "I'm sure they'll want this for evidence."

"You're really leaning into this whole getting-suspended thing, aren't you."

She shrugged. "They won't suspend me."

"Your family are major donors, then."

"You knew that," she said. "But yeah. Short of killing someone, I think I'm fine."

I could hear the scrap of Anna's voice talking to someone in the hall, almost as though this was our cell and she was our warden.

"Elizabeth got an email telling her to be here," I said, finally. "From my email account. But I didn't send it. That's what I was doing in the hall, talking to her. This was planned. This was going to happen, or something like it was."

Lena sat up a little straighter. "I heard about your laptop from Tom."

I frowned. I hadn't told him about the soda explosion, though maybe Elizabeth had. "Well. I guess I'm saying that I'm not surprised. She had a baggie of pills with her—brightly colored, they were shaped like stars, moons. This money thing is so vague, I wonder if she meant to hang me with those, and then found them missing, and went for something else instead?"

"I don't know, Jamie."

Outside, Anna's voice fell silent. "Hold on," I said, and opened the door. "Can you come back in, so I can ask you a question?"

I got a good look at her, then, for the first time. She was wearing bright colors, a choker around her neck, her hair long and straight and blond and glossy, and the look on her face said she'd rather eat a box of scorpions than talk to me a second longer.

"No," she said.

"That's fine. We can do it here." She was trembling a little, and while I didn't really want to frighten her, a part of me was glad someone else got a turn at being scared. "How long have you been taking money from Lucien Moriarty?"

Anna set her jaw. "You're crazy."

"No? Let's try this. How long have you been taking money from someone—anyone—to ruin my life?"

I could feel Lena draw up behind me. "Jamie," she murmured.

I whirled on her. "She dropped the bag in front of me. On purpose. With witnesses. You're sure you don't know this girl? I thought this party was invite only. Did you know her friends? Have you even seen them before?"

"I didn't know any of them," Lena said, and to my surprise, she sounded furious. On my other side, Anna was inching away from me like I had pulled out a gun. "But I wasn't going to throw out some poor freshmen in front of everyone. Jamie— you should probably, like— You should go. You brought this with you, didn't you? There was shit going on with you and you came to this party and—"

"And I had to do my English homework, and you wouldn't give it to me, and fine, maybe I should have said something to you but *what*, exactly, that didn't sound crazy? 'All these bad things are happening to me but they have loads of plausible deniability'? 'If it seems like I'm really clumsy lately and an asshole, I'm actually not'?"

To my surprise, she said, "How about, 'Hey guys, I think I have PTSD,' or 'Hey guys, more of that messed-up shit is happening to me which obviously isn't pretend because you've seen it for real when it happened to me before.' Maybe we could have helped you."

"We who? You and Tom? What could you have done? I didn't want to drag you into it. And Tom? Seriously? Since when does Tom want to get involved in my shit?"

"Well, *I* would have! I was in Prague, Jamie. I was in *Berlin*. I watched you get taken away on a stretcher—I bought all that goddamn art!" To my shock, Lena shoved me. Not hard. Not to hurt me. Just enough that I staggered backward into the hall. "I could have done something. Maybe gotten you to do some therapy. Tom goes to therapy! Tom could have talked to you about it! But you just pretend . . . God, you're just selfish. You think you're the only one who misses her."

"This isn't about—"

"Don't pretend this isn't about Charlotte!"

"Why the hell does it matter to you, Lena? I was her best friend!"

Lena stared at me, eyes dark and angry. "Well, she was mine."

"I can't— Lena, there's only so many come-to-Jesus moments I can have in a single night, okay?"

"Guys?" Anna cleared her throat. "I have literally zero idea what you're talking about."

Lena took her ridiculous hat off her head and swept it under her arm, like we'd come to the end of a performance. "Jamie, you, like, don't want friends, you know that? You just want to float in your little misery bubble alone. Then you walk around being all like I'm *miserable*, I'm so *alone*. Well, you do it to yourself! I've seen what this Lucien guy is like, okay? I was there. We would have believed you."

The police would be here soon. There would be questions, and handcuffs, and an interrogation room, and questions from the dean, calls from parents who thought I was a thieving scholarship loser, a killer, a boy who stuffed jewels down girls' throats, and I had put on so much speed in the last year that I had thought I'd left this all behind me. Now I'd been suddenly slammed into reverse.

And fine. Fine. If it came to that—I missed her.

God, I missed her. Especially now.

"Yeah," I told Lena, and she was right, she was right about all of it, and it didn't matter, because maybe I didn't want any other friends. Maybe I didn't want anybody but Charlotte. I couldn't cure the poison with anything that wasn't also poison. Missing her was sick, and pathetic, and made me a fucking fool, and maybe I hated myself so much for it that, even now, I couldn't look Lena in the face. "Yeah, that's totally how it went down the last time."

THE POLICE ARRIVED, YAWNING AND BORED, AND IMMEDI-ately took Anna away with them to be questioned. Lena trailed behind them, for whatever reason; she was saying something about an ambulance. That took care of two of the uniformed officers, but left one behind to glare at me alongside my old friend Detective Shepard, who looked like he'd rather have swallowed a hive of bees than to be back on this campus again. By now he and I knew the drill; he didn't even try to question me without my father, just left me to wallow while he examined the scene. The uniformed cop knocked a bike off its hook, and when it fell, it took down another, and another, slow and unstoppable, like a rhinoceros playing slow-motion dominoes. Then the dean of students arrived in pajamas and robe and a pair of neon trainers, and my father after that, bright-eyed and,

134

as always, horribly bushy-tailed, and after a huddled conference amongst the adults, the whole awful parade of us walked up to the headmistress's office in the clock tower on the hill, our shoes tracking slush and dirt into the paisley-carpeted entryway.

"Like I said, I'd rather question him at the station," Detective Shepard said, as we stomped the snow off our feet.

The dean shook her head. "You already took away the girl. I'm lucky I got here before you vanished Mr. Watson here."

"It's not how it's done—"

"They got me out of bed," the dean said darkly. "After last year, with the Dobson boy, we've come up with a new way of handling these . . . situations. And that 'new way' hauled me out of my house at midnight on a weekday, so yes, we are handling it here. I have no idea why that child called the police. This is an internal matter."

As everyone started up the stairs, bickering, my father hung behind. He looked as energetic as though he'd just drunk a pot of coffee and run a triathlon. I hated him a little bit right then. But I guess I had a lot of frustration to go around.

"So perhaps I should have picked you up when you asked me to," he said.

"Probably." I took off my gloves and stuffed them in my pockets. The clock tower offices were surprisingly warm.

He lifted an eyebrow. "No 'Dad, why aren't you taking this more seriously'? 'Dad, why aren't you cursing my name and wailing over our misfortune'?"

"Honestly?" I said. "I've been . . . pretty shitty, lately. I'm not going to tell you what to do. Just go ahead and be your weird self."

"Thanks," he said dryly. "But the detective looks a bit like he wants to disembowel you"—Shepard was waiting on the landing, watching us—"so shall we go on and be our weird selves in front of the firing squad? They might appreciate some of your wailing, if you want to try it out."

The head of school's office took up the top floor of the tower, and we clustered inside of it, everyone waiting for their cue to sit. The headmistress herself was an imposing presence in a crowd of exhausted adults. She was scrubbed clean, perched at the edge of her desk in a suit, while her assistant poured coffee out into ceramic cups.

"Ms. Williamson," my father said, extending a hand. "James Watson, Jamie's father. It's a pleasure. I only wish we could be meeting under better circumstances."

"Yes," she said simply. She had been head of school last year as well. I don't know how often she actually encountered "better circumstances" when it came to dealing with me. "Please sit, all of you. Harry, hand around the coffee, then go handle the phone. We'll have calls before tonight is over."

"Can you update us if they find the money?" I asked, sitting down on her settee. "Once they find out what happened?"

The headmistress and Detective Shepard exchanged a look. "We'll see," he said, finally.

"Jamie." The dean of students pulled an iPad from her bag. She had a rattle sticking up next to it; she'd left small kids at home. "I've pulled your records. The events of last year notwithstanding—"

"He was cleared," my father interrupted. "That matter's handled. We have the good detective here to thank for that."

The good detective rolled his eyes up to the ceiling, and said nothing. I thought, not for the first time, that maybe we should have had him help us bring in Bryony Downs. Instead of, well, telling him about it. Two days after the fact.

"Notwithstanding," the dean said, peering over her glasses, "Jamie's had a good academic year. APs, high grades. And then the last few days. I've looked at your teachers' gradebooks from this week—it says here that you did very poorly on a presentation that was nearly half of your semester grade for physics? The note says that you went off on a three-minute tangent about space elevators."

"Space elevators?" I searched my memory of the presentation to find that I didn't really have one. "Oh."

"Oh," the dean said. "Yes. And you skipped your classes yesterday—you didn't hand in any of your work? You had a response paper due in AP English. You missed a quiz in AP calc. Your French teacher says you sent him a bizarre email about him eating snails that looked like you put it through a translate program a few times—Monsieur Cann's note under 'discipline' expresses his dismay, and he also would like to know if you're a vegetarian and were offended by last week's lesson on French delicacies. Does any of this ring a bell?"

My father clapped a hearty hand on my shoulder. "Eating

snails *is* barbaric, isn't it, Jamie?"

I really, really should have changed my email password. How had I been so stupid? How had I been so in my own head that I hadn't taken the one practical step that was actually in my power?

"This is erratic behavior, you see," the headmistress said, more gently than maybe I deserved. "And now a girl's been stolen from. Did you have any contact with her before tonight?"

I shook my head.

"Anna was attending a party thrown by Lena Gupta, your friend—"

Detective Shepard muttered something like "known associate."

I sunk my head into my hands. "She sat at our lunch table the other day, but I didn't talk to her," I said through my fingers. "The girl, I mean. Anna. I didn't send those emails. Someone broke into my room and deleted my physics presentation so I stayed up all night redoing it, and so I didn't sleep much, and . . . okay, yes, I think space elevators are really cool and so that part is completely my fault, or my subconscious's fault maybe, or I was like, lack-of-sleep hallucinating, but someone broke into my room the next day while I was napping and hacked into my laptop—"

"You didn't tell me this," my father said.

"—they sprayed Diet Coke all over my room and into my laptop and now my girlfriend hates me and Lena wouldn't give me the AP English homework until I went to Tom's party, and I am really, really tired, I have no idea what day it is, and honestly

I know Lucien Moriarty is behind all of this, it's all his fault."

The dean and the detective and the headmistress all peered at me.

"You're saying that a man named Moriarty ate your homework," the dean said. "So to speak."

Detective Shepard cleared his throat. "It isn't totally impossible."

"And then you attended an illicit party, on a school night, at which a girl is claiming you stole a thousand dollars of her money," the headmistress said. "I should remind you that that's the reason why we're here. I don't usually call emergency midnight meetings about space elevators."

"It isn't totally impossible." Shepard was in apparent psychic pain from having to say the words again.

"The space elevator?" my father asked.

"That it was a Moriarty."

"See!" I pointed at Shepard. "You were there, last year. You remember."

"Can someone please just bring in Charlotte Holmes?" he asked. "Where is she, anyway? Usually if something blows up or someone's hurt, the two of you are lurking together around the corner, talking about your feelings."

The dean of students' phone rang. "Rang" was a generous word; it was sort of a quacking sound. "That's my babysitter," she muttered. "How long will this take?"

"Miss Holmes didn't come back to school this year," the headmistress said shortly. "This is about Mr. Watson alone."

Her assistant knocked on the half-open door. "Ms.

Williamson? The museum curator is on the phone for you? And also there's a student here named Lena Gupta—"

"Yes," she sighed. "Of course there is. Show her in."

Lena swept in in her furry coat. She unwound her scarf as she spoke, around and around and around. "Anna is fine. You can call to check if you don't believe me. She says she bought the pills from Beckett Lexington in the cafeteria, and that he gave her a sampler, and that he said he'd see her in the access tunnels tonight to deliver the rest, so that's what the money was for." She frowned. "Anyway I had the cops call an ambulance once we got outside. I was really worried about her. Can I have a cup of that coffee?"

The room exploded.

"This is about drugs?" the dean asked, turning to Ms. Williamson. "Drugs? I thought this was about money—"

"Are you also on the E?" My father was studying my face.

Exhausted, the headmistress put up her hands. "Everyone, please. Lena. Are you aware that the issue here isn't what substances your friend was abusing, but that she had money stolen from her?"

Lena was a genius. An absolute genius. By the time this giant mess she was creating was cleared up, the money would be either confirmed missing or nonexistent, the freshman girl would get help for her drug issue or, at the very least, a stern talking-to—and in the meantime, while the police went after yet another Sherringford dealer, we might have a chance to investigate the situation ourselves.

Beginning with who Anna was working for.

Lena frowned. "You'll really have to check with her about that? I don't know. Mostly she was talking about E. Or MDMA? I don't really know the difference." She paused. "Maybe she did both? Jamie, you'd take a drug test, right? Neither of us took anything."

I hadn't done E, or anything, really, for that matter, except for the occasional drink when I was in Europe, where it was legal. Even if I'd felt some draw toward pills or pot, my personal history with the police was a long and storied one, and I hadn't really ever felt like adding another chapter to it.

"I'll totally take a drug test," I offered. That one, at least, I could pass.

My father's phone chirped with a text. He ignored it.

"Who was at the party?" the detective asked me, pulling out a notepad. "I need a complete list of names."

"The curator still wants to talk to you," the headmistress's assistant said. "He's on his way."

With a sigh she capitulated, stepping out to take the call.

"The party," the dean said. "Lena. Who was there?"

"Oh." Lena looked genuinely surprised at the question. "I'm totally not going to tell you."

"You're not."

"Social suicide," Lena said. My father passed her a cup of coffee. "I just ratted out Anna, and I can, like, feel my stock plummeting. Plus it's my senior spring. Not worth it. Do you have any milk?"

There was a long silence. The headmistress came back in, frowning. "Why aren't you taking Lena's statement?" she asked Shepard, who'd stopped writing.

"I can't interview her without a parent present," Shepard said. "Remember? It's *your* policy."

"Everyone is getting snippy, don't you think?" my father whispered to me. "Caffeine jitters, perhaps?"

"We might have to suspend you if you don't," the dean of students said to Lena. "Tell us who was at the party. Not the detective—"

"Shepard can interview Jamie, *his* dad's here," Lena said. "Do you all have any sugar?"

My father passed her the sugar. His phone chirped again. He ignored it.

"Aren't you going to answer that?" the dean asked.

"Everyone, please," the headmistress said. "Again, for the cheap seats—Jamie, who was at the party?"

"I can't tell you," I said. If I went to burn this building down with all of us inside, I didn't think anyone would stop me. We were all already in hell, anyway. "Social suicide."

"Lena—"

"My dad was talking about donating a new dorm," she said, idly. "I know you all like the three he's donated already."

"This isn't about the party!" I said. "This is about Lucien Moriarty! Look, I'm doing it right this time. I'm telling you about it. You are *literally* the authorities. Can we just actually get ahead of this shitshow, for once?"

"All of you. Please." Ms. Williamson crossed her arms over

her blazer. "I am very, very tired. Jamie, I have a curator coming in with a delivery that is about to make your life a lot more complicated—"

"Is that possible, though? For it to be more complicated?"

"—and I suggest you stop telling tales about some Mori-whatever scapegoat and actually cooperate."

"Ma'am?" Harry said, sticking his head in. "The curator's here, with his assistants."

"It is *midnight*," the dean said loudly. Her phone was quacking again. "Midnight. I am a single mother. I have four children, and my neighbor is watching them. My neighbor, who I woke from an actual dead sleep. How many more people are we going to pull from their beds because the students are cavorting in the access tunnels again? How is this in the least surprising? Which janitor did you pay for the key code this time, Lena?"

Lena opened her mouth like she was going to answer and then thought better of it.

"We all have children," Shepard said grimly. "We all have responsibilities. A girl's been stolen from—"

The dean stepped between him and the headmistress, physically cutting him off. "Really, what is the point, Headmistress. So this boy is having a bit of a nervous breakdown in his senior spring. Stop the presses! It doesn't make him a thief, or a—a *druggist*—"

"Druggie?" my father supplied. "I think 'druggist' is actually the word for pharmacist. Or perhaps you meant dealer?" He stopped short. I had clamped my fingers around his arm.

"Dealer," the dean said. "Yes. Fine. Can we please go home."

"One moment. Send Bill in, please," the headmistress said to Harry-the-assistant, who was still helpfully holding the door open.

Bill the curator turned out to be a harried-looking man with white hair and a pair of assistants who looked like Harry's fraternal twins. The two of them were dragging along giant framed portraits with such carelessness that I was shocked; one smacked his against the doorframe, swore, and kept on going.

The headmistress, to her credit, didn't look surprised. "I assume these are the portraits we had commissioned for the Sherringford centennial? And that something awful has rendered them un-showable, since you're treating Headmaster Emeritus Blakely's face like that?"

The blond assistant blinked rapidly. He had the painting turned in to face him so that Headmaster Emeritus Blakely's face was resting against his crotch. "I'd left my glasses—I'd been wearing my contacts to work, but I had my glasses back at the museum and it was late, and I needed them because of the eye strain, and I went back and someone had *defaced* these."

Bill raised a bushy eyebrow. "A bit confused, but that's the long and short of it. These were delivered this afternoon from New York. I'd expected professional art handlers, but they had come in a truck, in a stack. I hadn't unwrapped them yet. My assistant here came in tonight to find the wrappings every-where, like some art raccoons or something had gotten in, and the portraits looking like *this*. I brought the most, er, eloquent ones along here to show you. Didn't figure we'd have to handle them gently anymore."

The other assistant turned his portrait around. It was Headmistress Joanne Williamson, cut large and magisterial, beautiful shadows on her face and neck, and in her arms a bound copy of the Sherringford honor code. It had a certain mood to it—windswept, romantic, a bit melancholy. It was a terrific portrait. It looked, in fact, just like the Langenberg forgeries we were hunting down in Berlin.

Except that someone had scratched out her eyes and written in hot-pink spray paint WATSON WUZ HERE.

"I have to go to the bathroom," Lena said, abruptly, and left.

"Seriously?" The words flew out of me. "Are you serious? Are you actually, totally serious?"

My father looked faintly worried. "Jamie," he said.

"'Wuz.' They spelled it 'wuz.' 'Wuz'! I'm in AP English! I read a lot! I read *books*. Big fucking books! I read Tolstoy, and Faulkner, and—'wuz'?"

Detective Shepard bit his lip. "You haven't been anywhere near the museum?" he asked, busying himself with his notebook. "Recently?"

"I didn't even know we had a museum!" I was sounding sort of shrill. "Why on earth do we have a museum?"

Bill the curator looked nonplussed. "We have a rotating historical exhibit, normally. This being the centennial—"

"Right," I said. I'd had it. I was in some kind of farce. Any moment now, I'd be handed a rubber chicken and a knife and told to dance. "Well, I'm sure if you go back to my room right now, you'll find that someone has left fifty-three cans of hot pink spray paint on my floor and, like, a grammar book open to 'to be' conjugations. I don't care. I didn't do it! I didn't do any of it, but that obviously doesn't matter, because I'm being framed, and pink spray paint? Hot pink? Are you kidding me—"

Harry stuck his head back in. "Ms. Williamson? There's a call for you. From a place called Just So Occasions." He adjusted his glasses. "Do they know how late it is?"

"We hired our artist through them," Bill said. "I'd gone to them for some framing work and mentioned the project, and they'd recommended Mr. Jones's portraiture skills to us. Very reasonable rates."

"Put them through," the headmistress said, rounding the desk to her phone. "Hello? Yes. Yes, this is highly irregular. Midnight? Oh—oh. I see." She frowned and scratched something down. "Yes. Yes. Well, thank you. I do appreciate it."

"Well?" the dean asked, after she hung up.

The headmistress sighed. "Apparently Just So has caught their clerk vandalizing outgoing deliveries, and wanted to warn us. Former clerk, I should say; apparently this vandalism was in retaliation for his termination. His name was Frank Watson. He defaced their store, as well. This sounds like a case of mistaken identity on our parts."

The detective gave me a hard look. I smiled at him as blandly as I could, but my pulse had picked up the second Ms. Williamson had answered the phone.

"The owner had discovered it and thought to leave us a message, in case he'd done the same to our delivery." The headmistress sat down heavily in her chair. "I think she was surprised to actually reach someone, this late. Gentlemen, ladies, I am so very tired. Mr. Watson, why don't you take five days to get yourself and your . . . affairs straightened out?"

"Is that it?" I asked.

"Frank Watson." The headmistress stared at me. "*Frank* Watson. It . . . well. I suppose it adds up. I'm sorry to drag you into this."

"So I'm not suspended, then?"

She sighed. "I don't know yet. We'll see what the police say in the next few days about this supposed theft. And about these drugs, apparently. Take five days off campus. Stay with your father. If your name is cleared, we'll call it a leave of absence, for health reasons. You're clearly not doing well—it's hardly a stretch. And if you *are* found culpable . . . then yes, it'll be a suspension, and we'll have to notify those colleges you've applied to of this new development."

Five days.

It was a challenge. And I was already making my plan.

I'd speak to Anna. Bargain with her. Get her to talk. I'd corner Kittredge and Randall, find out if either of them were holding a grudge, if someone on my hall had been hurting for money or hanging around Mrs. Dunham's desk too often, by the locked drawer where she kept the master keys. Mrs. Dunham could tell me who'd she seen come in and out of the dorm, midday, faculty or students or maintenance staff. Elizabeth could tell me if she saw anyone fleeing the scene once she'd gotten topside at Carter Hall.

And Lena could give me the invitation list to the party, as soon as she'd finished pretending to be the clerk from Just So Occasions on her phone in the bathroom.

"It's suitable," the dean said, already halfway out the door. "I'm done here. Headmistress, until tomorrow."

"Yes, goodnight, and my apologies. Bill, why don't you . . . honestly, I don't know what to do with those paintings. I think they look sort of avant-garde, don't they? Keep them. Maybe the performing arts elective will want to shoot them out of cannons or something. Detective, I imagine we can pick this up tomorrow? And Jamie—"

I was still reeling from all of it—the party, the emails, the exploded soda can, the brocade of the sofa scratching against the back of my neck, the defaced paintings, the parade of friends calling me out, the way Shepard was x-raying me with his eyes. There was so much to dread, and God knows I'd been a master of it these twelve months. I'd tangled myself so much up in the what-went-wrong to forget why I'd gotten involved with Holmes in the first place. There was danger here, loads of it, and my future at stake.

There was a case to be solved.

God help me, I was excited.

"Moriarty?" the headmistress was saying. "Do I know that name from somewhere?"

Just then, Lena slipped back in the door, face flushed and nakedly triumphant. "What did I miss? Anything good?"

"Miss Gupta," Shepard said. "Do you mind if I use your phone?"

twelve
charlotte

WHEN I WAS FOURTEEN I DECIDED I WAS DONE. FUCK IT. My mother was ineffectual, my father pathetic. I was the idiot child who thought I could mold myself into their image, that it was a worthwhile endeavor.

I had taken them sporadically at first. The pills. When all the white crushing nothing got to be too much. When a new book or a game of chess with my brother couldn't take me from myself. I had a sort of dread all the time, a feeling that an ax was going to fall, and if I could hide myself behind a buffer, why wouldn't I do that? I halved them. To be safe, I told myself, but I knew really it was to make them last, and when my mother slipped at work and fractured her leg, I knew they'd send her home with more, and it was lifting those from her bathroom cabinet that finally got me caught.

"Caught" is a prosaic way of saying it. Really I was sent to rehab. *The nuclear option,* my father had said, the man who'd taught me to spot a lie and clean a gun and make myself into another person because I myself was never quite right, would never be. Better then to be another girl. He always was so disappointed that I was still his daughter underneath the disguise.

At Paragon Girls San Marcos I learned how to play five-card stud underneath the bolted-in television playing *Days of Our Lives.* I developed an interest in *Days of Our Lives.* At night, discussing *Days of Our Lives* with my current roommate, Macy, we taught ourselves how to fill a syringe and then how to flick it to expel the excess air. The syringes themselves were from the married orderly who was sleeping with the team's lead psychologist (unbuttoned fly, ten minutes late from lunch; I cheerfully blackmailed him for months); the contents were from my former roommate, Jessa (a hole cut into the heel of her boot, a trick I soon adopted myself) who visited us every Sunday when not filming the detergent commercials that were her bread and butter. This arrangement lasted for four rather transcendent weeks. They weren't *friends*—to make friends, one had to share oneself and one's past, and I would do neither. Conspirators worked with you in the moment. We were conspirators, and good ones.

Then Macy ratted us out and was rewarded with a single room. Jessa was readmitted. I was summarily thrown out, and I took my habits with me.

I thought, like a child, that I'd be allowed to go home.

At This Generation Now! Petaluma, I tried. I did. I did everything to keep myself off it, the thing that crept under my skin like a pulse. Wanting, wanting, wanting. I was never anything if not in control of myself and now I was a current for something else's electricity. I took up smoking; it was, as they said, an acceptable alternative. I was forced into yoga classes, which made me both limber and furious. I cried for the therapists who wanted me to cry. I wanted so badly to escape into myself, felt it like an itching in my gums, in my skin, a real burning fire in my blood that was not in the least metaphorical and instead of crawling under my bed to die I lined the girls up from my hall and told them each their shoe size just by looking at their feet. I told them what sort of pets they had at home. I looked at their palms like a fortune-teller and told them if they'd ever had a job. None of us had, never, in our lives. Modeling didn't count.

I did it, all that they asked.

But my parents never came to visit. My uncle never called. My friends rotated in and out, and it wasn't friendship, it wasn't even conspiracy, it was them looking for an ear and I was the silent sort who would listen. The Funfetti cake they'd eat when they got out, the radio station they'd play on the way to the beach, the prom, the ex-girlfriend, the ex-boyfriend, the relentless pushing toward a future that they could see and I couldn't. What future? If I "got better," where would I go? What did my next year look like?

My resolve faded. I am, of course, human. I couldn't find a reason to change without any conceivable reward, and anyway, the teachers in rehab were wretched. I didn't need to relearn the periodic table. I had mental energy to spare. I put it to use. Taught the other girls how to palm their pills, how to cut holes into their mattresses. Did it in plain sight. I wanted to feel bigger, louder, stronger, so I took stimulants. Took cocaine. It was the easiest thing to find. It was the most obvious drug I could do. I had a mission: at Petaluma, as with most places, it was far easier to be dismissed as a destructive influence than to ever "graduate."

So I was dismissed. I went back to Britain for my mother to evaluate my progress; as with all things, I'd been given an opportunity to go home right after I'd stopped wanting to. They didn't send me away this time. At home I had my lab. At home I had my violin. I had Wi-Fi and a driver and silence, so much silence, and no one to speak to and no lessons, no school. Demarchelier had gone off to work at a lab in Tunisia. No one thought to replace him. I took an online organic chemistry course. I finished it in three weeks, studying sixteen hours a day, and then when I finished I had four college credits and still the itching in my veins. I took a week to paint my walls black. I repainted them navy. Black again. Bone white. I ran endless miles on my mother's sad little treadmill, and there were good things, too, there were the plants I kept, there were the uninterrupted hours with my violin, and the plants again, the lab table, the sifting and mixing, the motions of my hands. Doing my work reminded me of my body. It gave me a modicum of control. Then I'd look down and remember my skin, the *fact* of it, and the burning would begin again.

I woke up one morning to find I was content. I would feel this forever, I told myself, stretching my arms above me in bed. I could be alone. I could stop being a creature made of want.

The next day, I began feeling the itching inside of my mouth.

In short order I had a supplier in Eastbourne. It was easier than breathing.

I had my tells. Watson could never see them, though he looked for them every day. Maybe they were only there when I was using. Maybe without the drugs I was a blank. My mother always knew when I was back on; she raised the alarm straightaway. She was "done," she said, watching the house-keeper empty my drawers; she would never touch my things herself. My father, of course, wasn't there. He was consulting at Whitehall, now, in London; one of his contacts from Milo's school had finally wrangled him a position. When he'd been caught out at MI5 double-dealing information, his reputation had suffered, and without his good name he had had no work. My father had steadfastly refused to take any job that didn't make him the lion at the top of the food chain. The charismatic megafauna. He had chosen not to work, for years, rather than feel that lack of power. We had suffered for it.

And now he had wriggled his way back in. He was being groomed for office. It would be the first thing written down if he were vetted: *junkie daughter a liability.*

I would get help. Or, at least, the appearance of help.

I was sent to the cheaper places, the stranger ones, the ones that threw all of us addicts in together indiscriminately.

The one in Brighton—I couldn't think in all that white. Girls in sweats with dirty hair, painted nails, and none of us allowed sharps so our leg hair grew long. There was nothing to do so I taught myself German. All day and night I spoke it in my head: *nichts, danke, nichts, danke, nichts, danke.* I told myself I'd go to see my brother and I would know the language. I graduated. I went, and he looked at me like I was an object to wrap in glass. Went back. I had my schoolgirl French; now I was fluent. It was easier to learn since I still had my Latin. Learned euchre, whist, cribbage, Texas hold 'em, played cards all day at a table full of girls trying not to *want*.

I wanted. I couldn't stop. I took it and buried it in the ground beneath me and when I couldn't I found another way. I would try anything so I didn't feel like I was wrong. I grew like a plant would in the dark, twisting in on itself in search of any bit of light.

I kept my own company. That was a polite way of saying that I was my only friend and if I wanted to be alone I'd have to get rid of myself.

I didn't.

The money ran out, or their patience did, and my parents finally pulled me home to stay. There was about to be a scandal. They were marshaling their forces. They'd hired August Moriarty, you see.

I SPENT THAT EVENING IN A LUXURY HOTEL IN MIDTOWN Manhattan taking money from dilettantes.

The girls I was playing poker with tonight, Jessa Genovese

and Natalie Stevens and Penny Cole, were actresses. They were also models, and hawkers of diet tea on social media, and girls who had very expensive athleisure wear gifted to them by brands. As Watson would say, they had a hustle. I could respect that. For some, the most thrilling chase had a bag of gold at the end, not a criminal.

If I sound disdainful, it was because I was jealous of them.

There was the matter of the acting. Any good detective worth her salt knows that to winnow information out of someone, you need to play a part. The all-consuming roles I'd been playing, like Rose, the fashion vlogger, were the extreme version of this; as I didn't have a badge and so couldn't compel answers, I had to resort to more underhanded ways of learning information. But even when being "themselves," a good police detective needed to know when to intimidate, when to cajole, when to make promises, when to lie.

I'm also sure that if you asked those police detectives late at night, when they were wistful and a little bit drunk, if they thought they'd do a bang-up job at some Shakespeare given the chance, the majority of them would say yes. (I'd often thought I'd make a good Cordelia. But I digress.)

The other girls at poker night were doing something I'd always longed to do. They could play poker passably well. They were very beautiful and rich and no one wanted to kill them, at least not that I knew of, and so yes, I was a little jealous.

I was there because I needed the money.

Jessa Genovese was hosting us in the junior suite she'd been living in while filming *The Hollows*, her new art-house horror movie. She'd moved up from the detergent commercials she'd been doing when I first met her, back when she was my roommate at Paragon Girls San Marcos. Jessa had been three years older than me, which I'd known from the orderlies letting her smoke, and she was an actress, which I'd known because, when she talked, she talked quite loudly and with her hands, projecting her voice, watching her plosives, scanning to see who was looking and changing her presentation accordingly, and she was Italian, yes, which would account for some of the volume and vivacity—I quite liked Italians, actually—but did not account for the way Jessa jumped at any small noise when she thought she was alone. She jumped also when she was reading and one surprised her, and as she was reading constantly, endless romance novels set in Scotland, she was constantly spooked. One might assume she had a quiet home growing up and was used to silence. But no—she smothered her reaction, kept it to a jerk of the lips, a stuttered hand on the bed.

As though she was habitually afraid of someone creeping up on her, and whatever they'd do to her then. As though she'd had to hide that fear in the past.

One night, stoned in our room, I'd told Jessa the full extent of what I'd learned just by looking at her. She cried. She told me some things about her mother. And then she began to sketch out a plan for how my abilities would keep me in cash and her from ever having to go back home.

Hence, the poker.

In New York or London, whenever Jessa and I overlapped,

we would meet for a game. She would bring along some friends; different ones every time. I would win their money, slowly, and then very, very quickly. And Jessa would make sure they were having enough fun that they didn't really care.

Then, after they left, I would tell Jessa every last scrap of information I'd gleaned about them that night, for her to do with what she wished.

Six months ago I had had quite a bit of fun pulling this scheme in London. Tonight . . . it made me feel a bit ill. But I was broke, and Watson was in danger, and there was currently two thousand seven hundred dollars on the table, and Penny Cole and Natalie Stevens, the two girls tonight, could leave whenever they wanted to.

And they didn't want to. Jessa was seeing to that. She'd ordered champagne and chicken fingers and fries and foie gras, and she was playing the kind of cool-toned, echoing hip-hop that made one feel sort of sexy and important, and she was telling endless stories about bad behavior by musicians I hadn't heard of but that made Natalie and Penny howl.

"Then he zipped up. And by zipped up, I mean the back of his unicorn costume. It was incredible." I didn't really understand this story, but I could tell Jessa was telling it well.

"And was that how you guys met?" Natalie was giggling. "At a show like that?"

"No, Charlotte and I go way back," Jessa said. "Rehab."

The girls shot each other a look. Penny had her own Disney channel sitcom. Natalie was a Lifetime movie veteran turned Christian recording artist. If Jessa and I were drug addicts and this night of ours went public, their public image would suffer.

"Eating disorder," I said, to make myself seem like a safer prospect. It wasn't exactly a lie. Still, I hated the implication that that was intrinsically "better" than the addiction, or "less my fault." "I don't really want to talk about it. I'm doing better now."

Penny relaxed completely. "Oh, you guys," she said, and it was genuine. "I'm so sorry." But Natalie looked more troubled, a sort of troubled I was familiar with, and that put together with the state of her right index finger gave me more information for the file I was building on her in my head.

My phone chirped. I looked at it under the table; it was from my source at Sherringford. *Things are getting worse for him,* it read. *How soon can you come to Connecticut?*

I realized, dispassionately, that I would rather be nearly anywhere else. Even my old boarding school. But it was the final hand of the night, and I was closing in on my kill.

"The river," Jessa said, while Penny dealt. The game was Texas hold 'em. "And it turns! Final bets, ladies."

Penny raised, but she was bluffing; she was tapping her foot under the table, the way she had the last three times. Natalie had better cards than Jessa did, to be sure—she had a way of too-nonchalantly eating fries when she was sure she was going to win—but I had better cards than Jessa, too, who was big blind. Since she had to put money down, she'd stayed in. (And anyway, she'd split her winnings with me at the end of the night.)

My phone sounded again in my pocket. It would be poor

manners for me to duck out now.

But I looked, despite myself. *Jamie needs you,* it said. *It's only going to get worse.*

I gripped my phone under the table.

I needed to win this round rather desperately.

Natalie studied her cards. "Charlotte Holmes," she mused. "That's so funny. I've been thinking about this all night—you know, I loved the Sherlock Holmes stories when I was a kid."

People liked to add that tag, "when I was a kid," as though there was something childish about them. "That's great," I said, because while I didn't particularly want to hand her secrets over to Jessa, I also didn't care about her, or what she had or hadn't read. I only wanted her to bet, so I could leave and contact my source in private.

I tried not to think about the implications of that last text. Watson, dead. On his dorm room floor. Watson dead, shot in the snow, like—

"You know, I met a Moriarty recently."

My pulse quickened. No one noticed, of course, except for me, as I have a very good poker face. "It's a common Irish last name," I told Natalie. "You meet a lot of them."

"No," she said, and she tapped her cards against the table. "Like, a real, storybook Moriarty. I go to the Virtuoso School—you know, for working young actors and singers or whatever—and he was getting a tour. They had him sit in on my songwriting class. I guess he'd invested some money in the program."

Lucien Moriarty's consulting firm's client list. The new

additions: a large posh hospital in D.C. A wilderness rehabilitation facility for teenagers in Connecticut. And a Manhattan
prep school for the arts.

"You gotta bet, lady," Jessa said, sensing the turn in the
conversation. "Then we can order up more champagne. Maybe
I can call DJ Pocketwatch, see if she wants to come over."

My phone chirped again.

"Did you ask him if he'd committed any crimes recently?"
I asked lightly, but with just enough edge to let Natalie know
I was bothered. It was a tone that drew people in, made them
want to know the story behind your upset. It rarely failed.

It didn't now. She leaned in, fascinated. "Whoa, do you
guys still have run-ins?"

I shrugged. "Of a sort. What was he like?"

"Not very interesting. He had on a slouchy hat, like he
thought he was cool. Big glasses. He liked the song I played."

"Are there a lot of people in your songwriting class?" I
asked. "I mean, anyone I've heard of?"

Natalie snuck a peek at her cards. "Not unless you follow folk-rock? I mean, Annie Henry's a big-deal fiddler. Penn
Olsen and Maggie Hartwell have been playing together for a
while—"

"Come on, guys," Penny said. The music had stopped, and
she was staring at all of her money piled up in the middle of
the table. "Can we, like, get this over with?"

I pulled my chips toward me, and I found I didn't care
about my winnings.

Maggie Hartwell.

Michael Hartwell was one of Lucien's fake identities.

My phone chirped. *You know you can stop this before it happens,* it read, and just like that I was elsewhere, gone. August's eyes taking me apart on the plane back to England. August ducking his head into my room in Greystone, my violin in his hand—*Will you play for me?* August in the snow.

Things I could have stopped before they happened. I could get on the train. Tonight. I could be at Penn Station in an hour. I—

You need to feel *it,* DI Green had said. *Or else, every now and then, it'll happen anyway. And you'll continue to do very stupid things.*

I forced myself to breathe.

Jessa and I had played together enough at this point that she could read me across the table. A distant part of me thought it was a pity she and I weren't bridge partners. "Penn Olsen and Maggie Hartwell?" she asked, picking up my slack. "Are they on YouTube?"

Natalie laughed. "I guess. They're not big or anything. They do covers, mostly. Maggie's a sweetie, but Penn has a really big head."

Breathe. I was breathing. "Huh," I said, and it didn't sound strained.

"She has nothing on you, girl," Jessa said to Natalie. "Have you *heard* Natalie's new single, Penny? It's so effing good."

"It is so. Good." Penny kissed Natalie's head. "You need to talk to the producers of my show. Maybe we can write you into an episode? I think we're doing a musical one soon!"

They were looking at each other, so they didn't see the flash of jealousy in Jessa's eyes.

We sorted the money quickly, changing out the chips for cash. The champagne had run out. "God, I'm tired, and now I'm super broke," Penny said, packing up her bag, "and I have call at seven tomorrow morning. We're shooting a pool scene first thing. Maybe I shouldn't have eaten those chicken tenders, oof. Love you, love you"— she kissed her hands and blew at us—"but let's not do this again till I get paid, okay?"

Girls could be so profligate with their love, as though by spreading it wide, they would induce the world to love them back. As though the world wasn't going to take that love and beat them with it. Still, I blew a kiss at Penny. I waved goodbye to Natalie. I checked my winnings carefully—nearly three thousand dollars, I had taken almost the whole pot—and then faced Jessa across her notebook.

In that moment, I worried that I would open my mouth, that it would all come pouring out. How horribly I had behaved, and for how long. How much damage I had done. As though I would confess to the first person who asked.

Jessa saved me from myself.

"That was useful for you." When alone with me, her way of speaking had begun to mirror my own. She was clipped, precise, hoarser. It was clear that she was taking a new acting class, and that I was the current object of her study.

At that moment, I couldn't imagine why anyone would want to pretend to be me.

Imagine your father is sitting across that table, I told myself.

Be bloodless, and just like that I was again. "The information about the Virtuoso School? Yes, it was useful to me."

"Did you learn anything about them? Penny and Natalie?"

In fact, I had learned quite a bit. I opened my mouth, then hesitated. "Is it too much for me to ask how you plan to use this information?"

"I imagine the way you use money. As currency." She waited for effect, then blinked her blue eyes rapidly. I wondered if I did that too before launching into an explanation. "These girls are my competition. A rumor can be useful. Knowing their flaws, their foibles. I hoard the best ones, though, and if I'm short on money, I sell those secrets to TMZ."

We regarded each other. To be honest, her imitation of me was unsettling enough that I was having trouble thinking.

Was this what I seemed like to strangers?

I put that idea on to simmer while I told Jessa what I'd learned. That Natalie believed in God and prayed silently when she felt she was losing at cards; her faith was personal enough that she kept a small cross necklace not around her neck but in her pocket, where her hand returned to it like a worry stone. Penny had an older sister she worshipped. It was clear that the boots she was wearing had a previous owner, and they were (1) half a size too big; (2) made too recently to be vintage; (3) five years out of fashion. The sister had worn the boots for something practical, perhaps horseback riding (the sole was worn in the place where something like a stirrup would go) but Penny wore them for love. Perhaps the sister was dead. I couldn't tell from the data at hand.

"That's it?" Jessa said, when I'd finished. She was frustrated enough to revert back to being herself, much to my mixed disappointment and relief. "No habits, or addictions, or exes, or . . . ?"

Natalie was bulimic. Penny had a girlfriend back home she wanted no one to know about. Natalie, at some point in her life, had lost over a hundred pounds, and quickly; she had stretch marks, slight ones, when her crop top rode up over her pants. Penny wanted to quit the business after her contract was up, perhaps (this was a surmise) to spend more time with her beloved sister. (Perhaps the sister was not dead, but dying? I needed more time to observe her.) Neither of them ever wanted to play poker with us ever again.

Jessa made her own money now, through royalties and residuals. She was not "short on cash" in any meaningful way, despite what her selling secrets to tabloids would suggest. At the very least she didn't need me to ruin two girls' lives to keep herself away from her mother and her own ruined past.

"No," I said to Jessa's disgruntled face, "that's everything," and I knew I would never play poker with her again either.

How much damage I had done. How much damage I would continue to do.

On the street, I checked my phone again. My Sherringford source had written me one last message. *It's on your head,* it said. As though that was a new thing.

My heart rate had slowed. I wouldn't go to Penn Station tonight. I wouldn't head into Sherringford, guns blazing, on some supposition. I would go home and force myself to "feel things" about my past for thirty minutes, on a timer, and I would continue with my plan, as it was the best way to keep Jamie Watson safe.

Safer than August had ever been.

Safe from me.

I lit a cigarette, the first I'd allowed myself in weeks. I had money. I had eaten food I hadn't had to pay for. It was late, and I was actually tired, and in the morning, I had an interview with Starway Airlines. I had quite a bit of prep to do.

thirteen

jamie

DETECTIVE SHEPARD HAD GONE THROUGH LENA'S PHONE while she stood there, arms crossed, rolling her eyes. "I thought you actually, like, wanted to make a call."

He scrolled again through her texts, her missed and received call log, her contacts, and then he tossed her mobile back. Because she was Lena, she caught it neatly with one hand. "Just was a little too good to be true," he said. "You disappeared. Then immediately, Ms. Williamson got that phone call from the gallery with a confession."

"Serendipity," she said, and wound up her scarf. "It's an SAT word. Look, since it's a school night and everything, I should go home. Jamie, text me or something tomorrow, okay?" She waved good-bye and left.

Everyone else had left too. My father was warming up the car in the parking lot. The detective zipped up his parka, looking out over the snowy quad. "I'm not going to say it's good to see you again," he said.

I shivered. "I'm sorry," I said. "I don't really want to be in this mess either. I am happy, though, that you're working the case." I meant it. I had always liked Detective Shepard; he was smart, and determined, and flexible enough to work with me and Holmes. I just wished I wasn't always the person he was investigating.

He stuffed his hands in his pockets. "You've made some real enemies, kid," he said. "Or she has. Charlotte. I don't know. I hope it's all been worth it. I'll call you in the morning. Don't leave town."

I told him I wouldn't, then got in my father's car.

You didn't make that call? I asked Lena.

She wrote back instantly. *Told you I was useful. You don't need to be a dealer to keep a burner phone in your bag. He didn't ask me for that one haha night Jamie xoxo.*

I laughed to myself. It was late, late enough that we were the only car on the road back to his house out in the country. It had been where I'd grown up, out here, playing tag in the yard with my father, eating dinner outside together in the summer, my sister and I locking each other in the closet below the stairs. My father lived there now with my stepmother, Abigail, and my half brothers, Malcolm and Robbie. They'd set aside a room for me, what had been the stuffy old guest room before. I hadn't decorated it, and I didn't sleep there much, but it was good to know it was there anyway. I kept enough clothes there, a razor, some shoes. I wouldn't have to go back to the dorm for my things.

When we walked in the door, Abigail was waiting up for us in the living room. She'd had a fire going, but it had faded down to embers.

"Jamie," she said, and pulled me into a tight hug. "You're okay. Thank God. And *you*—"

My father said, "Hello to you too."

"Will you tell me next time? Instead of leaving me a note saying, *J in trouble, be home late,* and then not answering any of my texts?"

"I'm sorry, things moved very fast." There wasn't a lot of apology in his apology. "Can we talk about this tomorrow? I don't want to wake up the kids."

"It's fine, they haven't seen you in days anyway." Abigail tugged on her nightgown. "Sorry, Jamie, I'm exhausted, and this—anyway. Go to bed. We'll figure it out."

"Your mum's coming in," he said to me. "I spoke to her earlier. She changed her tickets, she and Shelby—we'll figure out lodgings. Maybe you on the couch? We can talk more about it tomorrow."

"You talked to Grace tonight and not me?" Abigail said.

I took that as my cue to go upstairs.

They kept on quarreling quietly, the sound creeping up the stairs as I got myself ready for bed. My father wasn't an award-winning parent, to be sure, but I'd thought he'd grown out of some of his shittier habits. No matter how much I'd fantasized as a kid that he would give up Abigail and America and come back to us in London, it wasn't anything I wanted from him now. I'd wondered a little how he was keeping up with his work or the house or his two little kids, what with all the traipsing around with Leander, but my father was an adult, and as far as I knew, adults worked those things out.

I guess my father hadn't.

I fell into an uneasy sleep, and when I woke, it was late morning, the day half-started already. A kettle was whistling downstairs and the door to my room was open. In the kitchen, Abigail was nowhere to be found. Malcolm, my toddler brother, was missing too, and my father, and Robbie, who was school-aged. Was it a school day? I was too tired to remember.

In lieu of any members of my family, Leander was perched at the counter, scrolling through a news site on his tablet. His dress shirt was pressed, and he was freshly shaved. "Good morning, troublemaker," he said.

"Please tell me that's not going to be my nickname." He'd switched off the whistling kettle, but the water was still hot. I made myself a cup of tea. "Though I guess I'm a wanted thief. And possible 'druggist,' if the dean has me pegged right."

"How much of it do you think is Lucien?" Leander asked, setting down the tablet.

"The paintings, for sure. My father filled you in on that?" At his nod, I said, "I thought at first the phone call from the shop was Lucien toying with me. Like, showing how easily he could reach into my life, and how he had the power to fix it, if he were inclined to. But it turned out to be Lena Gupta instead, getting me off the hook."

"I always liked that girl," he said.

"Yeah, Lena's great." I leaned back against the counter. "As for the rest of it—my dad doesn't know this, but the laptop sabotage? Someone emailed Elizabeth, pretending to be me, and asked her to be there for it. And for the party, too."

Leander nodded. "Do you want to walk me through it?"

"All of it?"

"I could help."

"And you won't tell my dad?"

He hesitated. "No. I'll let you do that. Deal?"

"Deal."

He picked up his tablet again. "Let's start with times, if you have them, and places, and where everyone was when it happened." When I finished, he said, "My thoughts: we'll approach the problem from two separate sides. If you feel comfortable asking questions around your school, I'll keep on with my investigation in the city. I have an appointment today I'd like to keep."

"Is my father coming?" I asked.

Leander looked uncomfortable. "He and Abigail are taking a day," he said. "It's important, especially with your family coming in, that the two of them have a moment alone to . . . recalibrate."

"Oh." I studied him for a moment, the man I'd come to think of as my own uncle. He had a careless sort of elegance that he wore like a cloak, and every now and then, if he let you get close enough, you saw how deliberately it had been woven, what he hid beneath it. "Has this happened before?"

Leander hadn't ever been one to mince words with me. "With your mother, quite a few times. Never before with Abigail. If this isn't settled soon, I'll go back to London and try to do my part from there. I . . . might be putting some strain on the situation."

When I called up an image of my father in my head, he was cheerfully rumpled, in his usual corduroy and blazer, and in that imagining, he was never alone. Leander Holmes was there beside him. Not my mother and not Abigail, but his best friend, one I'd only known in person now for a year. But I'd never really considered what a problem that would be for the woman my father was married to. When your life was split that way, how could you ever have everything?

Maybe some of us weren't meant to.

I thought, like a reflex, about Holmes. My Holmes, that night in the hotel in Prague, determined and afraid and her arms around my neck, whispering words I couldn't hear, words she maybe thought I could read from the shape her lips made against my skin, and it wasn't something I ever let myself think about, much less in front of her uncle who was like an actual reader of minds, or after I'd just been thinking about my *father*, and I flushed, and then flushed again when Leander gave me a startled look—God, he was *deducing* things—and then I hurried away as fast as I could to pour myself more hot water.

Leander cleared his throat. "Want a ride up to campus?"

he asked after a moment. His voice was very, very neutral.

"No," I said, fanning the steam away from my face. "Nope. No, I can walk."

It was a very long walk. In the end, Leander insisted, and I was back at Sherringford by noon.

fourteen
charlotte

STARWAY AIRLINES WAS ONE OF THE OLDEST IN THE BUSI-ness. They'd been one of the few not to go bankrupt in the early years of the new century, and they had responded by doubling down on their luxury offerings (leather seats, free checked bags, a steam room in the airport lounge) while the other airlines cut their costs. They specialized in long-haul flights, nonstop to Dubai and Melbourne and Kyoto, trips that took days and were expensive to begin with, and they decked out those planes with beds and masseuses.

Which is to say, one couldn't look cheap for an interview to work as a Starway gate agent, not if one wanted to represent their brand. I slicked my hair back into a high bun and put on false eyelashes. I put on the skirt suit I'd pressed and prepared for the occasion. In short, I looked the part. There was plea-sure in that.

At the airport, I gave my credentials at the Starway infor-mation desk.

"The recruiter will come and walk you there in about fif-teen minutes," the kind-eyed clerk said.

I asked him the exact time, and then where the toilets were, scrubbing out my accent into the Queen's English. For what-ever reason, Americans love the English. The clerk smiled and pointed the way, and now I knew he would remember both me and exactly when we'd met.

I had spent some time with the airport map these last few weeks. Starway had the smallest presence of any airline at this airport; their desk was at the far end of the terminal, and there was no one in line for the kiosks or for an agent, not at 9 a.m. on a Wednesday for an airline that had so few commuter flights. I waited until the only agent on duty stepped off for a break, and then, in my skirt suit and pumps, I stepped behind the counter and up to their monitor.

Thankfully, the agent had left himself signed in. I didn't have to try the clearance code I'd watched an agent enter at Heathrow; it had been the weak point in my plan, and I was relieved to dispense with it.

Once in, I needed a moment to get myself oriented. The screen was black, with scrolling white text, and the only way to navigate was with keyboard shortcuts. It took several false starts before I even got myself into the right system. Above me, cheerful pop music was playing, and I tapped my foot along with it to steady myself.

There. Future reservations.

From the corner of my eye, I saw the desk agent approaching, hands in his pockets, looking out the giant windows at the end of the terminal. And then he focused his gaze on his destination. He saw me at the monitor, and he began to walk faster.

I'd assumed this would happen. I'd styled my clothes as closely as I could to the existing Starway employees so that, from a distance, any employee would have a moment of doubt that would keep them from immediately calling in the police. I knew I had about two minutes.

But I only had one hand to type with now, because with the other, I was pressing the desk phone up to my face and crying.

Reservations. I ran Michael Hartwell, then Peter Morgan-Vilk. Quickly I put the names into the system, and the results began to scroll downward. I'd watched hours of tutorials online, but there were a number of keyboard shortcuts I hadn't quite mastered. When I pressed what I thought was the Page Down button, the screen went blank. I pressed it again, and the screen returned. Quickly with my index finger I punched in the three-key sequence to bring me back several pages, and I put the names back in again with that same finger, the phone against my face, my face itself in tears, my body angled away from the screen to make it seem as though I was a harmless young professional girl who couldn't possibly be hacking into their system.

The agent was talking into his radio. By the door, the

security officer perked up and turned my way.

Moments. I had moments. I needed a flight record, a complete one, and to know the next time Moriarty was arriving. Today was Wednesday. The day that Lucien always flew to New York, from what I'd seen from my weeks at Heathrow in London.

"Hey," the agent said gruffly. "Hey, you! What are you doing?"

I'd found it.

Quickly I hit the Print key. The results tumbled out onto the carpeted floor. The agent was in sight of me now. "Stop! Stop what you're doing!"

I gasped, dropped the phone, and crumpled to the floor.

He rounded the desk to find the screen blank, and me sobbing. "What—who are you? What are you doing? Young lady?"

"I'm having a panic attack," I said, through the tears. "I have a Starway interview today—I couldn't, I—I had to call my doctor. I couldn't breathe. I'm so sorry. I'm so sorry, don't arrest me."

Crouching, he picked the phone up off the floor and put it to his ear. I could hear the cheerful message. *Press eight if you need to make an appointment. Press nine to hear these options again.*

"You don't have a phone?" he said, helping me to my feet.

I smiled at him shakily. "Not one that works in the States," I said, my accent posh and plummy. "I'm just getting myself set up."

The agent's eyes went again to his monitor screen. It was

blank. He relaxed, infinitesimally. Let him think he'd signed himself off.

"This might not be the best job for you," he was saying, steering me back toward the information desk at the center of the terminal. "It gets pretty stressful here."

"Does it? I bet it's awful around the holiday."

It was enough to get him telling a funny story, something about a girl in a reindeer suit, and when the bewildered clerk at the desk confirmed that I was, in fact, there for an interview, that I'd checked in five minutes ago, that he had spoken to me himself, the agent said, "Listen, Charlotte, don't worry about it—but maybe don't take this job," and before either of them had another thought about calling the police, I was outside and in a taxi en route to Manhattan.

The driver raised an eyebrow at me when I fished a sheaf of papers out from under my skirt. I'd barely had the time to stuff them into my tights.

I flipped through them slowly, trying to make some sense of what I was reading. Michael Hartwell wasn't flying to New York. Peter Morgan-Vilk wasn't flying to New York. They weren't flying to Boston or D.C. Nothing confirmed, nothing in the reservation system. I checked it through again to be sure.

That left the last page. The contingency search I had done at the last possible second. We bumped along in traffic, thick now as any London rush hour, and as the driver rode his brakes, I took a deep, steadying breath, then held the last page up to the light.

There.

Lucien Moriarty was flying to America. Tonight. As Tracey Polnitz.

I had waited for this for the last year and still I wasn't ready. I—I couldn't quite breathe. Why couldn't I breathe? I needed to speak to someone, to someone who knew me well, and from before all this, someone I could trust.

Without even really thinking about it, without considering the repercussions, I picked up my mobile and called the only number I had thought to save.

fifteen
jamie

I'D ARRANGED TO MEET ELIZABETH OVER HER LUNCH break; I'd called her, so she knew for sure this time that it was me. The parking lot was near the far end of the quad, at the bottom of a slope, and I could see her walking toward me long before she arrived—the red flag of her blazer under her parka, her legs in tights, the scattering bright of her hair.

She was beautiful, and magnetic, and I was wasting her time.

I knew it especially when she passed me a hot paper cup from the cafeteria. "Cocoa," she said. "I figured you wouldn't want anyone to see you in there, since you're sort-of suspended."

"Thanks," I said, cupping it in my hands. "I don't think

they have a watch out for me, but yeah, I'm trying to lay low."

We looked at each other for a long minute.

"You're not a good boyfriend," she said, like it was simple. Maybe it was. "Someone is playing on that, I think. They want me to be mad at you. I am, but for different reasons."

"I'm sorry," I said.

"I know."

"I thought that I could—I really like you. You're really cool, and really pretty, and—"

"I know," she said, a bit despairingly. "I think I am too."

"And I just have my head somewhere else. I'm graduating, and last year was a mess, and I know I haven't been good to you." I had this urge to reach out to touch her, but I didn't know what that would accomplish. "I don't know if it's because of that, or if I'm just not a good guy."

Elizabeth shifted her weight from foot to foot. "Just because you know something about yourself doesn't mean you should be forgiven for it."

"I'm sorry," I said, again.

It was over, then. It was for the best.

"So stop."

"I'm sorry—what?"

"Stop," she said again, louder. "If you know it, just stop. Stop. You like me. This shouldn't be this . . . hard. I can't believe you're so hung up on someone you never even dated, not really—was she ever your girlfriend? She broke your heart anyway. Maybe that makes it worse. Do I need to break your heart? Is that how I can get in there, under your skin?"

An hour ago, I'd been thinking about Holmes in my bed. Even the memory now made me feel claustrophobic, too hot, and whether it was the way love should feel, I didn't know. "I don't know," I said aloud. "I don't want that to be true."

"I'll help you clear all this up," she said. "This mess."

"What mess? The Moriarty mess? Elizabeth—"

"Stop it with the pity voice." She crossed her arms.

"Why would you put yourself in that kind of danger? What would any of this prove?"

"That I'm a better person than she is?"

I took it like a knife to the gut. No matter how many times I'd thought it to myself, that Holmes was a garbage human, a real piece of work— "Don't say that. It isn't true. This isn't a contest of who's less of a fuck-up. I think I'd lose, if it was."

"Stop," she said, shaking a little with the force of what she was saying. "I'll help you clear this up, because it involves me, and I hear things around here that you don't, and God, Jamie, you need a little help, I think."

"It has to be over, though," I said. "Between us."

"Okay. Fine. So we'll fix this. Then we'll see."

I should have said no. I had Lena's help. I had my father and Leander. I had a five-day maybe-suspension lighting a fire under my ass. But Elizabeth was so adamant, and so cracklingly smart, it felt wrong to refuse her help.

"Where do we start?"

We walked slowly back up the hill toward school. "Anna's in the hospital. Word is that Lena put her there, what with the ratting her out for the MDMA." Elizabeth's mouth twisted.

"No one's really sad about that. Anna's not a prize."

"I don't know her that well."

"She's Sherringford swine," she said with a bitterness I didn't expect. "Lots of money. There are these amazing scholars who teach at this school, people who've written biographies of Elizabeth Bishop, who worked at the White House, who worked at NASA, and Anna doesn't take notes and pays her hallmates to write her essays. Money gets you a lot here. But a thousand dollars is a whole 'nother level."

"Did it exist in the first place? Like, did she bring it to the party?"

Elizabeth gestured with her cup. We were approaching the student union. "Let's go find out."

The union had a restaurant inside, the Bistro, where for ten dollars you could have them make you a sandwich with the same ingredients they had in the cafeteria. Students went in the evening, if they'd had to miss dinner for sports or studying, and the faculty had lunch there if they hadn't packed their own. I hadn't heard of any students going during school hours. It seemed sort of pointless.

But there they were, Anna's friends, in pleated skirts and snow boots, eating their sandwiches next to the fireplace. Three of them had their hair up in high cheerleader ponytails, but the girl at the center had her long red hair loose and wavy. They sat almost as if arranged.

"They've been watching too many CW shows," Elizabeth said, and determinedly started forward.

"Elizabeth," the redhead said, placidly. "Hi. Oh, hi, Jamie."

I didn't know any of their names, but I guess I had just supposedly scammed their friend, so. "Hi," I said.

"Was the money real?" Elizabeth asked.

I blinked. I was used to Holmes maneuvering herself in with a suspect, building trust and planting bombs. She never went for the jugular this soon.

"No," the redhead said, and took another bite.

There was some history between the two of them that I was missing. "I don't remember you at poker night. Were you there?"

The redhead regarded me over her sandwich. "I wasn't invited. *I* don't have an upperclassman boyfriend."

"We don't either," one of the girls said.

"You wish you did," the redhead retorted.

The other girls looked at each other. One shrugged. They went back to their conversation.

"Jamie's not a status symbol," Elizabeth said. "He's—"

"Something you wanted and went out and got. I was there. I was your friend, before you dumped me."

"I'm sorry," I told her, backing away. "I sort of feel like I shouldn't be here—"

"So the money wasn't real," Elizabeth was saying. "Did you put her up to it? Who did? Why was she there?"

One of her friends piped up. "She wanted to be there. We all did. Kittredge was there."

"Kittredge?" I asked.

"Yeah," she said. "He's gorgeous."

The redhead shrugged. "Don't go thinking it's all about

you," she told me. "It's not."

"No," I said, trying not to laugh. They were talking about a guy who had farting contests with his roommate that you could hear all the way out in the hall. "It's all about Kittredge, I guess."

"And the money—"

"Look, honestly? I don't know. You'll have to ask Anna," the redhead said. "She spends a lot with Beckett Lexington and his stash. She spends a lot at Barney's online. Maybe she overspent and was embarrassed. She told Lainey and Aditii and Swetha that she was going to stake them"—the other girls, if their expressions were any indication—"and maybe she didn't realize she was too short on cash to do it. Got to the party, decided to blame you. I don't know. I think there's more to it than that."

"If anyone knows, it's Jason Kittredge," said Aditii. Lainey? "He was on her from the second she showed up. He'll know if she had it to begin with."

"Thanks." Elizabeth lingered there for a beat. "Marta," she said to the redhead. "Your hair looks really good."

"Thanks," Marta said. Her eyes didn't soften. "I like your boots."

"Thanks."

This strange ritual complete, we left.

"What's the story there?" I asked, pushing the union door open.

"There isn't one," Elizabeth said. "They wanted things from me they couldn't have."

I stared at her, washed over with the strangest déjà vu. "What?"

"It's pretty simple. Undying loyalty." She pulled out her phone. "Which means, no fuckboys. And everyone's a fuckboy. Crushes are fine, boyfriends aren't. Dinner with the group every night at seven. Those are the rules."

"Wait. They think I'm a fuckboy?"

"You have a fuckboy haircut," she informed me, rapid-fire texting someone. "And no, I've been dating you for too long for anyone to think that. You were famously in love with a junkie who'd dropped out of school, you'd been framed for murder together and now she was gone, and they thought it was all crushingly romantic. Marta told me you'd break my heart. And we stopped being friends over it."

I didn't know what to say. "Why didn't you tell me?"

Elizabeth put her phone away. "Because I didn't want you to tell me it was true. I have to go to Biology. I'll see you later?" She kissed me on the cheek, and trotted up the hill.

There was so much about this girl I still didn't know.

Three hours to kill until the end of the school day, when I could corner Kittredge in his room. I ducked into the library and hurried quickly up into the stacks, to the PQ–PR section. It was silent—most students didn't have a free period, and almost no one had it after lunch—and smelled overwhelmingly like old leaves. The heater, as usual, was working overtime. I shed my outer layers into a pile and sat down at a carrel.

On the ride back to my father's last night, I'd finally changed my email password. I pulled the account back up to go through the sent messages again. The remarkable thing was that the fake emails sounded so much like me. Whoever had been forging my mail had read through my old messages, listened to the tone, noted the way I'd signed off. The final one "I'd" sent yesterday, to Elizabeth, read:

> E,
> I'm so sorry about before. Maybe it's best if we meet somewhere public, and then we can go talk? Come to Tom's party—I'll be there. J x

It was stupid to be unnerved by it—the template was literally right there, in the hundreds of samples I'd sent just this school year—and still I was. The initials (E, J) were easy enough to copy, and the one-or-two-x sign-off was standard practice for any email you sent in Britain. But the long-short sentence combo, the statement that ended in a question mark, the dash—they were all things I did all the time and hadn't realized until now.

There wasn't any clue there, at least not that I could tell. Nothing to learn except this wasn't a slapdash job. They would have taken at least a few hours to learn how to convincingly sound like me.

It had to be Lucien. Who else could it be? But I'd seen firsthand what you got from forming conclusions before you had the facts. You dragged in Moriartys, Milo Holmeses, you threw your weight around trying to make your guess right. You ended up with a friend shot dead in the snow.

On my phone, a text popped up in my international app. I was grateful for the distraction. *I'll see you soon,* Shelby said. *Checking out that school, then headed to Dad's house. Lots to tell. Hear you're in trouble again. Shock-er.*

I sent her a line of vomit emojis and a *see you soon.*

I still had time to kill, so I did my best to begin a response paper for AP Euro on one of the school computers. It was hard to feel focused. If I was suspended for stealing in the spring of my senior year, it didn't matter what grades I got; I wouldn't be going to college anywhere.

I felt a weird sort of calm about it. Maybe it was fatalism. Maybe it didn't matter if it was. I was good at writing papers—not amazing, but good enough—and we had been reading about the causes of the First World War, and I found myself getting into the rhythm of it, laying down sentences, rearranging them, contradicting myself, and then stopping to figure out what I actually thought.

I was so engrossed that I didn't notice Kittredge was sitting next to me until he leaned in and breathed, hot and disgusting, into my ear, "You were looking for me? Because I have a lot to say to you."

sixteen
charlotte

I HAD MADE THE CALL. I WAS WAITING FOR A RESPONSE. I was receiving three text messages a minute from my Sherringford source, saying *Why aren't you responding? Where are you? Don't you even care?*

I was too anxious to go inside, too anxious to stay put. I paced up and down the steps of the building where I was staying, and I thought, *Lucien could find me here, I'm only one degree removed from DI Green, he knows I work with her, I am an idiot for staying in this flat.* I thought, *There are places in America where no one could find me;* I thought I could change my name and move out to Oklahoma. *I would be safe,* I thought. Safe. Safe, safe, safe. Moriarty had paid for two other plane tickets; I didn't have their names on the reservation, I hadn't known

189

how to look it up. Phillipa, I thought, and perhaps another henchman, another tattooed man to hunt us through the woods like deer.

Why was I feeling all of this now? Was this what happened when you carved a door into the dam—that the water eventually blew it out, came rushing through?

I wasn't safe. I had never wanted so badly to be safe. I had been chasing this man for so long, and now I would give anything to be in Switzerland with my mother, accepting whatever comfort my mother was capable of giving me.

But if Lucien Moriarty didn't already know where I was staying, he would if I kept on causing a scene, in daylight, dressed as myself. I was making a spectacle of myself. Already an elderly woman had stopped to ask if I needed help. Did I need to make a call. I was fine, I assured her. I was just locked out and very badly had to pee.

That excuse had a ninety-eight percent success rate. She nodded, then walked away.

I ran through Latin declensions in my head; I started listing the bones in my legs out loud, first alphabetically and then by size; I named the stars I knew by heart. A long, unrolling scroll of data in my head. Things I knew. Things that could be put into tables, and lists, and studied. Things that you learned that wouldn't change, no matter how the world did.

I'm changing, I thought suddenly. I had wanted to, and so I was. Last year I would never have behaved this way if I knew Lucien Moriarty was coming.

What would I have done?

Smoked, for a long time. Considered Watson's capabilities. Thought about what I could stand to lose. I would have gambled big on a plan to snare Lucien and leave him helpless, using my brother's money and my father's connections, and after I saw him hung I would have washed my hands of it completely. Put him in a black box. Sunk him to the bottom of the sea.

That was, of course, before August's death.

Again I was thinking about it. I never let myself think about it, and now, in the last twenty-four hours, I had to create a litany to keep myself in the present. What safeguards did I have left? I went back through my list. The quadratic equation. Fermi's paradox. Numbers and letters, in concert, balanced. I thought about—

I thought about the day that August Moriarty knocked on my bedroom door the day after my fourteenth birthday.

I was in bed. I was in bed quite a lot, after that stint at rehab. I'd gone back to my old supplier the moment I'd returned home, and then tried, unsuccessfully, to cut myself off. It had been a week. The symptoms were the same as they always were. There was a strange comfort to the nausea, the burning, the accompanying black mood. I knew them like they were old friends.

"Charlotte," he'd said, then knocked again. "Ah. Do you mind . . . coming out? So I can meet you? I realize this is rather awkward."

I was still in bed. I was spending rather a lot of time in bed. "Yes," I told him, and rolled my face back over into the pillow.

"Yes, you do mind? Or yes, this is awkward?"

"I'm—" What was the word I wanted? I had read it in a book once. But I was blurry. The walls were raw. The walls of my head. I was having some trouble with it, the thinking. "I'm indisposed. Come back tomorrow."

A sound, like him putting a palm against the door. Then the door opening.

"Oh," he said. "Do you want some light?" And before I could protest, he'd gone into a flurry of motion—flicked on the lights, pulled open the blinds, retrieved my blanket from the floor, and folded it up at the foot of my bed.

I heard all of this, rather than saw it. I still had my face pressed to the pillow.

"Charlotte." I finally turned to look at him. He had a lock of blond hair that curled up and away from his face, like a decoration. Later I would find it beautiful. "Your parents aren't here?"

"No," I said, then realized that might be a lie. "Maybe. I'm not sure."

"And you're ill?"

That was a simple explanation. I took it. "Yes."

I watched him come to a decision. "If this is to be our first day, then we'll have a first day." He fidgeted for a moment, looking at me (I did look back, though I'm sure I had all the affect and charm of a wall clock), and then looking around the room. Idly, with a finger, he scanned the bookcase that housed my library.

"When I was ill, I used to like to have someone read to me," August said, quietly. Then: "Do you like to be read to?"

"I don't know," I said, because I didn't. What did he have in mind? A calculus textbook? That seemed difficult. "I can try to find—"

"Ah." His finger had stopped. "How about this?" he asked, pulling a volume from the shelf.

"I can't see it, so I can't offer an opinion."

"Hush," he said, but kindly. "I'll just sit in this chair, then, and we can begin here. You'll find it illuminating, I'm sure."

"I'm sure," I said. He was hiding the cover with his hands.

He thumbed it open, flipped to the back of the book. "'It is with a heavy heart,'" he said, "'that I take up my pen to write these the last words in which I shall ever record the singular gifts by which my friend Mr. Sherlock Holmes was distinguished,'" and that was how I came to know August Moriarty: his slow, steady voice reading *The Memoirs of Sherlock Holmes* to me, as though I was his younger sister, or his beloved, or both.

He wouldn't ever do that again.

I realized then I was crying.

That was how Leander found me, on the bottom step of a brownstone, my arms around my knees.

"You came," I said, and then I cried a bit harder.

He got me upstairs and into the apartment. Sat me on the overstuffed sofa, put a blanket around my shoulders, and left me there to cry. Moments later I heard him running water for a bath.

"Up," he said, "come along," and led me to it by the hand, as though I were a child.

"It has bubbles," I said, numbly. "Pink bubbles." They were foaming up out of the water. They smelled like roses.

"It does," he said. "Go sit in that for a while. At least twenty minutes. Understood?"

I nodded.

"Okay then," he said, and pushed me inside and shut the door.

I sat in the bath, as instructed. I pulled the pins out of my hair and laid them out in a row. I took off my makeup with a cloth and put my head under the water for a long, warm moment, and when I surfaced, I realized I hadn't had a bath in ages. I didn't like the waiting of it, the patience needed for the tub to fill.

Leander had gone out. I heard the front door open again now, and his particular footfalls as he returned. He was exaggerating them on purpose so I knew it was him. My breath started coming faster—perhaps Lucien had tracked me here; perhaps Lucien knew Leander and me both well enough to know how Leander walked and—

But then he started singing. He never sang, but he was singing now, some Irish folk song about a man named Danny. It was unmistakably my uncle, sweet and resonant and sad, and I wanted to cry again. *Whatever is making me like this is wretched,* I thought, *and ends now,* and I got up and toweled off my hair and put myself into a robe.

I realized then that I had spent the last hour in emotional turmoil and not once thought about the pills stashed away in my coat.

"You have a terrible singing voice," I told Leander in the kitchen.

On the kitchen island, he had laid out a paper bag of giant pastries, a pair of salads, and a well-polished sawed-off shotgun.

"I can't be completely perfect," he said, and offered me a cronut.

We ate. It would be more honest to say that Leander bolted his food and then watched me eat. I made it through a pastry in my usual way, slow bites and sips of water and tearing the thing into pieces to give my stomach time to settle as I went.

"It's still like that for you?" Leander asked.

"Yes," I said. As a child, mealtimes had been difficult. I didn't like food then. I didn't now. *Verbum sap.* "What is that shotgun for?"

He inched the salad toward me. "One bite for one answer."

"I'm not a toddler. I don't need to be bribed."

"Really." He opened the lid. "It's a salmon salad. From Dean and DeLuca. And if you eat it, I'll get you oysters for dinner."

I smiled a little, despite myself. "Fine. Hand me a fork."

Leander talked at length. He paced as he spoke about the past twelve months, up and down the narrow aisle between the kitchen island and the sink. What he told me about Watson I had largely already known (though I obediently ate a forkful for each fact), but he filled me in on what he'd learned from his research into Peter Morgan-Vilk, after his and James Watson's interview with him in the stairwell.

"Morgan-Vilk's father, the one Lucien left in the lurch during his political campaign, isn't hiding out in Europe with his mistress. Not anymore. Merrick Morgan-Vilk is back in New York." Leander gestured at my salad, and I took a bite. "He's putting together an exploratory team for political office—though which office, or why a British politician is doing so in the States, I don't know. What I do know is that he hates Lucien Moriarty, and he has a fair deal of money and influence, and you owe me at least two bites for that."

I took my time with them, thinking. "Do you think Merrick Morgan-Vilk knows Lucien is working with his son? Peter?"

"Probably not. And Lucien has his son's passport for a reason. Peter Morgan-Vilk might just think he's gotten a good deal—he gets to piss off the father he hates while making a paycheck, and all he has to do is stay in America—but Lucien has to have a plan, and I doubt it has anything to do with foreign travel. If you have someone's passport, you can steal their identity. Take their money. There are even cases of people's houses being stolen."

I laughed. Then I realized he was serious. "I'm sorry?"

"I dealt with a case last year," he said, fishing out another pastry. "It's absurdly simple. The con downloads a transfer of property form, makes copies of the stolen passport and forges the signature, and signs the house over to his actual name. A woman I worked for paid her mortgage for months, not realizing she was lining someone else's pocket. I found the thief in Vancouver, after a long search, and . . . persuaded him to come back to the States with me. I'm not saying this is exactly what

Lucien has planned. But you can do quite a lot with someone else's identity, and I imagine that he plans to."

"And he has Merrick Morgan-Vilk's son involved. Merrick, who has no love for Lucien Moriarty." I thought for a moment. "Do you think we should approach him directly for help? The father?"

Leander laughed, surprised. "Not unless you want to announce our presence with a bullhorn. I'm sure Lucien knows about Morgan-Vilk's current political plans—it isn't public, but it isn't on lockdown, either, and he'll have eyes on the campaign. No, I think we have to convince Morgan-Vilk more indirectly."

"Put that on hold for now," I said. "I had an idea for this afternoon. You know about the Virtuoso School?"

"I do. Spent any time on their website recently?"

"Why would I? I've been reading New York's private school forums."

Leander began to smile. "And?"

"Hartwell," I said. He wasn't listed on the official website, or on any of the provisional pages I could find online. The only connection of his name that I found with the Virtuoso School had been a man named MHartwell43 asking a question about paid vacation leave. He was a new employee, too new to be officially listed, and already he was looking to switch jobs.

But he hadn't yet.

"Hartwell." His mouth quirked up. "Good work."

As we'd been talking, I found myself warming from the inside. Perhaps it was simply the bath, or the food, or the presence of an adult I admired. But there was more than that. I had that feeling of being known, of having all my dark corners illuminated. It wasn't a new feeling. I'd had it in the past, with Leander and Watson and once even with my mother. But it had been a very long time.

"I've been—" I struggled with saying it. "I think I've been impossibly awful to you. I won't be again."

Leander nodded. His eyes were bright.

"Thank you for sharing what you know, and for trusting me. I know I don't deserve it." The words were coming easier now. The dam door blown open.

"Darling girl," my uncle said, a bit hoarsely, "of course you deserve it. How would you like yourself a partner?"

THE VIRTUOSO SCHOOL WAS IN THE MIDDLE OF MANHATtan, on a surprisingly serene street in Chelsea. We weren't far from Peter Morgan-Vilk's apartment, in fact, and I put my umbrella up against the rain, not out of worry for my hair or clothes, but because I wanted a shield ready against recognition if I needed one.

The school itself was quiet, furnished in the spare style my mother had always liked, and yet there was a hominess to it I hadn't expected. Natural light. Wooden rafters. A pair of girls holding hands, running late to class. It made me nostalgic for a school life I'd never had. Somewhere in the background a girl was playing her cello, but I didn't recognize the piece. It might have been of her own devising.

We were shown to the admissions suite, where we were

greeted, to our disappointment, by a girl in a smart dress who had us fill out a dossier. "I thought Hartwell worked Wednesdays," I whispered to my uncle, but he shook his head imperceptibly.

"Don't worry," he said at normal volume. "We'll get you in, you belong here," and the man walking into the suite laughed a bit to himself.

"I admire your confidence," he said.

Leander stuck out his hand. "Walter Simpson."

"Michael Hartwell," he said. "Why don't you come into my office and tell me a bit more about your daughter?"

"My niece," Leander said, with his thousand-watt smile, and this time when he reached out to guide me into the room, my hesitation was all pretend.

"This is such a gorgeous place," I said, sitting down and smoothing out my skirt. "I keep hearing music! It's wonderful."

"I know it's late in the year for a transfer," Leander said.

"Of her *senior* year. Miss Simpson will have already applied to colleges, by now, yes? I don't know how much we can help her." Hartwell flipped through my file again, then shut it. He gave me a sympathetic smile. "May I ask why you're looking to change schools now?"

I stared down at the shiny tops of my Mary Janes. "My tutor died," I said. "Unexpectedly. My parents thought I should come be with my uncle in the States for a change of scenery. And besides, I didn't apply to conservatory yet. I thought I'd perhaps take a gap year."

"Her tutor's loss has been quite the blow. They'd worked

together for a long time." Leander stole a look at me. "She's going to hate me for this, but—"

I colored. "No, don't! You promised you wouldn't!"

"You should play for him." He reached into his bag and pulled out my violin case.

"Uncle," I protested.

"No. Show him what you're made of. Show him why you're a good fit for this school." Leander turned to the counselor. "That's the idea, right? She'll be able to pursue professional opportunities, and she'll have the finest instruction. Play for him!"

Hartwell sat back in his leather chair. "I'm no judge. She'd have to play for the music faculty, at auditions." Then the corners of his mouth turned up indulgently. "Is she any good?"

I drew my instrument up to me like the living thing it was. It hadn't been in my hands now for so long—an extravagance and a danger, lugging it around with me, a hobby of mine that I couldn't hide. I could almost feel it breathing there under my fingers.

"That's a Stradivarius." Hartwell's eyes glittered. "Interesting."

I put it up under my chin, arranged my fingering. I always thought a little about the sky when I held my violin. A bird wheeling. The sun. That sort of thing. It was difficult to explain.

A very, very cursory Google search had found that Michael Hartwell was a significant donor to both the Metropolitan Opera and the New York Philharmonic. Hence, the violin.

Leander gave me a moment to settle. Then he said, "Mr.

Hartwell, I think she'll make you weep. Play him an original, Charlotte?"

Had my eyes not already been closed, I would have startled like a hare. This hadn't been in the design at all, which already skewed far closer to the truth than I wanted it to. I had proposed that Leander play my father. We'd be Americans recently returned from abroad. We would say that I wrote songs on my guitar about our quaint life in Surrey and how I missed it so. I would ask Hartwell to introduce me to his daughter, the songwriter; I would be a fan. He would be flattered, he would feel appreciated, perhaps be more willing to talk.

Leander had refused. *Bring your violin. Be my niece. Let me take the lead.*

I never let anyone else take the lead, not when I was involved. I never deviated from the plan unless I had to, and "had to" had a very narrow definition. (I could comfortably bluff my way through having a gun put to my head.) But I didn't trust my instincts today, not with all that fear still rattling around in my chest. I'd taken a step back.

Was this willingness to give up the lead maturity, or hesitation? I didn't know. It had been one thing with DI Green, who could give me directions but wasn't there to see me follow (or not follow) them. This was something else.

And now Leander was calling me Charlotte when the name on my form read Harriet Heloise Simpson, and he was telling me to play a composition that I hadn't, well, composed.

Had Hartwell noticed the name? He must have. I couldn't risk opening my eyes to check. Whatever my uncle was playing at . . . but more than a moment had passed now, long enough for an eighteen-year-old girl to believably compose herself, but anything longer, and—

I began to play, pulling from a folk tune I remembered from a village concert as a child. My parents had never taken us. There wasn't much art in their blood. But I had been eight and obsessed with my fiddle and Milo had been home for the summer, and when our housekeeper told us about the festival, he'd seen the longing in my face.

"You're indulging her?" my father had asked. Not judging, not surprised.

Milo shrugged. "She wants to hear the band," he said, the only time I could remember him pushing back against my father, and he hoisted me onto his skinny shoulders and took me into town.

We didn't have much down there—a Tesco, a wine bar, a few nebulously purposed shops that sold "gifts," the usual lineup for a tourist haunt by the sea. But that night, we had a gazebo on the village green, and a quartet playing folk airs, and my brother kept me on his shoulders as we watched. People weren't used to us being out, as a family. We Holmeses were the vampires up the hill. But I clapped my hands along to the music, and my brother bounced me in time to the beat, and soon an elderly gentleman approached and asked me if I wanted to dance with him. Milo heaved me down and watched, bemused, as I was spun and spun and spun in my dress and then sat dizzy onto the ground.

"Did you like that?" he said, when it was over. The old man

had bought me a taffy apple at the stand, and I held it out on the walk back to our land, too afraid to eat it.

"Yes," I remember saying. "I liked how sad it was."

Because the day had ended. There would be no more days just like it. If I ate the apple, it too would be gone, and soon enough Milo would be back at the school that was changing him.

My brother didn't press me to explain.

I took that day and laid it under this one. I spun those two parallel moments into a song and then played it, and I played for some time.

When I opened my eyes, Michael Hartwell was weeping.

"Charlotte," he said, and the hair on my neck stood up. "That was beautiful. I'm so—I'm so sorry."

I set down my violin on my lap. Then I said, "You know who I am, then."

Hartwell said, "I've been shown photos of you, yes."

"But not me," Leander said, standing.

"No. Only the girl. Charlotte."

My uncle put himself more fully between me and Michael Hartwell. "You're here," he said, as Hartwell wiped his eyes, "but you did your residency at Washington Mercy in psychology. Is that right?"

Hartwell, I noticed, was shaking; perhaps it was an aftershock from his tears. "Yes."

"What does Moriarty have on you?"

"Nothing," Hartwell said, "nothing."

I cleared my throat. "Then what is he offering you? He's

using your passport to get into the country. Why isn't he just using a dead man's identity?" I wanted to hear what his answer would be.

Hartwell looked at me with red-rimmed eyes. I didn't think this show of emotion was for my music. I think the music had reminded him of something. Someone. His daughter, by the way his eyes kept straying to the photo on his desk of her in a blue dress, holding her guitar. The frame said *MY MUSICAL GIRL*.

"It's a deal," he said slowly. "I have—I have connections. I know people, at Washington Mercy, at— I know people, okay? He wants me to use those connections to arrange something for him. And if I don't, he's going to . . . I can't talk to you about this. I have children. I have a family to protect."

A posh hospital in D.C. A wilderness rehab in Connecticut. A prep school in New York.

Hartwell turned to Leander. "If you're really her uncle, you'll get her far away from this. As quickly as you can. Okay? Pack your bags. Get on a flight, go somewhere inaccessible. I don't even know if this office is bugged—"

Leander took a step forward, his finely made hands in his pockets. "When's the last time you swept it?"

"Swept it?" Hartwell stared at him. "I'm a psychologist. I— Mr. Holmes, I'm not like you. Any of you. I don't know how to sweep an office for bugs."

A helicopter buzzed the roof. The sound came on like a swarm of bees.

"Is there a helipad nearby?" I asked, tracking it.

"It's not—he doesn't—he isn't *here*," he managed to say. "Not yet. So go. Leave town. And if you don't, I can't be held responsible for what happens."

There was nothing else to be said. We bundled up our things quickly and ran outside, my violin case banging clumsily against my leg. It was wretched outside, the rain turned to sleet, and we held on to each other, pulling ourselves up the block step by sleety step.

"You called me Charlotte," I said to him at the corner, as we waited for the light to change. "You outed us. Why?"

"What are the markers of a good man?" he asked me.

"I'm sorry?"

"The markers," he said. "Of a good man. How can you tell if a man is someone you can trust?"

"I don't," I said. "I don't trust—well. I trust you."

I thought, strangely, that Leander was going to laugh, and that it was a laugh that I didn't want to see. His hair was slicked back off his face, and he was hatless, and the sleet was beading on him like pearls. His greatcoat was beautifully tailored. His boots were a soft brown and quietly handsome. And he had a look on his face so wolflike he would have driven any sheep back to pasture.

He could be terrifying. I realized it now.

As I watched him, Leander carefully put his expression away, as though he were folding it up like a jacket. The light changed. He was benign again, a benevolent gentleman, a lamb.

"You'll learn," he said. "But not yet. I don't want you to trust anyone again until this is over."

"Even you?"

He looked at me. "Perhaps," he said.

I put my hand in the crook of his arm and said nothing. Someone was close behind us, slipping on the snow to over- take us, and I took a breath, and Leander steeled his shoulders, and then he was passing us, an older man with a cane who wished us a good afternoon and disappeared into the fading light.

Even now, Lucien Moriarty could be playing back our con- versation with Michael Hartwell.

New York was a trap, I thought, and we'd walked right into it.

Leander was nodding as though he could hear my thoughts. "When we get home, you're packing. We're leaving. Tonight."

seventeen
jamie

THE RUGBY PLAYERS I KNEW WERE MASTERS AT A CERTAIN kind of intimidation. It had everything to do with their bodies—drawing their shoulders back to call attention to their size, or yelling and hollering with their friends until the veins in their neck stood out. Licking a guy's forehead to make him squeal "like a girl"; pissing in a guy's shoes to see if you could make him step in them and scream "like a girl"; coughing up shit from their lungs and spitting it, breathing heavy in each other's faces, then howling; pushing each other over on the field between plays, all to see if their macho macho-ness would break someone down into what they saw as feminine weakness.

Being a girl was their worst fear, and they chalked up all kinds of behavior to "girliness," things that didn't make sense.

I don't know why they were so specifically afraid of it. From what I could tell, most of them liked girls, had them for friends, wanted so badly to date them or screw them that it was all they could talk about after practice. But when we were all in a pack together, practicing a game where we tackled each other into the ground like beasts, there were the guys who liked the game, and then there were those who lusted for it, the hard takedown, the feeling of pushing someone else down into the mud. It bubbled up outside of practice in physical ways. Not all my teammates were like that. Barely half, if I had to count. But it was more than enough for me. I'd learned to go stoic and invisible when this kind of shit started so that I didn't become its target. It was a strategy Kittredge took too.

Not today.

I turned in my chair. "You have things to say to me? Say them."

He licked his lips. "You're trying to blame this on me," he said. "Marta told me. She told me everything."

"Blame *what* on you, exactly? What are you being blamed for?" All I did was berate people, anymore. I might as well be my ex–best friend. "I don't see you being threatened with suspension, or anyone pointing their finger at you for a thousand goddamn dollars. So what? Because Elizabeth and I asked questions about who Anna talked to last night, I'm suddenly putting your ass to the fire? I don't think so."

Kittredge shook his head. "I didn't take her money," he said.

"Her alleged money—"

"Stop saying that," he interrupted. I had taken this strategy from Holmes, and it rarely failed—people could always be provoked to correct you. "You act like you know what happened, but you don't. I *saw* it. She had this fat wad of bills in her pocket, she took it out to show me."

"She did? Why?"

He looked around carefully, but the library stacks were empty except for us. "Because she said someone gave it to her. She was laughing, like, in disbelief—it's not like she needed the money, she said. But she was giddy about it. I couldn't tell if it was the MDMA. I don't do that shit, so I don't know."

"I don't either."

"Listen." He spread his hand on the table, then balled it up. "If I were you, I'd be talking to Beckett Lexington. He sold her those pills. Maybe he was giving her a cash advance on some sales she was going to do for him. He does that, sometimes—Randall was telling me."

It was a better working theory than anything I had. My estimation of Kittredge went up a notch. "I will," I said.

Kittredge stood. "We didn't talk about this. Okay?"

"You don't want Anna to find out," I said.

"No." He eyed me cautiously. "But I also don't want someone suspended for shit they didn't do. Beckett works at the school radio station. Start there."

He stuck out his hand. I clasped it, and just like that we weren't animals anymore.

"Let's just get out of Sherringford before it eats us alive," Kittredge said.

But Beckett Lexington wasn't easy to find. I checked the radio station, a poky little warren in the basement of Weaver Hall, and found the system on autoplay, records scattered across the floor. The cafeteria wasn't open for another hour, so I couldn't corner him at dinner. Finally I looked up his room in the online directory. Apparently he lived on the first floor of my dorm. But I hesitated at the steps up to Michener. Mrs. Dunham would be at the front desk, and she would have heard about my forced leave of absence. I wasn't sure I wanted to risk being thrown off campus, especially by someone I respected.

My phone buzzed. *Your mother's getting in tonight,* my dad had texted. *What time do you want me to pick you up?*

Can I let you know? I wrote back.

I was standing in the shadows, debating, when Mrs. Dunham came to the door. "It's freezing," she said, ushering me in. "Come on, I'll put the kettle on for you. Isn't that how you say it? 'Put the kettle on'?"

"Are you sure?" I asked.

She waved a hand. "I won't tell the administration if you won't," she said, walking back up to her desk. "I'm just icing some cookies I brought from home. Do you want to help?"

There were worse things to do on a stakeout.

I dragged a chair over from the lobby. Mrs. Dunham's desk was a riot of cheerful uselessness. Her knitting was in a basket, full of the bright scarves she made to send off to her daughter at school, and a series of dala horses she'd brought back from Sweden, red and blue in a line, that she said were for luck. She kept her coffee mug on an ever-rotating stack of poetry books, Mary Oliver and Frank O'Hara and Terrance Hayes, and beside that a tablet that was always streaming something mindless, a buddy cop show or a British baking program. All of her projects could be abandoned at a moment's notice if she needed to run off to put out some small fire in the dorm.

Today, she had sugar cookies in a giant plastic container, and a number of smaller ones full of red and blue and green frosting. She handed me a knife, then started back up her baking show. I watched the door and tried very hard not to eat every cookie I iced.

Guys came in and out, on their way back from practice or the library or the union, and I steeled myself against the looks I'd get if the news about Anna's money and my "leave of absence" had spread. But they didn't. A few said hi, or asked if I was sick, since I hadn't been in class, and I told them, yes, very sick, not contagious, no, I'll see you guys next week.

When things were going wrong, it was so easy to imagine that everyone knew, that everyone was talking about it. But nobody cared nearly as much about your life as you did.

We finally came to the bottom layer of cookies just as the 4:30 lull hit, the moment before everyone came down to go to dinner. No sign of Beckett Lexington yet. I looked again at Mrs. Dunham's desk, but this time my eyes drifted down to the place she kept the master key.

"Something strange happened to me the other day," I said.

"Oh?" she asked, only half-listening. A girl on the baking show had burnt her English muffins.

"Yeah," I said. "Someone got into my room and sprayed a can of soda everywhere."

Mrs. Dunham turned to me, shocked. It looked genuine. "That's terrible, Jamie. Are your things okay?"

"Not really. But, you know, I lock my door. I was just wondering if anyone came through and asked for the master key yesterday afternoon." I was starting to feel a little sick from everything I'd eaten.

Frowning, Mrs. Dunham pulled out the maintenance record. "A carpenter at seven a.m., fixing a broken window sash—"

"Too early."

"And of course Elizabeth when she came up to find you after dinner." She glanced at me. "Do you want me to stop doing that? I do know that you like to keep your door locked even when you're in there, love, but she's your girlfriend—"

"It's fine," I told her. "I appreciate it."

"You two have been through enough. I like to make your lives easier in little ways, if I can," Mrs. Dunham said, stoutly. She returned to her record. "Otherwise, I gave it to a student at bed check when he locked himself out. Do you want his name?"

"No." I was starting to feel really nauseous, actually, enough that I was starting to sweat. "No, that's too late. It's okay." I pushed the cookies back toward her. "Thanks for looking."

"You know," she said, "you actually don't look very well. Do you want to go to the infirmary?"

I reacted to the word "infirmary" the way you would to being hit in the face.

"Oh! Oh—you know Nurse Bryony doesn't work there anymore, it's fine to go if you're ill, you'd be safe—"

"I'm fine," I said, gasping a little. *PTSD,* Lena had said. Was it true? I hardly even knew what that was.

"Jamie," she said, reaching out to touch my forehead. Unthinking, I jerked away.

Because the week I was having wouldn't allow for anything else, Beckett Lexington chose that moment to walk in the front door.

"Watson," he said, stomping his snow boots on the mat. "You look awful, man."

I couldn't deal with it right now. "I feel awful," I said. "Can you hold on a second? I think—Elizabeth said she wanted to talk to you—"

He brushed his asymmetrical hair out of his face. "Yeah," he said. "That's cool. Hey, can I have one of those?"

"Of course," Mrs. Dunham said, holding the container out.

I hunched over my phone, trying very hard not to look at Beckett stuffing a red-and-green cookie into his mouth. *SOS,* I texted Elizabeth. *Beckett Lexington at Michener. Kittredge thinks he gave Anna the money. Having an Incident, like an asshole.*

You're not an asshole. There in five, she wrote back, almost immediately.

I wasn't sure what information she could get out of him,

especially if she went after him with a hatchet like she had the girls at lunch, but I was in no state to try to interrogate someone. All I could really do was call my father. "Dad," I said, as soon as he picked up. "You need to come get me. Like, now."

"I'm just in town running errands," he said. "I'll be there in a minute."

I waited for him outside on the steps, breathing in and out, slowly, trying not to immediately assume that I'd been infected with a nanovirus. Ever since the run-in with Bryony Downs where she'd stuck me with an infected spring, I could work myself up into a panic any time I felt ill.

Panic, or fear, or was it trauma, or maybe Mrs. Dunham was poisoning me—

No. The cold air felt good on my face. I shut my eyes for a second, swaying, and when I opened them Elizabeth was staring at me.

"You okay?"

I gestured inside to Beckett scrolling through his phone, cookie in hand. "Talk to him?" I asked.

Unexpectedly, she grinned. "You have frosting on your face," she said. "Blue frosting. You look like a snowman. Did you eat cookies for dinner?"

I hadn't eaten lunch, I remembered; we'd left the Bistro without me ordering anything. In fact, I hadn't eaten anything all day. The thought made the nausea lessen, a little. *It's just panic,* I told myself again.

"Jamie," she said, starting up the steps toward me.

"I'm okay," I said. She had a knit hat on, and the color

matched her eyes. In that moment I was so grateful that I could cry. "Thank you. For everything you're doing to help. You don't need to be doing it."

She took off a glove, then reached out and, with a finger, took a bit of icing off my lips. "Well," she said softly. "Of course I'm helping."

My father's sedan pulled up to the curb.

"That's my cue," I said.

"I'll go talk to Lexington. Find out what he knows. Will you call me later?"

"Yeah," I said, and on impulse, I kissed her cheek. "Talk to you tonight."

I popped the trunk of his car and made room for my back-pack amidst a cluster of grocery bags. There were fancy things spilling out of them—goat cheese, a few bottles of wine, some pickled Italian things I didn't recognize. I swallowed down my nausea and hopped into the front seat.

"You're excited to see Mum, I take it," I said. "Big dinner plans?"

My father shrugged. "Just trying to be a good host."

The car was warm, too warm, and I cracked the window as he pulled out of the school gates. "Sorry," I said. "I'm feeling kind of gross."

He gave me a look. "Apparently not that gross. How's Elizabeth? Are you two back on?"

"No. Maybe. No. No, we're not." I knew it wasn't a good answer. I thought about saying something like *I can only solve one mystery at a time,* and then cringed. What was it that

Elizabeth had said? Being aware of it didn't excuse your crappy behavior?

My father didn't say anything else until we'd made it out of Sherringford Town and into the cold, white fields beyond. "It isn't nice to leave people in the dark," he said, finally, with an odd vehemence.

I looked at him. "Am I leaving you in the dark about something?"

"Elizabeth," he said, gripping the wheel. "That poor girl. She has expectations, you know, and I don't want you jerking her around. It's not very nice. I don't like to see that kind of behavior in you."

I didn't like it in me either, but it was sort of beside the point—my father never came down on me like this for anything. "Are you all right? Is everything okay with Abbie?"

"You don't need to get yourself involved in that."

"Okay," I said, unsettled. I'd groused a lot over the years about my father's relentless good humor, but I was discovering I didn't know what to do when it wasn't there.

The night got darker, streetlights winking out as we drove further into the countryside. It wasn't proper farmland, with farms and turbines and hay for miles and miles; instead, the road wandered through little towns, none of them any bigger than a gas station and a couple of bars, surrounded by ancient farmhouses. During the day it was unremarkable, but at night, with the snow turning into sleet, those old houses were strange and sad.

"Then again," my father said, out of nowhere, "it isn't fair for her to expect things from you that you can't give her. Has she even said anything to you about it?"

I blinked. "Yes?"

"Well, that's good. Good. Good for her. That's better than—than just wanting things and never saying anything about it and hanging around, feeling tortured, instead of communicating your feelings like an actual adult."

We were definitely not talking about Elizabeth. "Dad." I swallowed, then said, "Is everything okay with Leander?"

He almost swerved off the road. "What are you talking about?"

"I think you know what I'm talking about," I said, not unkindly.

More silence. More farmhouses, standing like sentinels in the dark. My father pounded his hand against the wheel once, twice, three times. "Your stepmother doesn't like Leander hanging around so much, looking at her like—she says, and I quote—'like he's just waiting for James to realize how much more he likes him than me.'"

"He's been at the house a lot, I take it."

"He's renting a place down the road," my father said. "I haven't gotten to see him this much in ten years! We'll usually put together a few weekends in the summer—run around Edinburgh like we used to, tidy up the ends of some case he's solving—but you know, it was never enough. It was the best when he lived so close to us, in London, but that of course made your mother furious. I—ah. I shouldn't be telling you this."

"Probably not," I said.

"Abbie is different, you know. More adventurous. We have a lot of fun." He nodded, as if talking himself into something. "She thinks he's in love with me."

There it was. "Is he?" I asked.

"No." He sounded almost relieved that the conversation had made its way here, as though this had been the end point all along. "No! No. No, he's not. Just because he's gay doesn't mean he's in love with his straight best friend. I hate when people insinuate that. You know, that's insulting to both of us, and anyway, I'm just—he's brilliant, you know? Leander is the life of every room, and he's obviously a good-looking man. He could have anyone he wanted, he's not just hanging around pining after *me*. Of all people! That would be absurd. That would be . . ."

He trailed off.

"It would be really sad for him," I said, looking down at my hands.

"Oh, God," my father said.

The sleet was coming down harder. Little dots and dashes of hail were bouncing off of the windshield.

"Yeah." I paused. "He's your favorite person?"

Mechanically, he put on the wipers. "I've never—I'm not attracted to men. He's not an exception to that."

"But he's—"

"He's my favorite person." He was talking almost as if to himself. "Don't you wish sometimes that who you—you spent your life with was determined just by that? Wouldn't that make it less complicated?"

I was seventeen years old. I was dating-or-not-dating another girl who was right now questioning the campus dealer about a crime I hadn't committed, and I was in love with my best friend, who I hadn't seen for a year but who lived on in my day-to-day like a splinter in my goddamn heart. I thought about the rest of my life a lot more than I'd like to admit.

"I don't think that makes it less complicated," I said.

Our house came into view. Despite the weather, the garage was open and lit up, and inside it, figures were hauling in suitcases from a rental car.

"Your mother's here," my father said happily as we pulled up into the drive. He was doing that adult thing that I hated, where he pretended an uncomfortable conversation hadn't happened. "Go in through the front, will you, and make sure the cat hasn't gotten out? And see if your stepmother needs help."

I grabbed my backpack and a few of the grocery bags, trying not to look inside them (my stomach still wanted to pretend that food didn't exist), and fought my way through the sleet through the front door.

Abbie wasn't anywhere to be seen. Neither was the cat. I was checking inside the pantry, looking for it, when my phone rang. It was a number I didn't recognize. "Hello?"

"Jamie, it's me."

"Shelby?" I said, moving around some bags of potatoes.

No cat. "Where are you? Aren't you here? Are you okay?"

"Are you alone?" Her voice was urgent, ragged.

I grabbed the pantry door and shut it. "I am now. What's wrong?"

"Jamie, everything is seriously so messed up, I don't even know where to begin, and I think I only have a minute—"

My heart was racing. "What's *happening*, Shel?"

"That school? In Connecticut? It's not a school, Jamie, it's like some kind of rehab, and I have no idea why I'm here but I'm *here*, I'm in the infirmary because I fainted, I guess, when I figured out what was going on, and I'm using the phone here because they took mine, but the doctor might be back, and Jamie, you have to do something, you have to come get me—"

"Rehab?" I couldn't quite believe what I was hearing. "What was their justification? What the hell is going on?"

"It was Mum. I don't even understand it. She's super furious about the stuff going down with you, *still*, which is weird, first of all, because usually she, like, rages but then gets over it, and then she was going through my things and she found a bottle of vodka in my drawer, but it wasn't mine, I swear, I'd never seen it before!"

"I believe you—"

"And Ted tried to talk her down and then— Footsteps. I hear footsteps. Wait."

I stood there in the dark pantry, clutching the phone to my face, listening to my sister's frightened breathing. I'd never felt so helpless in my life.

"They're gone," she whispered. "I don't know when they're

coming back. But the school—I can't. It's like a wilderness camp, and there are horses, but it's like *survivalist*, they put you in the woods for days, there's no school at all, and Mum insisted—and she and Ted got married—"

"*What?*"

"It was supposed to be a surprise." Shelby had been talking so quickly I could only half-understand her. "In the middle of the day yesterday. In London, at the courthouse. So like . . . meet your new stepdad?"

"Are you serious—"

A rustle, a man's voice. "No *no*," she was saying, and then the line went dead.

The nausea hit me again, full force, this vertiginous feeling like I was crashing, and I was sure now that all of it was panic.

I made myself breathe. *Be logical,* I thought. *Be a grown-up. Shelby could be lying about the vodka, it could have been hers. The school could just be more severe than she was used to. It could be homesickness. Ted could be a nice guy.*

Breathe.

From the garage, I heard my father saying a hearty congratulations. Laughter. The garage door groaning to a close.

They staggered in through the door, then, laughing—my mum with her hand on my father's arm, chatting excitedly, my new stepdad hauling a pair of bags behind them.

"Jamie," my mother said when she saw me, rushing forward. "I swear you've gotten taller—hello, sweetheart." She grabbed me by the shoulders; she was never this effusive. "It's so good to see you."

"Hey," I said, forcing myself to sound friendly. "Where's Shelby? Thought she was coming."

"Loved her school," Ted said, behind my dad. "Just loved it. Wanted to start right away." He had a wonderful speaking voice, a round tenor with a Welsh accent.

"She did," my mum said, and turned back to me. "Just loved it. And we have news!"

"Gracie, not so fast," Ted said. "I haven't even met the boy yet."

"Hi," I said, stepping forward to shake Ted's hand. I was going to rewrite this conversation, take control. I'd figure out exactly what was going on. "I'm Jamie, it's nice to finally meet you."

He took it, scowling a little. Ted was tall, broad-shouldered, surprisingly bald. Maybe my sister had mentioned that to me before? But he didn't have eyebrows either—it looked almost as though he'd shaved them—and his eyes beneath were small and shrewd. He looked like someone, I thought, my pulse beginning to speed up. Who did he look like?

"Jamie," he said. "Hi. Ted Polnitz."

"His given name is Tracey," my mother said, coming up beside him, smiling. She'd had her hair done, her makeup. She was wearing a necklace that belonged to my grandmother, pearls on a long string. She looked beautiful. "Tracey! Isn't that cute? But he prefers his middle name. Theodore. More *serious*. And we have plans for tonight—a reception!"

"A wedding reception," my father said, bemused. "We're doing a dinner thing in New York. Tonight."

222

I was hardly paying attention. "You remind me of someone," I said to Ted, slowly.

He grinned at me. "I get that a lot."

"Jamie?" my mother asked. "Are you okay?"

When he smiled my new stepfather looked just like August.
And Phillipa. And Hadrian.

"I'm fine," I said to Lucien Moriarty. "Really. It's just so
good to finally meet you."

eighteen
charlotte

BACK AT THE FLAT I WAS THROWING THINGS INTO MY SUIT-
case, not bothering to fold them. I could hear Leander on the
phone, pleading with someone. "Tonight," he was saying, "it
can't wait," and had I wanted to I could have gone to the door
to listen.

It didn't matter now what he was saying, not really.

"We'll regroup from a distance," he'd told me. "We don't
have the time to bag him when he arrives, and God knows
what he plans on doing when he gets here. We'll find some
high ground, girl. Pack your bags."

There was a kind of relief in it, the giving up. We would
plan, and in the meantime Leander would let me live with him.
He hadn't offered, not as such, but for the rest of the walk

home he'd been listing places we could go.

As the eldest of his siblings, my father had inherited our house in Sussex; my aunt Araminta had been formally given the cottage and apiary where she'd taken to spending her days; my uncle Julian our flat in London, and presumably leave to never talk to the rest of us again. (A smart decision.) My uncle Leander had been too peripatetic to be given land, the will had read. He'd been granted my grandfather's money instead, our intelligently invested takings from the life rights of Sherlock Holmes.

In his early twenties, back when he was rooming with James Watson in a tiny flat in Edinburgh, Leander had socked away his inheritance in smart investments and lived like a churchmouse. (My uncle, despite his well-groomed appearance, had always been a frugal man.) When his investments brought him returns, he bought property, and with the income from letting out those, he purchased new places, sold others, tailored his portfolio.

All of this to say, we had some places to hide.

"They're largely under my name," he'd said. "The flats in New York and Edinburgh, the house in Provence. Those are the ones I've kept."

"We can't go there, then."

"No. We can't. But London—London is another matter. I bought a flat there a few years ago through a dummy corporation. I was on an undercover case—I needed a bolt-hole for quick-changes, a place to stash my things that couldn't be traced. I never did sell it. I worried that it might be useful again." He gave me a grim smile. "And here we are."

Here we were.

Good-bye to New York, I thought, stuffing my wigs back into their wooden box. Good-bye to Connecticut. Good-bye to America; who knew when I'd have reason to be back here again. Good-bye to picking locks, prying doors with crowbars, to putting on doe-eyed masks to learn what I needed to know. I would help him research. I would help, and I would stay out of the way.

My mother hadn't called me once since I'd left home. I thought again about the argument she and my father had had in Switzerland, where she pled my case to him for five minutes and then, as far as I knew, never did again. Any love my mother had for me was bound up in the frustrations she had with my father, and now, with him absent, it was as though I'd ceased to exist as well.

There had been so many losses: My parents. August. Milo, gone radio silent during that never-ending murder trial. And while I had always imagined Jamie Watson leaving me bit by bit, he'd instead done it all at once. Pulled the bandage off while the wound was still bleeding.

Had it been wild denial or self-destruction that had sent me running headlong into the jaws of the beast that was hunting me? Why really had I spent the last year chasing Lucien Moriarty, except to put a speedier end to it all? I had diligently photographed my pills each night. I had eaten and bathed and traveled and plotted, I had pretended to be looking to the future, and all the while it looked like I was living.

But the moment I knew I wouldn't kill Lucien Moriarty was the moment I wrote my own ending. I saw that now. I didn't know another way to be rid of him, the spider that had built a web over the world. Chasing him down without a gun in hand would ultimately end with my death.

I didn't want to die. Not anymore.

My box of wigs, my lockpicking kit, my recording equipment, my dress blacks, my casual blacks, the makeup lockbox that held all my other faces. All of it into the suitcase.

I put on a set of old sweats I'd found in the chest of drawers. They were too big on me, but I did them up anyway. I'd leave fifty dollars, more than enough to replace them; I had three thousand dollars to burn. More than enough for a plane ticket across the pond and a dye job when I got there. Enough to pay the fee to change my name, to make myself disappear.

I hauled my suitcase into the kitchen, enjoying the sound of my footsteps on the tile. My boots looked ridiculous with the sweats, I was sure, but after weeks of walking silently, I needed to hear myself move.

"I'm charging your laptop, and the phones I found in your bag." Leander was rummaging through the pantry, throwing dry goods in a pile. There was quite a lot of peanut butter. "Who lives here? I'll reimburse them for the food, but I want to have supplies in case we need to hole up before our flight. Ideally, we'd leave late tonight, but if we miss our window, I don't think it's safe to try until three or four weeks have passed."

"Late tonight?" I asked. It was barely four o'clock in the evening. "Why not now? We can go straight to the airport, get the red-eye to London."

Leander had his back to me. He spread his hands out on the counter. "I'm going say good-bye to James Watson before I go, and you're going to come with me."

"You're *what*?"

"God help me, Charlotte, don't argue with me on this—"

"No. I categorically refuse. That man cannot keep a secret to save his life, and the last thing I need is for him to see me when his son—his son—I *can't*."

My uncle bowed his head. "You can do this one last thing for me."

"This last thing—"

"Dammit," he said, "I am not leaving you alone in this flat with that man loose in this city."

I bit my lip. "I'm sorry."

"I know." I watched him breathe out.

"If it's important to you—"

"You should probably change," he said. "James called it a wedding reception."

I dragged myself back to the bedroom. At home, in Sussex, we dressed for dinner, but that was an exercise I'd never taken seriously. It was another disguise, one masquerading as the self. Long skirts my mother bought me, elegant and expensive, and dark lips to match their dark colors. Done up like that, I looked years older than I was.

Here, I had nothing that didn't belong to Rose the fashion vlogger, and I didn't want to wear her right now.

I flipped through DI Green's sister's closet, wondering idly if she'd have anything that would fit me. Cardigans. Blouses with high necks and buttons on the cuffs. And then a row of cocktail dresses. Two were in my size; the second of those was red. I shed my clothes and put it on and walked over to the mirror.

Watson had once described me as a knife. It's true that I have no "curves." If we are speaking geometrically, I am a line. This dress didn't change the fact of my body, but then I didn't need it to. I took a pair of shoes from the closet and a silver evening bag from the hook on the closet door. I stuffed it with necessities. We would return for our suitcases if we could; if we couldn't, I would make do with what I had.

"Charlotte," Leander was saying, almost as though he were being strangled.

I found him bent nearly double over a mobile phone on the kitchen counter.

"What happened?" I asked, panting, and then I really got a look at him. "No. You're not—you're laughing. Why do you have my old mobile?"

He'd said he was charging both of my phones. I'd been keeping the one I'd used at Sherringford at the bottom of my bag, turned off so that the GPS couldn't be used to track my location. It was always a good idea to have a spare.

It was almost always a good idea to have a spare.

"It says you haven't booted it up in eleven months," my uncle said, wiping the tears from his eyes. "Eleven months! In that time, you received zero messages. Zero texts. Until today. Until quite literally just *now.*"

I snatched my phone from his hand.

Four new texts:

Holmes.

Holmes.

Charlotte.

Where are you?

nineteen
jamie

CHARLOTTE HOLMES PUT HER HANDS TO HER FACE. SHE was crying. "Milo," she said. "Milo. Milo, no. No, you didn't."

In the distance, a car started up. There was yelling, someone crying out, *Don't touch me, don't touch me,* and then wheels on loose gravel. When I turned to look, a lone figure, a man, was standing in front of the Holmeses' dark estate. Like someone locked out of their home, or a drifter looking for a place to spend the night.

Holmes's mother was gone. Hadrian and Phillipa—where were they?

"I—" Milo was shaking. He held the gun out in front of him. "Is August—and Hadrian—God, Lottie, I can't do this anymore. Lucien disappeared. He disappeared. There's no footage, no intel, no . . . *I can't keep doing this.* How could I, and succeed?"

The master of the universe, asking us this question.

Holmes wrenched the rifle from his hands. Without looking down, she stripped the gun of its clip and dropped it all on the ground.

"Leander's *done*," she said. "August is *dead*. Is this it for you too? Are you leaving the two of us here to pick up this mess?"

"It's your mess," Milo said. "Isn't it time you did?"

I was only half-hearing it, what they were saying. In the distance, the ocean raged louder. The cold bit at my hands. August Moriarty was spread-eagled, and it wasn't a dream, I could see the outline of his coat in the snow. I couldn't look at them, either of them, Holmes or Holmes, two faces of the same terrible god staring out in opposite directions. Passing their judgments. Firing their guns. And the figure in front of the house—he was gone, the field empty now, and the ocean was deafening.

But it wasn't the ocean. It was sirens, a cacophony of sirens, and by the time the red and blue lights reached the top of the drive, Holmes and I were alone.

Milo had gone. One moment he was there, and the next there weren't even footprints, as though he'd erased himself where he stood. I looked for them, for a sign. There were animal prints, deer and fox, the low slide of a rabbit, a dog's muddy paws. Even in the winter this was a place that breathed with life.

"Watson," Holmes was saying.

The man lingering near the house was looking at us. He held up a hand and then pointed his finger, like a teacher calling on a student. Then he pulled his coat more firmly around himself and walked away from us toward the house.

"Watson," Holmes said. "Watson. *Jamie*. Look at me."

I wrenched my eyes toward her. I felt slow, and heavy, as though someone were holding me down underwater. The up-down-up-down wail of the siren beat against us like a current. It was an ambulance. Someone must have called one. Was there a house close enough to hear the gunshot and call 999?

I almost asked Holmes. But she was looking at me like I was a cancerous growth she needed to have removed.

"What now?" I asked, half-laughing. "What's the plan?"

Her eyes were always colorless. Now they were cold. "I need you to take the fall," she said, turning to look at the paramedics jumping out the back of the ambulance. "I need you to confess."

Had it been any other day, any other situation, I might have agreed. I might have flung myself into it after her. Maybe it was desperation for connection. Maybe it was delusion. Folie à deux. Maybe for the last three months I'd had a death wish, throwing myself off bridges, not caring if any net hid at the bottom.

Not this time.

"That's what I'm here for, then. To take the blame."

"Watson—"

"That's the big reason behind me coming along with you. I'm the fall guy. The person you pinned it on. You've had weeks. Weeks, Holmes, to explain! If you'd said *anything* at all. Anything! I could have changed your mind! But you maneuvered me here just to—"

She whirled on me. "This is love," she snarled, her pupils pinned, her eyes all dangerous light. "This is what love looks like."

"Then no one's ever loved you," I said, "including me." The paramedics—I would get their attention. There was a police car right behind them, men pouring out of its doors. A detective, unmistakable in her plainclothes and sunglasses, a radio in her hand.

"Hey!" I yelled. "Hey! I need help!"

"Watson," she said, grabbing my arm, "what are you doing?"

"Telling the truth."

She didn't have an answer for that.

I shook her off and ran to meet the approaching officers. "There was a man here—he's tall, he has glasses, he had a rifle with a scope. He shot our friend. He's still out here somewhere."

The officer looked past me, to August's cooling body. "Where?" he demanded. "Which way did he go?"

I pointed helplessly at the copse of trees where he'd been

hidden, hoping they'd find something I'd missed, something to point the way. The policeman took off at a run, the others behind him.

Holmes stared after them, wild-eyed. "Wait," she said, "wait. Wait. I did it."

It was soft. So soft that only the officer at the back stopped, and turned to see.

"I did it," she said again. "It was me."

"Miss," he said, a bit pleading. "I know that isn't true—"

She stalked forward. "I used a .338 sniper rifle from the top of that elm. I've been practicing at the range in Eastbourne for years; take my picture to them, they'll identify me. I've been away for the last two years—"

The officer took an involuntary step back. "Backup," he said into his radio. "Backup."

"—but I've been planning this all this time, because that man over there?" She jabbed at finger at August's body. "He broke my heart. He *lied* to me. He proposed to someone else. He belonged to me, and he proposed to Bryony Downs, and I will be damned if I see him go. If I saw him go. Past tense. We're past tense now."

The officer put his hands up, nodding, the way you would with a tiger in a center ring.

"And this?" Holmes jerked her hand at me. "This pathetic, sniveling boy thinks that if he gets me out of this mess, he can have me, like I'm some prize to be won. Look at it. Look at me. How much is it worth to you now?"

"DI Green," the officer said gratefully, as the woman in

the long coat approached, picking her way through the snow. "We have a confession—I haven't cautioned her, it's an excited utterance—"

Her sharp eyes went from Holmes to me and back again. "Which one?" she asked.

"Her."

Did I imagine it, the DI's disappointment? "Fine," she said. "Cuff her. Caution her. Then ask her again. You too, boy, come along."

Cautiously, the officer took Holmes by the arm. Despite everything, despite the way she'd all but spit blood in his face, he treated her like she was spun glass. He put the cuffs on her wrists, and the DI put a hand on her shoulder, and the three of them walked back to the car.

I made to follow them. And then I saw that I had missed the paramedics taking August's body away. From a distance I saw them hoist the gurney up into the back of the ambulance. They would take him to the morgue. They would cut off his clothes and lay him on a slab, like an object. Like a doll. I wondered who they'd call to identify him. Who was left to come and say his name?

Beyond him, the police were putting Holmes into the car. They were taking their time with it, like they were paying her a courtesy. I knew she had worked with the Yard before, in London; she'd helped some detective whose name I'd forgotten solve the case of the Jameson diamonds. The one that I'd heard about, all the way in America. But we were far from London, now, and America too, and the police here would only know the Holmes name and not the girl who wore it.

I hadn't realized until I registered the wet on my knees, but I had bent down to kneel in the snow. I didn't think I could walk. Time had gone slow; the police were milling around now, putting up tape, taking out a camera and tripod from the car to photograph the scene.

It didn't matter. I would just stay here, in a place where I didn't have to think.

Someone put a hand on my shoulder. "Come with me, boy," he said, and I nodded and got up and followed. He led me around the house and to the cellar door, still open, the floor below it dirty and covered in straw. "Down," he said.

I turned to look at him. It was Holmes's father. Alistair. "Why?" I asked him.

"They want you to wait down here," he said. "Come along."

He was kind about it, in practice. He gave me an arm to help me down the stairs, and once I was down there, he produced a chair—one from the dining room table, it looked like, from its high, carved back—and let me get myself settled before he pulled out the rope.

I didn't remember what he did with it. I only remembered the after, the rope wrapped around me like a snake.

Looking at me, there, he steepled his fingers under his chin. "I'm sorry to have to do this," he said. There was something in his face that had been snuffed out. "I'd much rather have my daughter here, with you. I think it would give you some comfort to have her beside you. Do you want me to put out a chair for her too? As a symbol?"

"No," I said. I had the vague sense that something was wrong. I wiggled a little against the rope, but it held.

"Oh," Alistair said, watching me. "You're coming out of shock. That'll make this harder."

Behind him, the wall was hung with weapons—a pair of fencing foils, a set of knives with the edges dulled. This was their practice room. I looked back at Alistair's face. His eye was bloodshot and bleeding from where I'd kicked him, crawling out of the cellar. I had the insane urge to apologize.

It *was* insane, that urge. Wasn't it? But so was being bound up to a chair in the cellar of a house where your friend had just been murdered.

"Will you let me go?" I asked him cautiously.

"Do you have a compelling reason?" he asked. "I always made my children give me a compelling reason. Why do you think I've led you here? There are several pretty points to be made. Biblical. Isaac and Abraham. You could start with those."

"Okay," I said. "How about, you're a right bastard?"

But Alistair had already lifted up the gas canister. That was when I started struggling in earnest.

"Help!" I yelled. "Somebody help me! I'm down here!"

"Make no mistake," he said, "this wasn't my first choice of action, but it's the only logical one remaining. Lucien has no reason anymore to keep our—our financial situation a secret."

"Your financial situation," I said, gasping, as he doused my legs in fuel. I hardly felt it. They had already been wet from the snow. "What the hell does that mean?"

Now he was washing his own legs with the gasoline. "It

means I've been taking payouts from the Russians. Convincing my friends at MI5 to be in certain places at certain times. Leaking the information. Letting them get picked off. Like chickens in a little house, waiting. There's a song about it, I think."

I was the architect of some small international conflicts, he'd told me, on the day I'd met him. "I thought you worked for the Ministry of Defense."

"The MoD. I started there. I spent some time in Whitehall too. Home Office. MI5. I came back. Where on earth do you think my daughter learned her skill set? She certainly didn't intuit her abilities. But it's over. Do you know how Lucien Moriarty escaped his surveillance in Thailand?"

I didn't say anything.

"No guesses? Pity. Do you know what my country does to traitors? Lucien Moriarty does. And when he found he couldn't control my actions—when he couldn't control my *daughter's* actions—he stopped mincing words. I would call in the last of my favors. I would go out there myself, have a word with Milo, a drink, I would wait until he slept, and then call on those men loyal to me in his company."

"You have spies? In Greystone?"

"Of course I do," he said, impatiently. "Why on earth wouldn't I? It pained me to do it, of course, to help that man. He's a blunt instrument. Much like my daughter. I'd always thought she'd come to an untidy end, but at Lucien's hands—

"Well. I suppose it's no use now. Lucien is 'on the loose,' as ridiculous as that sounds, and no matter what promises he made me I know he'll leak the information anyway. What loyalty does a man like that feel? None. It'll all come to light. The only real recourse I have is to erase the evidence. I, myself, am evidence. You're evidence as well—and Leander, of course, and my wife, though those two are beyond my reach. This is the best I can do. The insurance policy should leave a nice nest egg for my son, if he ever decides to settle down."

From his pocket, he pulled a lighter. Not a metal-plated one, as I'd expected, something precious and small, but a plastic one, the kind you bought at the gas station.

"No," I said. "No, no—no, absolutely not—"

"Or he could just buy himself another war," Alistair said, squinting at the small fire in his hands. "I swear, that boy has more influence than I'd ever dreamed of—"

I kicked my feet against the floor, skittering my chair back. I was yelling now, wordlessly, an endless stream of sound.

And then something on the stairs, something hollow-sounding, a knocking, almost, and I wasn't sure if I was seeing right when Hadrian Moriarty came around the corner. He didn't say anything. He just grunted, and did something with his arms, and then Alistair Holmes was laid out cold on the floor.

Hadrian bent and picked up the lighter, then pocketed it.

"Hi," I said, dumbly.

He jerked his head, a greeting.

"I thought you'd—run."

"I did," he said. "Behind the hedges by the house. It's best to stay close for as long as you can, before you make a break for it."

"Oh." I didn't know what else to say.

"I smelled the petrol," he said, by way of explanation. "Here," and he pulled a bowie knife from his pocket. Flicked it open.

I wrenched myself away from him, panting. From the spit to the fire—

He rolled his eyes. "No, kid. Stop," and he got to work sawing the rope off. "Next time this happens to you, you shimmy. Like you're dancing, okay? He didn't even tie your hands."

"Next time. Okay."

"Yeah." He tossed the ropes to the concrete floor. "Get up," he said, "and get lost."

On the ground, Alistair Holmes was already beginning to stir.

I rubbed my arms, trying to coax feeling back into them. "Why did you help me?"

Hadrian looked down at Alistair. "He deserves to rot in a cell. He doesn't get to pick his ending. He doesn't get to burn down the house I'm hiding in, either, even if it is his own." With that, he spat on the ground. "As for you—"

I waited for him to say it. *You're just a dumb kid. You've been conned. Used. You're in over your head. Go home to your mother.* The things that had been scrolling through my head since we landed back in the UK.

"You're not done yet," he said, and tossed me the knife. "Now get out of here."

The detective said later she found me wandering outside,

dazed and covered in gasoline, holding a blade in my hands. I told her someone had done it to me, that I didn't know who. I don't know why I lied. Maybe I couldn't face the idea of more of this day, this week, unending, stretching out into court dates and arguments. More battles in this war.

Maybe that was what you did—bent the truth open until it made a big enough hole for you to escape.

They asked me to describe him, the man who'd tied me up. I said I couldn't. I said it wasn't a big deal.

I still don't know why they believed me. Maybe they thought I'd done it to myself.

They kept me at the hospital overnight, for shock. Alistair's diagnosis had been correct. I stayed another half day there, my mother sleeping in the hard plastic chair by my bed, and then after another round of interrogations, my father arrived, and they released me to London into my parents' care.

What haunted me most wasn't the ropes, or the chair, or the gasoline, though those played recurring parts in my nightmares. It wasn't Alistair, or Hadrian's crisis of conscience. It was that we'd had the time, Holmes and I. Three long minutes before the police made it to us, enough for her to turn to me and say, *This is what you have to do, and why you have to do it.*

No, what haunted me most was that I knew, had I confessed to August's murder there on the lawn, Holmes would have found a way to clear my name. But she was letting her brother walk free for his mistake. She'd given up Bryony Downs to God knows what fate. She'd played judge and jury for Hadrian and Phillipa. And now she was letting herself be led away for a crime she didn't commit, and she would walk away from it unscathed, and there would be no one doing time for August's death.

It wasn't hers to decide. It wasn't mine, either. Charlotte Holmes had told me once that she wasn't a good person. That day I'd begun to believe it.

twenty
charlotte

WILL YOU BE THERE? AT THE PARTY TONIGHT? I TOOK A
breath, and sent it.

A minute. Then: *Yeah.*

Watson, I thought. Something was buzzing in my head. He
was there. He was talking to me. Even now, he was typing—

He's watching me. I have to go.

I asked four times for a follow-up. Received none. I hesitated, then switched the phone back off.

Watson, I thought, *and Lucien Moriarty,* and I turned the
volume down on what I was feeling until I couldn't hear it
anymore.

"Put your shoes on," Leander was saying. "I hope you two
are all set to kiss and make up."

"Uncle."

"Where did I put my jacket?"

"Uncle. I think Lucien's at the party."

"Cold feet?"

I tried very hard not to stamp my foot like a child. "I'm serious."

He sighed, and got back up to finish stuffing his bag with dry goods. "That really is the lowest excuse I think I've heard you use," he said. "I don't have time for this."

"Leander. Look at me." Grudgingly, he did. "Watson said he was being watched by someone. A male someone, and then he stopped responding. On the off chance that I'm right. That that *is* what Jamie is saying. What do we do?"

My uncle set the duffel bag aside, and hoisted up the shotgun he'd left sitting on the counter.

"I don't know," he said. "Any ideas?"

twenty-one
jamie

I COULDN'T GET MY FATHER ALONE.

We were at a fancy restaurant in SoHo, in New York City, that my mother had researched and booked the week before. All of us were there: my father, my mum, Lucien Moriarty. The whole happy gang. Abigail drove out with us too—she'd been upstairs when we'd arrived home, setting up the guest bedroom—though she'd left Malcolm and Robbie with their grandmother.

It was for the best. I didn't know what would happen tonight, but two small children had no business being in the middle of it.

Lucien—"Ted"—kept calling the waiter over for more wine, more cocktails, more lobster, more filet mignon. He did it in a way that was unobtrusive, conspiratorial. The food arrived at his elbow like it would at a king's, and he would smile at the rest of us, a bit sheepishly, and say, "Do you want to try this? I hear it's very good." They'd put us at a round table in a small private room so we could hear each other better, but Lucien was dominating the conversation.

He told my father he liked his coat, then wrote down the name of the shop where he'd bought it. He asked Abigail endless questions about Malcolm and Robbie—did they like their school? Their teachers? What scamps—what sort of trouble did they get up to? Then he pulled my mother in and asked if I had been like them as a child, and I watched as, for the first time, my mother and Abigail had a conversation that wasn't stilted and awful and loaded with resentment. *Jamie had taken that long to toilet train too*, my mother was saying, and Lucien held my mother's hand, running his thumb over the silver wedding band on her finger.

He was terrifying.

He was so much more terrifying than if he had been obviously cruel. That would have been confirmation. I would have had certainty. Would have felt justified in doing what I needed to do.

And now all I could think was, *I'm going crazy.*

I'd been staging an investigation into the wrongdoings against me like I was . . . Batman, or something. But I'd been having panic attacks. I'd been lashing out at Elizabeth; I'd been hiding things from my friends; I'd been accusing people of conspiring against me, as though I were so important that

247

people would go out of their way to mess my life up.

As though they enacted some grand scheme against me, and the *pièce de résistance* was spraying a can of soda onto my laptop.

But what if . . . what if I had done it to myself? What if I'd deleted my physics presentation by accident? What if I'd never written it in the first place? I was sleep-deprived, on high alert, I was throwing up whenever I even thought about last year, and maybe I was doing all this to myself, I was manufacturing situations to match the panic in my head. What if I was hallucinating? Blacking out? What if my sister was just a girl at a perfectly fine new school who hated it, who wanted her brother to take her home?

I was paranoid, I had been ever since I met Charlotte Holmes, but—why on earth would Lucien Moriarty take the time to woo and *marry my mother*? As though I needed so badly to treat my mother's remarriage as a personal affront to me that I'd decided her new husband was the boogeyman.

It wasn't far-fetched. I'd treated my father's remarriage that way.

Oh God.

What if my mum had just found a really nice guy who wanted to make her happy?

I spent the whole dinner staring at him. I couldn't even be subtle about it. When we'd first sat down, I'd been texting Holmes under the table, when Lucien—Ted—had put a hand on my shoulder. "This is a bit embarrassing," he was saying, "and I don't want to boss you around, but do you mind if you put your phone in the middle of the table?"

Confirmation. Confirmation that I wasn't losing my mind. He knew I was reaching out for help, he wanted to get my lifeline out of my hands—

Desperately, I looked up at my father. He was switching his phone to silent. Abigail was too.

"It's a game we've been playing on nice occasions," my mother said, "out with our friends. It helps us stay present. Everyone puts their phone in a stack in the center of the table, and the first person who caves to check theirs has to buy dinner."

She and Lucien shared a conspiratorial look. "Not that I'll make any of you pick up this tab," he said. "But I've been so eager to get to know you all."

I watched as he placed my phone at the top of the stack.

"There," my mother said. "Isn't that better?"

I sat next to him at dinner, this man who had orchestrated murders, told lies for politicians, blackmailed, cheated, infected me with a deadly virus and then dangled the antidote out of my reach. I refilled his wineglass. I listened to him tell my parents, at length, about how he'd gone to a wilderness school just like Shelby's. "I'd always loved horses," he said. "I was so happy when I found out we had that in common."

My mother squeezed his hand. "Shel loved her new school when we first arrived, you know. We'd signed the paperwork and everything. Such a beautiful campus! Impressive buildings. They even had a full medical facility—I imagine in case there's any riding accidents."

"And then the poor girl calls when we've hours away and begs us to come back and get her."

"Homesickness," my father said, shaking his head. "It's very real."

"She'll adjust soon enough," my mother said.

I was clenching my jaw so hard I was sure it had gone white.

As the waiters brought out shrimp and steak, my mother told stories about how the two of them had met—they'd bumped into each other in front of a grocery store; he'd helped her pick up her fruit and veg; just like a film!—and about their whirlwind courtship. "Ted is always traveling for work," she said, "and I found every time he went away I missed him more."

He caught up my mother's hand and kissed her palm. My own hands seized under the table.

"My first wife died," he said quietly, more to my mother than anyone else. "It was slow, and it was painful, and I—I spent a lot of time by her bedside, thinking. I didn't want to waste any more time. And when I met Gracie—I decided that life was too short, that I needed to take a risk."

My mother held their clasped hands to her lips. "From everything you've said, Betty was one hell of a woman."

Across the table, Abigail's eyes had filled with tears. My father was diligently cutting up his steak, nodding to himself, as though Ted was some kind of minor prophet.

That was what got me—what I couldn't figure out. How

much did my dad know? How much had he figured out? Did he look so studiously polite because he was celebrating his ex-wife's marriage to someone new, or because he knew he was sitting across from Lucien Moriarty, and was biding his time before he acted?

I tried desperately to catch his eyes across the table. But my father kept staring at his plate, sawing away at his food.

And my mother—my mother was so happy, her hair done up in curls, her nails painted, a modest ring on her finger. Wouldn't Lucien Moriarty have gone the whole nine yards? Stuck a giant rock there just for show? But no, there was just the dainty band on her finger, and Ted's gaze kept returning there, then flickering back up to her face, and I'd be damned if there wasn't actually affection in his eyes.

I was officially losing my goddamn mind.

"Does anyone need anything?" my mother asked, smiling. Everyone shook their heads.

"I think we've had everything on the menu," Abigail laughed. "It was so wonderful! Thank you."

"Do you think it's time for the cake, then?" Lucien asked, as the waiter appeared in the door to our private room. He made a hand signal, and the man nodded.

"Ted." It was the first time my father had spoken in a good half hour. He had on his bluffest tone, the one he reserved for toddlers and criminals and his in-laws. It was clear that, even if he didn't know who Ted really was, he didn't like him much. *Thank God for that,* I thought. *Not everyone's falling for him.*

"How about you and I sidle over to that excellent-looking bar, and I buy you a drink?"

"Oh!" Ted said. "I'd love to, but I don't want to leave Gracie—"

"No," my mother said, and beamed at her ex-husband. "Go. I want you and James to get to know each other."

And there. There it was.

Lucien paused.

It was natural to need a moment before a one-on-one with your wife's ex-husband. But this wasn't that. Holmes had taught me a lot of things, and I'd mastered very few of them, but I was getting better at reading people.

He didn't look hesitant. He didn't look scared. He looked, for less than a half second, furiously angry.

Watching Lucien's reaction, I had the uncanny feeling that I was watching Holmes at work. The clockwork gears spinning along so quickly the whole thing looked natural. But he must not have seen a way out of it without displeasing his new wife—and without her largess, he was powerless here.

Well, as powerless as Lucien Moriarty could be.

"Of course," Lucien said, pushing back his chair. "Of course, James."

"I'm just going to call and see how my boys are doing," Abigail said. She took her phone from the pile in the center of the table. From the look she shot me as she walked away, I could tell that she thought my mum and I needed a moment alone.

With her fork, my mother chased her lobster tail around

her plate. "You've been very quiet," she said.

"I know," I told her. "It's all been a bit of a shock."

She looked at me. "I'm happy, you know. And I'm allowed to be happy."

I knew what she wanted from me. The words I should have said. I should have hugged her, should have asked her to tell more stories about her and Ted—*What was the courthouse like? Was it really romantic? How did he propose?*

I couldn't make myself do it.

"Good," I said, instead, like an asshole, and we sat there like two strangers, sipping our water.

Who knew how long my father and Lucien would be? I'd find a way to sneak away. I'd take my phone with me; Abigail had taken hers, and so what if my mother was mad at me for it, it was nothing compared to the alternative. Maybe I was stark raving mad, but I had to know for sure.

The waitstaff began tidying around us, making room for the cake. I helped them make a stack of dirty plates to take away, more to avoid my mother's sad eyes than anything else. Lucien had dropped his napkin on the floor when he'd gotten up, and I pulled back his chair to replace it.

There. On his seat. My phone.

How had it gotten there, on his seat? I hadn't seen him take it. I hadn't seen him look at it.

How much did he know?

I had it in my hand and up my sleeve before my mother could see it. "You know, I should use the restroom too. It's a long trip back home."

My mum wasn't looking at me. "Do you want any dessert?" she asked, quietly.

"No," I said, standing up. "Thanks, though."

Inside, I locked myself in the restroom stall and hurriedly turned my phone on. I couldn't tell if he'd gone through my texts, my emails, if he'd slipped something in there to track my messages and calls. I tried to remember what Holmes had told me. A tiny earpiece? I peered into the receiver, but saw nothing.

And my phone was pinging, over and over, with messages. A long text from Elizabeth: *Lexington has been selling to Anna since he got here, but he didn't front her the thousand dollars. She was flashing it to him too; he said she said something about some kind of daddy. Sugar daddy? Is that what it's called? Disgusting. I got all of this out of him by telling him I would do his English homework for the rest of the semester. I'm not writing a word.*

Then: *Lena says that she thinks she has a lead on where the money ended up. I'm meeting with her in a minute, I'll report back.*

Then: *The money's real. The crime is real—Lena says that Anna is doubling down on her story. She's scared of something. She must need the money back.*

Then: *Jamie? Are you there? Can we meet tonight after bed check?*

Then, twenty minutes ago, four words from Holmes. *We're on our way.*

Her and Leander, I imagined. So that had been his errand in the city today. I wasn't surprised.

I'll meet you on campus at midnight, I wrote Elizabeth.

Inside the Carter Hall tunnel entrance. And to Holmes, I wrote: *Where are you?*

The door opened. Someone came in and started washing their hands.

I'm here, Holmes wrote, and I stood and deleted all of the messages I had, row by row, person by person, painstakingly, and when I opened the stall door Lucien Moriarty grabbed me by the shirt and pulled me through it.

twenty-two
charlotte

WE DIDN'T TAKE THE SHOTGUN. WE TOOK TWO PISTOLS instead. I had mine in my purse; it was the only thing that would fit in there, other than a lipstick. I didn't bring a lipstick. I brought my lockpick kit, belted to my upper thigh, and I put in my hair clips that could be used as a Phillips-head screwdriver if I needed one, and I thought for a moment about bringing a duffel bag along with us so I could in fact bring the shotgun—it was sawed off expertly, it was a thing of beauty— but that seemed like it would perhaps draw attention.

It was clear that Leander thought I was taking a ridiculous series of precautions. I hoped very much that he was right.

The restaurant was crowded when we walked in. I imagined it was always crowded; it was the sort of place where no one wore their wealth ostentatiously, but wore it all the same. Cashmere. Driving gloves on the table. That sort of thing. Leander pointed the way to a series of small private rooms, off past the bar where James Watson was drinking, alone.

"You go on," he said. "I'll say good-bye to James, and you can go talk to Jamie, and we can leave. Ten minutes, yes? There's a flight leaving LaGuardia at eleven. I mean to be on it."

I watched him as he walked toward James. It was voyeuristic to do so. But I thought I might learn something, maybe, about myself.

He approached silently—that wasn't hard to do in a restaurant this crowded, I deducted points—and sat down beside James all at once, as though he'd stepped through an imaginary door. It was the sort of thing that would usually get me a delighted smile, I thought. The show of effort, the neatness of it.

James Watson looked up at Leander, and then he put a hand over his eyes. Was he weeping? The trick wasn't that good.

Oh, I thought. *I should not be watching this.*

But I didn't go to the table, either. It was a fit of vanity more than anything else that led me to the restroom instead. I'd told myself I wanted to make sure my lockpicking kit wasn't showing beneath my dress. Wasn't it interesting, the interplay between our verbal thoughts and the currents that ran beneath them? In actual fact I wanted to assure myself that I looked pretty before I saw Jamie Watson for the last time, and I knew that was why I was going. (Good-byes are difficult; let me have this one thing; *qui multum habet, plus cupit*, et cetera.)

I looked passable for someone who suspected that the man trying to kill her was in the same restaurant.

Fine. I bent to wash my hands.

Noise from the other side of the bathroom wall, like someone beating a wet sack with their fists. More accurately, like someone was trying to kill someone else in the men's.

Watson.

I didn't stop to think about it. To consider the decision. It only took a moment to take the gun out of my evening bag.

twenty-three
jamie

LUCIEN MORIARTY HAD NO INTENTION OF KILLING ME. I knew, because he was telling me that verbatim.

"But I want you to know," he said, throwing another punch into my stomach, "that I have no problem hurting you until you listen to me."

He had his other arm against my throat, keeping me pinned to the wall. I'd fought against him at first, but I couldn't get any purchase, my feet sliding on the tiles as he cut off my air. All I'd managed to do was claw some of the buttons off his shirt when he'd first grabbed me out of the stall.

"You'll do what I say," he said, and pushed that arm harder against my neck. "If you don't, I'll stop. I'll stop giving you orders. And I'll start giving them instead to the people who have your sister. Do you understand?"

"What's your plan?" I croaked out.

"Wouldn't you like to know. Nod. Nod if you understand."

I couldn't manage to nod. I croaked out a "yes" and watched his awful shiny face smirk.

Ted. Ted with his charming accent, with the eyes only for my mother. Ted, bashful, brilliantly happy, Ted who had won everyone over.

Ted with his arm against my windpipe.

I took a shuddering breath. Then I pushed back hard and surged forward, shoving him down onto the floor. He skidded backward until his head hit the concrete wall.

I'd been playing a lot of rugby this last year.

"I want you to know that I'm not going to kill you," I said, putting my knees down onto his chest. He was conscious, breathing, but there was blood spilling down his forehead into his eyes. "But I want you to know—I don't have any problems hurting you until you listen to me."

His breathing was coming hard. "You little shit," he gasped, and at that moment the bathroom door flew open.

Charlotte Holmes was standing there in a red dress, pointing a pistol at Lucien Moriarty with both hands. The door snapped shut behind her.

"Oh," she said. "I didn't know you had this covered." She put the safety on and slipped the pistol into her bag.

There was a commotion in the main dining room. One lone voice, yelling, *I saw her, I saw she had a gun—*

Calmly, Holmes flipped the lock behind her.

There were so many things I could have felt in that moment, but the only one I could muster was relief.

I grinned at her. "Hi," I said.

"Hi," she said. "What are you going to do about that?" She pointed her toe at Lucien Moriarty. He was struggling to get up, but he was still groggy enough that I could keep him pinned for another few minutes. I told her so.

"Do you have a plan?" I asked, and then I blanched. *The last time I let Holmes make the plan—*

She must have seen it. "No," she said. "The gun was my plan. But—it's not the plan anymore. There's a window. A small one, up there."

"So we climb out it. Then what? Remember that he can hear us."

"Of course I can bloody well hear you—"

I punched Lucien in the mouth. "That's for my mother," I informed him. "Or for my sister. For both."

Holmes raised an eyebrow. "That's going to leave a mark."

"But the bleeding head wound, that's just going to disappear."

"I didn't say I wasn't okay with your decision."

"You should be," I said. "The head wound was for you."

There was someone hammering on the bathroom door. "Come out, we've called the police, come out—"

"Get my phone?" I asked her. "I think it's under the sink."

"Screen's cracked," she said, tossing it to me.

"I'll charge it to him." I scrolled through my contacts. "Here. Hold on."

"Detective Shepard."

"Shepard," I said into the phone. "I—"

Lucien shoved hard against me; two seconds later, Holmes had her gun trained on him again. *Check him for weapons,* I mouthed to her, and she started patting down his legs. "Hi."

"Is everything okay?"

"Yes. Well. No," I said into the phone, as Holmes pulled a sheathed knife out of Lucien's sock. "We're in the men's bathroom at Arnold's restaurant in New York City. Lucien Moriarty married my mother, and now I have him pinned to the floor, and Holmes is here with a gun, and someone's called the cops."

"You—you *what?*"

Holmes darted in around me and yanked a gun out from inside his blazer. Then she pulled out his wallet and his mobile and his passport, one two three, with the clean skill of a pickpocket. Her other hand was steady on the gun.

The hammering on the door was getting harder. "Police!"

"Like I said. Listen, Shepard, I want you to know that we're going to have to leave him here—"

"Police!"

"—but I can give you the full story when I see you." Holmes made an all-clear sign with her hands. I nodded.

"This isn't my jurisdiction," Shepard was saying.

"I sort of thought you should know anyway."

"Fine—then get down to the station."

"Later. We're kind of busy."

"Jesus, Jamie, get down there *now*—" But I'd already hung up. Holmes was stuffing Lucien's things into her tiny bag.

"Police! We're opening this door!" Someone throwing their shoulder against it. A splintering sound.

The adrenaline was starting to make its way out of my system. The glow of it, the sudden clarity, the confidence, it was going, and when I got up off Lucien Moriarty I had to wince when I kicked him to stay down.

I was going to do jail time, I realized. It wasn't even a question anymore.

Holmes nodded to the window. I clambered up onto the sink, then pulled her up next to me, and for a moment, she was flush against me, warm, her hair just under my nose, and I bent to make a cradle with my hands to hoist her up, the way I did when we first met, when I was helping her climb into Dobson's dorm room. We were better at it now. On the first push up she had the window open; on the second she was out, and reaching a hand down to help me.

The bathroom door cracked, like lightning striking a tree. Lucien Moriarty was stumbling to his feet. Outside, people were screaming.

But I grabbed Charlotte Holmes's hand, and I scrabbled up the wall with my shoes, and she pulled me out onto the corner of Broadway and Prince. The second we got to our feet, we started to run.

twenty-four
charlotte

WE NEEDED A BOLT-HOLE, SOMEWHERE WE COULD HIDE. They would check the trains. They would check the taxis and the toll stations and the rental cars. They would check the airports now too, and so I supposed if going to London tonight had still been on the docket, it wasn't anymore.

Possibilities:

Return to the Green apartment.

Fall on my sword in front of Hadrian Moriarty, ask for sanctuary.

Locate an empty Airbnb, break in.

Hide temporarily and call DI Green for assistance.

Leander might be back at the Green apartment; we might

lead the chase back to his door. I didn't dare contact him in case he was currently being questioned. The second option was suicidal, and the third, if we misjudged even slightly, would involve us waking up vacationers by breaking into their rental. That meant more police. The fourth—the fourth had possibility.

I dragged Watson into an alley, down behind a Dumpster at the far end. A moment passed, and then a police car raced by. The next one got stuck behind a snarl of traffic. Its siren bayed on and on, like a hound.

"I'm calling the Yard," I whispered. Watson nodded.

It was the middle of the night in London, but DI Green was awake. "Hi, Stevie," she said.

"Yes. Hi. I need a bolt-hole in Lower Manhattan."

"What did you do to Lisa's apartment?"

"Nothing. We just—we had a physical altercation with Lucien Moriarty in a public restroom in SoHo."

"We who?"

"Watson and I."

"Yes. Brilliant. Well done."

"Help or don't," I hissed, "but spare me the smart remarks."

"I hear sirens," she grumbled, but I could hear her typing. "Fine. Listen, I meant to speak to you anyway. We made contact today with a new source."

"Who?"

"Merrick Morgan-Vilk. He's in your area. I'll call him to

say that I'm sending you to him. Here, I have an address, do you have a pen handy?"

Watson made a horrible strangled sound. A rat had made its way out of the Dumpster and was now crawling across his shoes.

"No," I said. "But I have a fairly good memory."

twenty-five
jamie

I REALIZED, AS WE WERE USHERED IN THE BACK ENTRANCE
of the Morgan-Vilk residence, that my shirt was covered in
Lucien Moriarty's blood. Or maybe my own. It was hard to
tell. Holmes, who was always so fastidiously clean, was filthy.
Her red dress had gone brown and ragged at the bottom, and
her legs below it were all-over cuts and dirty-looking bruises.
She and I stood together in the kitchen like a pair of murderous orphans in the thick of the Black Plague.

The kitchen itself was unremarkable—cabinets, table, a
stainless steel sink. From what I could tell from the stairs leading upstairs, Morgan-Vilk was renting the bottom two floors
of a brownstone.

The girl who let us in eyed us warily. "Mr. Morgan-Vilk has

just gone to get some documents."

"Yes," Holmes said. "Fine. Who are you?"

"My colleague," said Milo Holmes, sitting at the kitchen table, as his assistant exited quietly. I jumped about a mile. I hadn't seen him there. From the way that Holmes's eyes widened, then narrowed, she hadn't seen him either. Which was a first, as far as I could tell.

Maybe it was because Milo looked nothing like himself. A tracksuit. A massive beard. No glasses, and his hair long, tied up in a knot on the top of his head. An empty glass in front of him, and a bottle.

"No," Holmes said, edging back toward the door. "No, absolutely not," and for a hysterical moment I thought she was talking about his man bun.

"Sit," he said, and I was shocked to hear a slur on his words, as though he'd been drinking. "Sit, or I'll drag you back into this house and tie you to that goddamn chair."

I'd always been afraid of Milo Holmes—it would be stupid not to be—but in that moment I was terrified.

Holmes was impassive, but she sat down across from him slowly, as though he might lunge at her. "DI Green sent me. I'm here for Merrick Morgan-Vilk."

"You always assume I don't know these things," Milo said. He splashed more whiskey into his glass. "You never learn, do you."

I swallowed. "Why are you here, Milo?"

"Jamie," he said, with extravagant scorn. "I'm being so

rude, forgive me. Perhaps you'd like a change of clothes? Either of you?"

"No, thank you. Milo—"

"Stop looking at me like a pair of frightened rabbits." He brought the glass to his lips. "I wanted you here. I'm not going to hurt you."

Holmes watched his throat as he swallowed. "Are you in touch with DI Green?"

"Detective Inspector Green was the one who reached out to me, girl." That, from a voice booming down the stairs. "Hold on, hold on. Yes, hello." Merrick Morgan-Vilk was a bit out of breath. He had a document box balanced on his well-fed waistline, and he greeted us with a politician's smile. By habit, I jumped to my feet. Holmes extended her hand up from her chair.

"Merrick," Milo said. "Miss Holmes would like to know what's 'going on here.'" The air quotes were almost visible.

He dropped the document box down on the table. "Our friend Milo here—"

Milo saluted.

"—has introduced me to his friends on the United Nations Security Council. I'm here working with an exploratory committee."

"I see," I said. I really didn't see.

"That's neither here nor there," Milo said. "I'm here because I don't think the Americans will extradite me back to Britain. Well. They might not. Perhaps they will. Who knows! It's a party, really."

Morgan-Vilk's mouth tightened. "We've had some . . . new developments these past few days."

Milo took another sip. "Security footage. Of all things. Security footage from the camera on *my* property, that *I* set up, footage that I wiped so clean it was *sparkling*, and somehow it ended up on some idiot's desk at Scotland Yard, someone who didn't know the score—"

"Footage. Of you—of you shooting—" I couldn't make my mouth say the words. Say *August Moriarty*.

For a moment, Holmes put her head into her hands. "And what? Now you're feeling all the guilt that you'd been suppressing?"

"Guilt?" Milo held his glass up to the light. "Is this guilt? I just don't particularly want to go to prison."

Holmes looked like she was about to launch herself across the table at him, claws extended. I put a hand on her shoulder. "Hey," I said to her.

She stiffened, then relaxed. Then nodded.

Milo watched this with some interest. "Disgusting," he said, to no one, and drained the rest of his whiskey.

Morgan-Vilk cleared his throat. "Charlotte," he said. "We were talking about the UN?"

"Right," she said, her eyes still on Milo. "And your mistress, of course."

To his credit (or actually, maybe against his credit), Morgan-Vilk smiled.

"What? Wait. I'm sorry," I said. "I'm still sort of lost."

"Mr. Morgan-Vilk, in the interest of time, would you mind

terribly if I explained to Watson here your current situation, and what we're all doing here?"

Merrick Morgan-Vilk looked delighted. He would have liked my father. "Yes, go on."

"Where should I start?" Holmes asked, scanning him with her eyes.

"Well, not to put too fine a point on it, my mistress isn't my mistress anymore—"

"No, of course not," she said. "Your mistress isn't your mistress anymore, she's your wife. That's easy, the wedding band. But she's not here with you—I've noticed you turning it around on your finger, perhaps because you'd forgotten to call her today and now it's too late to reach her in Britain. What was your district, when you were an MP? Is she back at the old family pile? No—that would upset your children. A flat, then, in London, because if anyone is avoiding the countryside and has your means, they're there. And, by the way, you're not running for office, so I'm not sure why you insist on calling whatever you're doing here an exploratory committee."

"Oh?" he asked. "And how do you know that?"

"You're sleeping well, eating well, and you look like you're at peace." Holmes paused, her eyes tracking into the distance, and then she continued. "Any man who's running for office again after a sex scandal wouldn't be so comfortable. He also wouldn't be in America. It would be absurdly stupid to raise American money to run for British office. You're meeting with a member of the UN Security Council? You're done running for office. You're trying to drum up support for a nomination for an ambassadorship, which is not precisely legal but not precisely illegal, either. Hence the cloak and dagger."

Mr. Morgan-Vilk applauded. He had a wonderful, jolly smile. "Oh, excellent," he said to Milo. "I like your sister. How fun."

Milo shook his head. "She's missing all the important bits. Like telling us what on earth she's doing here."

Holmes scowled. "I phoned Scotland Yard in need of a safe house."

"Because you had just been beating Lucien Moriarty half to death," Mr. Morgan-Vilk said, with the same jolly smile he had on before. I inched away from him. Maybe I didn't want him to meet my father. "How did you manage that?" he asked me. "Brilliant work, really."

"Ah. Rugby?"

"I should have played rugby," he said. "Pity. Yes, anyway, Mr. Moriarty. I am very interested in Mr. Moriarty."

Holmes frowned. "I've looked at the records. You know, when I first spoke to your son—"

"When was that?"

"Monday," Holmes said. "In his stairwell." She said it so smoothly it took me a second to realize.

"You were there—"

"Later," she said, and gave me a look I couldn't quite interpret. "When I first spoke with him, I got the impression that perhaps Lucien had quit your campaign to deal with the matter of his brother August losing his job as my tutor."

"'Losing his job.' What a euphemism. Can't forget the

trunkload of cocaine, or you framing him," Milo said.

"I'm so happy to entertain you. Yes, me and my wretched mistakes, it's all very dramatic." Holmes's tone was acid. "But I looked them up, and the dates don't track. Your election was the summer before all that happened. So why did Lucien quit, just before your scandal broke? When he would quite literally have been needed to 'fix' your problem?"

The two of them locked eyes. Morgan-Vilk rested his hands on his belly. "After Moriarty quit, and I lost my seat in Parliament so dramatically, I had some time on my hands. As you can imagine, I had developed a bit of a . . . fixation with Lucien."

"And?"

"He consults for a number of clients, you know. Spins things for them in the news. He hasn't worked for Downing Street in years, it's all been in the private sector. You spend your days telling lies for a living—it's toxic. It can kill your sense of right and wrong, and if you didn't have one to begin with . . . do you want to know why he left my campaign?"

"Why?" I asked.

"He was having an affair with my wife," Morgan-Vilk said. There wasn't a scrap of emotion in his voice. "And I had no idea. It had been going on for more than a decade. Lucien was . . . what, mid-twenties when he started working for me? Young, handsome. He has that ne'er-do-well charm, or did, anyway. That Moriarty name. There's an odd glamour to it. I suppose my wife was drawn to it.

"He left my campaign because my daughter, Anna, was

thirteen years old, and the moment she hit puberty she began to look just like him."

Anna.

Anna Morgan-Vilk.

Anna with the missing thousand dollars.

"No," I breathed. "You have got to be—"

"Was there a paternity test done?" Holmes demanded.

"Of course," Morgan-Vilk said. "Lucien wore his hair longer, in those days. Anna did it herself—plucked a few hairs off his coat and sent them in through a mail service. She showed him the results the week before the election."

"And he rabbited," I said.

"Yes," Morgan-Vilk said. That smile again, like Santa Claus. "Yes, he rabbited. I quite like that term. And when the news broke the next week about me and my mistress—well. My daughter despised me. She despised her mother. And she began worshipping the 'father' she'd just discovered she had. She tried to live with him, you know, and he promptly sent her off to school."

"Our school. She's working for him now," I said. "Set me up pretty neatly earlier this week."

"Oh, I thought he might do something like that. Nasty business." Morgan-Vilk's smile faded slightly. "I hate that my girl is mixed up in all of that. You two—well. Like I said, the story about Charlotte and August and Lucien is the sort of nightmare fuel I've been running on, thinking about Anna. That man has it in for you, and he's using my daughter to do it."

"I'm sorry," Milo said, and to my surprise it sounded

genuine. Maybe it was because the bottle was almost empty. He stood, unsteadily, to open the document box on the table. "I came here originally to discuss certain actions Mr. Morgan-Vilk could perform to improve his public perception, both here and abroad."

Even drunk and disheveled, Milo Holmes had a certain sort of dignity that made you loath to talk back to him. But I couldn't let this one slide. "Right. You being here had nothing to do with taking down Lucien. With helping your sister."

She locked eyes with him. He shook his head almost imperceptibly.

"Come, now. Moriarty has his fingers in other pies. Yours isn't the only one." Morgan-Vilk indicated the files in the document box. "Let me put it bluntly. He's a brand-name criminal, and I'm in need of the recognition that would come from bringing him to justice. So I'd like to be the one to haul him in, if you don't mind. I'm working out the extradition details already."

"Mind?" I laughed, bitterly. "I don't know about Holmes, but yes, please, for Christ's sake, drag him home in irons. That fucker just married my *mother*."

"Did he?" Milo murmured, the way you would ask about the weather.

"That's a good reason to be wearing someone's blood down your shirt," Morgan-Vilk said.

"I actually don't know if I agree with that, but sure, fine. Look, he has some kind of plan. Who knows how deep this goes. And he's on his way to accomplishing it—Milo is hiding out, drunkenly giving you advice in a *kitchen*, and Holmes and I have our hands tied. I can't imagine what he's telling the police right now. The facts themselves are pretty damning."

"Which are?"

Holmes sighed. "We beat him up, stripped him of his weapons, his wallet, and his fake passport, and then we escaped the police through the bathroom window."

Morgan-Vilk whistled; Milo stuck his hand out. "His passport," he said. "And wallet."

"No."

"I'm sorry?"

"No," Holmes said again. "Why would I help you? Where would that possibly get me?"

"Oh, I don't know, Lottie. Closer to putting away your tormentor?"

"You don't help." She was struggling with them, the words. In her filthy red dress, she looked like a girl who'd wandered away from an explosion. "Milo, you don't know how to help. You take over, instead. You make things worse. I knew what I was doing! I knew where Leander was! I was going to *free* him, I went to Berlin to lure Hadrian and Phillipa back to our house. DI Green was going to 'arrest' them. Lucien would never let his brother and sister take the fall for something he'd done. He has that much loyalty. In order to spring them, he would have had to make a move! Come out into the open! It was a *plan*, a good one, and then you showed up with your *sniper rifle*? Didn't it have a scope? Didn't you stop to look before you fired? Did you—"

Milo had his hands up in front of him. They were shaking. "I was trying to protect you," he said, quietly. "I only ever wanted to protect you."

"You had years to protect me," Holmes said, defeated. "That was a piss-poor time to start."

They stared at each other.

"Charlotte," Morgan-Vilk said, into the silence.

"Oh, for crying out loud—fine," she said. "Fine. How about this? I'll give you *copies* of Lucien's forged passport and anything you find in his wallet. In exchange for the originals, I'll allow you to bring the bastard in when the time comes."

"And that time is?" Morgan-Vilk asked.

Holmes glanced at me. "Watson?"

She was asking my opinion. "We still have a few loose ends," I said, taken aback. "How does tomorrow work for you?"

While Holmes supervised the extensive photography Milo's assistant was performing on Lucien's things, I stepped aside to turn on my phone. It had been ringing so incessantly since we'd cut and run that I'd had to turn it off to save the battery.

I had nearly a hundred texts, almost all of which were from my stepmother, Abigail. *Jamie, what have you done? What were you possibly thinking?* and *Jamie, come home, it'll be okay, I promise,* a blatant lie, and *Your father keeps telling me to let the police handle this but I just don't know what's going on, what were you thinking, how could you do something like this?* I was horrified for her, but when I began to type out a reply, I realized that she might not be the one in control of her phone. In fact, I'd bet that she wasn't. If not Lucien Moriarty, then the police.

Nothing from my mum. Well—now that the adrenaline was beginning to leave my system, I had to come to terms with the possibility that there wouldn't be anything from my mother ever again. I'd just assaulted her new husband in a public restroom. I couldn't even wrap my head around it, what she must be feeling. Even if she found out that Lucien Moriarty had been behind it all this time, I'd beaten him so brutally that she had to think that I was a monster. How could she ever look at me again?

I realized I was shaking. Nauseous. I took a steadying breath. *Think about it later,* I told myself. *You can't deal with this now.*

Texts from Elizabeth making sure I was okay; she hadn't heard back from me. Texts from Lena, incomprehensible, thick with unicorn emojis, celebrating some kind of win she thought was coming when we'd meet up tonight.

And a single text from my father. *I want you to know that I'm proud of you.* Nothing else.

For some reason, that scared me more than anything else I'd seen tonight.

I was crashing, and hard, by the time that Holmes returned with the passport in her fist. "I'm going to have to sleep with this under my pillow," she muttered, as Morgan-Vilk chattered on a phone in the background.

I showed Holmes my text messages from her and Elizabeth. "What do you think? Should we meet up with Lena?

See what she has on the boil?"

"I'd think so. My plan had been to leave the country tonight—"

I stared at her. "Tonight?"

She hurried on. "—but I don't think it's safe for me to rejoin my uncle—"

"Wait, you were staying with Leander? For how long?"

"—or maybe it is safe, but why risk it, and then there's the matter of you being hunted by the police, and I—well. I'd prefer to be here. But Lena said midnight. That's still four hours until we're due back in at Sherringford."

"Jesus." It was only eight o'clock. I was shocked a whole week hadn't passed since I left campus this afternoon.

"Well." Holmes wasn't quite meeting my eyes. In the background, Milo dumped out a file folder on the table, and papers scattered like a rush of leaves.

"We haven't had a chance to— I haven't told you about Shelby," I said, remembering in a horrible rush. How could I have forgotten? Lucien-stroke-Ted, and our mad dash across town, and Milo appearing like the Ghost of Hangovers Past— all of it had pushed my sister to the back of my mind. "She started her new school today, here, in America, but I think it's another con of Lucien's. My mother's claiming that she's just homesick, but I trust my sister's judgment, and Holmes—Shel was scared, when she called. Hiding in a closet scared. That isn't homesickness."

Holmes's eyes refocused on me. "Where is it?"

"Somewhere close to Sherringford, I think? I don't know—"

"Get her out of there," she said, immediately. "Now. *Now*, Jamie. How long has she been there?"

"Only a few hours," I said. "Hopefully not long enough for anything terrible to happen to her."

"There are a lot of terrible things," Holmes said, "that can happen to a girl in a few hours."

"Can we get a car? How do we get out of the city? Is there—"

"Do you require my assistance?" Milo called.

"No," Holmes and I said together, and she dragged me away from him and Morgan-Vilk, out into the darkened hallway.

There, she paced, dragging her hands through her hair. "No. No, we can't be everywhere. We can't try to be. We have resources—yes. My uncle."

"My dad," I said, pulling out my phone. "I'll text him."

Dad, I wrote. *Shelby's in trouble. Her new school—I think it's a front for something.*

Holmes was watching my fingers. "Lucien consults for a school in Connecticut. A wilderness rehabilitation school. I've been to places like that, and they're awful, but generally safe. I don't know how true that will hold if Lucien is involved."

"She's just a girl," I said, almost desperately.

"I know," Holmes said. "I wish that made a difference."

Get Leander and get her out of there. Please, I wrote, and I powered down my phone, but even still I couldn't keep myself from staring at the screen, like some reassurance would appear there by magic.

"Wash your hands of it for now," she said, watching me. "Trust them. Your father. Leander. They've handled worse. And I know your sister. She's strong."

"Okay," I said, because it was awful and it was true.

"Okay," she said, and then, "Jamie. Can we talk?"

"Yeah," I said, "of course," because we hadn't yet, not really. She fidgeted a little, flexing her hands. "There's a bedroom upstairs," she said, finally. "If you want some privacy."

"Oh." The back of my neck went hot, then freezing cold. "Oh. Okay."

"Not 'oh,'" she said, the rebuttal automatic, and then, "I mean. Not necessarily 'oh.' Not 'oh' unless—dammit, Jamie, I am trying very hard here, can we please just go upstairs."

There was more house here than I'd realized. The room we'd been given was at the end of a long corridor, the floorboards chalky and warped, the walls paneled too in dusty white. All the other rooms were shut up, unused, and there was a musty smell in the air, like no one had opened a window all winter.

Our bedroom had the same haunted feeling. The bed was piled high with white down and linen, and there were chairs and a dresser, but they were covered in dust sheets. I wanted to snap them off and shake them out, see if there was anything below them worth salvaging. I didn't, though. They were beautiful as they were.

Holmes didn't care about that. Not that kind of beauty. "Someone might have bugged the room," she muttered, and immediately started dismantling it piece by piece, beginning

281

with the bed. Once she'd finished feeling up the mattress, I flopped myself down on it and watched her work.

It was the first moment I'd had alone with her in over a year.

I found myself looking for signs of change, ones I could see. Her hair was the same length, give or take, dark and straight down to her shoulders, her eyes still the same unfathomable gray. She was taking apart the dresser, now, removing each drawer to examine them, and she moved with the furious intensity she always had when we were on a case.

Like a missile, made of pylons and metal and rocket fuel, deadly and unstoppable, fired off to hit a tiny target thousands of miles away. That precise. That incredible.

I stopped myself there. A year of beating my head against a wall, alone, cursing her, mourning August, awash in guilt and shame. An hour together in Manhattan, and I caught myself admiring her?

Really?

I felt myself begin to shut down.

"What's wrong?" she asked, flicking the sheet off the last chair. It kicked up a storm's worth of dust.

"Nothing," I said, coughing. "Do you need help?"

"I'm almost done." She dug her hands underneath the cushion. "Wait—no. Hold on." Frowning, she examined the thing in her palms. "I think that's an actual bug."

"Maybe wash your hands, and—"

"Right."

I saw, when she returned, that she'd also made some effort to wash out the bottom half of her dress. "I think it's unsalvageable," she said, standing awkwardly by the bed. "I feel badly. I took this from the house where I was staying."

"Where were you staying?" I asked, because I didn't know what else to say.

"Ah," she said, gathering back up the sheets and pillows in her arms. She dumped them unceremoniously on top of me. "I don't—that is—do you remember Detective Inspector Green?"

It was hard to forget her. She'd been the one to arrest Holmes for killing August Moriarty. "I do," I said, neutrally.

"We've known each other for so long—no. I mean, yes, she was the Jameson emeralds, but I—her sister—"

"You're staying in her sister's place," I said, sitting up.

"Yes."

"By yourself?"

"I've been going it alone now for some time," she said, with an airiness that was obviously false. "But Leander's with me now—I didn't know if you knew that."

"I didn't. But it makes sense, since you showed up together tonight."

"Of course."

"I'm not stupid, Holmes," I said, and she recoiled. Why did I lob that one at her? Why was all this suddenly so hard? We could put down our worst nightmare in a restaurant bathroom and then escape across New York bloody City in the dark, but

I couldn't talk to her alone in a quiet room.

"I never thought you were stupid," she said. "Not ever. Which you know."

I'd been trying so hard to stay in the moment, to meet her where we were now. But her defensiveness—*which you know*—dragged it out of me. "I wasn't worth it," I said, trying to keep my voice even. "You decided that I wasn't worth telling the truth to. You couldn't even tell me where you were going. The police took you away, and you walked off without saying a word. You were gone. A *year* went by, Holmes. A year! For all I knew, you were—you were dead."

"You're my friend," she said, crossing her arms. "My only friend. If I would've told anyone what I was doing, I would have told you. But I thought that you would trust me."

"You don't get to pull that one," I told her. "We chased Hadrian and Phillipa across Europe because you lied to me. I should have trusted you after that? Leander was in your *basement*. You knew about it. You didn't tell me. I should have trusted you after that?"

"Yes," she said, automatically. Then she winced. "No. No, of course not. But can you blame me for not thinking clearly after what happened to—?"

"To August," I said. "Well, you were thinking clearly enough to give me orders."

She gave me a despairing look. "Not good ones."

"Clearly not."

Holmes shifted her weight. "Anything else?"

"Well." I pulled my knees up to my chest. "I— That's all."

"That's all?"

"I had— There's been so much I've wanted to tell you. I've made so many mistakes. I feel . . . I feel almost like you've ruined me."

"Watson—"

"Or maybe I was like this all along. I didn't know why you put up with me, for so long, and at first I thought, *I'm not as smart as her, I'm just her sidekick,* that you wanted me around because I—I admired you. I couldn't hide it, I felt it so much. I just didn't know what you wanted from me. What *you* got from the two of us together. And then you left, and I—I think I got lost, somewhere. I don't like myself anymore. I used to. Like myself. At least a little. And I've just been behaving like a monster."

"You think I've done that to you?" It was an honest question.

"Maybe," I said, and swallowed, and said the thing I'd been thinking ever since Lucien Moriarty dragged me out of that bathroom stall. "Holmes, I don't know if we're going to get out of this one alive."

Her eyes were shining. "I know."

I forced a laugh. "Any final words?"

She shrugged a shoulder.

"Holmes—" I pulled it off, the comforter, the sheets, all those mountains of white, clearing a space beside me. "Come here," I said, then winced. "I mean. If you want to."

She sat down gingerly at the edge of the bed. "Jamie—"

The word hovered in the air.

"I'm sorry," she said, all at once.

"For what?"

"I'm—I'm sorry, Jamie."

I waited. Sometimes I could read her as clearly as though her thoughts were scrolling across the sky, and sometimes she was the most unknowable creature in the world.

"When I met you, I was still . . . I *hate* this."

Words are imprecise, I remembered her saying once. *Too many shades of meaning. And people use them to lie.*

Holmes had this look on her face like she was trying to drag something up from the basement of her heart.

"Try," I said.

"I was . . . I think the only way to describe it is wild."

"Wild?"

As she spoke, she left long pauses between her sentences. "Or hungry. Like I'd been kept in a room for years, and given enough food and water to survive. Then I was brought out to a buffet, and there were all these people there who had been eating for years. I knew that I wasn't one of them. I was hardly even a person. I was . . . I just *wanted.* I was starving, but it had made me sharp. The world was too soft, too complacent. I hated it for that.

"This isn't right either. Maybe I was being held underwater. Maybe I held myself there. When I met you, I'd been thinking I was at the end of it all." She drew her knees up to her chest. "The end of me, I suppose. I think it was true, that I was at the end of whatever that self was. But I had to go off and end it myself, do you understand? Alone. I wanted . . . by the time

I saw you again, I wanted to have found my way back to a beginning."

I didn't understand her at all. I thought, *I'll never know anyone better than I know her.*

"I'm sorry," she said simply. Her dark hair fell down around her face. "I should have told you what I was planning. I panicked. August was dead, and everyone else had scattered, and there were weapons in play, and you weren't safe. All I could think was, *If I can get Watson to DI Green, he'll be out of harm's way. She'll know what to do.* I skipped all the other steps and went straight there. I get so impatient, but I was wrong, and I . . ."

"You let your brother walk." I tried to keep my voice firm.

Holmes shook her head rapidly. "He would have walked anyway. You couldn't arrest him, then. Maybe you still can't. Not with his money, not with his team of lawyers. Milo got sued maybe twice a week. He had a crisis team on twenty-four-hour call, he would eat the Sussex constabulary for breakfast. And now—I don't know. Maybe he'll see justice for it."

"I hope so. If not, there isn't going to be anybody left to hold responsible," I said. "For August."

"There will be. I might have started this, but I'll finish it with putting Lucien away. And even if he wasn't the one to kill August, I'll still consider that case closed. Maybe I'm the one responsible for him dying. But I was . . . I was a child, and I hadn't been given a compass, and I made a terrible decision. I thought I'd get him fired from being my tutor. I don't think that makes me responsible for his death. Maybe that makes me a bad person." She straightened her shoulders "But I . . . I don't think I am."

"I don't think you're a bad person."

"You did."

"I don't anymore," I said, and found that I meant it.

"I want to be good," she said. "I want to be good without being nice. Can I do that?"

I smiled, despite myself. "I like you best when you aren't nice."

I'd been holding out hard against the urge to touch her, but she turned to me now in a rush, buried her face against my neck. My arms went up and around her almost of their own accord.

"I *hate* this." She wiped at her face with an angry hand. "All week I've been crying, and why? Over you? Over Lucien Moriarty?"

"I'm getting his blood all over your dress," I told her. "I'd cry, too."

"You're not still dating that girl," she said.

I raised my eyebrows. "That wasn't a question."

"You're not wearing her scarf anymore."

"When did you ever see me wear that scarf? In that stair-well?"

Her quicksilver smile. "I have my sources."

"Is that what you've been doing all this time?" I asked, stroking her hair. "Watching me?"

"Would it be terrible if I had?"

I exhaled. "A little terrible."

She pulled back to see my face. "You don't think it's terrible."

"I don't."

"You think it's kind of hot, actually." That smile again, there and gone.

"Did you just say 'kind of hot'? Who are you?"

"Most recently, I was a fashion vlogger," she said, and then she kissed me, quickly, like an impulse, like an accident.

"Hey," I said softly, pulling back.

She tugged at my collar. I felt her hand trace its way down, and she undid the top button, slowly, sliding it between her fingers. It was like this with her. Fits and starts. Nothing I could ever see coming.

I'd never thought we'd be here again.

"Holmes," I said, reaching up to touch her hands, to fold them in mine.

"Do you forgive me?"

"You sound like you're making some kind of decision," I said, because she was scaring me a little.

"Do you?"

I paused, thinking. Not long ago, I'd wanted everything from her. For her to be my confidant, my general. My best and only friend. I wanted her to be the other half of me, like we together made a coin. She the king's head to my tails. I loved her like you would the person you'd always wanted to be, and in return I would have followed her anywhere, excused any action, fought to keep her hoisted high on her throne.

When that myth I'd made of her shattered, I didn't know

what to do. This last year, any thought I had of her felt wrong. Skewed. How could I understand what had happened, when I had put up so many lenses between my experience of her and the girl herself?

Holmes wasn't a myth, or a king. She was a person. And to have a relationship with a person, you had to treat them like one.

"Can I forgive you a little now?" I asked. "And then a little more tomorrow, and the next day? If there is a next day?"

"Yes," she said, quickly, like it was more than she had asked for. Like I might take it back.

"Provided you don't blow anything up, of course."

"Yes."

"Or try to look in my ears again while I'm sleeping—"

"Yes," she said, laughing. That look on her face, always, like she was surprised to be laughing, like it was something involuntary and slightly shameful, like a sneeze.

I couldn't take it. "I missed you," I said, gripping her shoulders. She was here. She was here, and I could touch her and God, how could I be so lucky? I said it again, like a compulsion: "I missed you, I missed you—"

"Jamie," she said helplessly. She said my name again, trying out the word's edges, almost like she was saying it aloud for the first time.

"Since when you do call me Jamie?" It came out soft, a little dangerous.

"Why don't you call me Charlotte?" she whispered. Her fingers went back up to my neck, and then followed an invisible line up to my cheek, traced my lips. "Why don't you call me by my name?"

Because she'd been a girl from a story I loved. Because when we first met, she told me to call her Holmes, and when Charlotte told me to do something, I listened.

"Do you want me to?" I asked.

"No," she said, urgently. "No, I only want to know why."

"Because I needed a name for you that was mine," I said, and her eyes went wide and dark with something I didn't have a word for. An hour later, I still had her in my arms.

twenty-six
charlotte

WE ROUSED OURSELVES, FINALLY, WHEN THERE WAS A knock on the door.

"You have thirty minutes before the car arrives to take you to Sherringford," Milo's assistant said, handing me a bundle. She had bought dark clothing in our sizes and then had it pressed. It was far nicer than anything I'd been able to purchase myself this past year; the shoes, in particular, were things of beauty. I thought that I might love her. I felt very loving, just then.

Watson and I took turns showering. Back in the room, I hummed a little to myself as I did up the buttons of my shirt. He laced up his new black boots. He was smiling—he had always wanted a pair like mine.

"How are you feeling?" he asked when he'd finished.

For me, anything done in a bed with a boy was a fraught prospect. I didn't know how long that would be true, if it would be true forever. Several times tonight we had had to stop ourselves, talk through what we were doing and how we felt about it. It sounded like a tedious exercise, and perhaps in some ways it was. I didn't care.

How was I feeling? Like one of my Aunt Araminta's beehives, buzzing, like I had a city inside of me. With Watson I had always been made better. I had spent the last year mourning our friendship, but knowing too it was better to be away. And now—

Now I'd have to keep on mourning our friendship, I supposed. He and I had been here once before, in a hotel in Prague, but before we could reconfigure what we were to one another, everything had disintegrated around us. Tonight, his dark, tousled hair was half dry, and he smelled the same as I did, as we'd used the same shampoo. He'd done the half cuffs on his trousers because they were, like all his other pairs, a bit too long, and there was nothing new about his shoulders, but an hour before I had mapped them anyway with my fingers. I loved them, his shoulders. He'd watched me, wondering, while I touched his wrists, his palms. *What are you remembering?* I fitted his hand against my hip and told him the three other times he'd put it just there (a bookshop in South London, by accident; on the flight back to England, to take my phone from my pocket; while brushing our teeth in the same bathroom in Sussex, because he needed to open a drawer and I'd been in the way). I was unmarked by what had happened tonight, but his torso was darkening with bruises where that bastard had driven in his fist and there was still a bit of blood under his fingernails and there was a look to him that was altogether new, wary and alert and impossibly sad, even now, especially now, one I'd first seen when I'd barged in on him beating the life out of Lucien Moriarty. I'd thought I'd come in to save him, but Watson had needed a partner, not an avenging angel.

He had a lovely left hook. He had a nick on his jaw where he'd cut himself shaving. How had I just seen it now? I wanted to examine it with my fingers, to put my lips there, and so I did.

He made a sound deep in his throat. He pulled me down onto his lap, his breath coming fast and warm and when the knock came I tried not to snarl at it.

"Hide the knives," Watson said, laughing at my expression, his hands caught up in my hair.

"Mr. Watson and Miss Holmes," the assistant said through the door. "Your car is here."

Nothing cut the feeling of it—not the dash out the door to the car, not the rain that had started to break up the snow, not the not-knowing of what would be waiting there for us at Sherringford. I had the pieces of a plan. Watson helped me rearrange them to my satisfaction, or something approximating it. So much of what we'd needed to know this past year had been in our separate hands—Anna Morgan-Vilk, for one. Had I stayed at school I would have known her for what she was. I could have done my work without leaving school, without leaving Watson, and if I told myself I'd gone away only to track down Lucien Moriarty, I knew it for a half-truth. Had I stayed I would have had to face the mess I'd made. Had I stayed, Watson would not have been wearing that scarf when I'd met him. It shouldn't have mattered to me, the idea that some kind, resourceful girl had been kissing him. Because I knew Watson well enough to know that in my absence, there would be another girl beside him. He wouldn't pine forever. Why should he? The thought gave me comfort. It made me furious. It made me reach out and take his hand more forcefully than I'd meant to. He raised an eyebrow, then intertwined his fingers with mine.

What was wrong with me? It was, as they say, the question. The lovely, buzzing feeling I'd had wasn't gone, but it was shifting into something else.

In Sherringford Town, all was seeming quiet. I counted three police cars lingering on side streets, their engines on and their lights off. No doubt Lucien Moriarty had mentioned that Watson would perhaps try to return to school. Still, our black car cut quietly through the night, and the cruisers stayed where they were. Getting through the school gates would be another matter.

"Would you please find an alley to pull over into?" I asked the driver as we drove through downtown. "We'll need to climb into the trunk."

It was an ignominious return to Sherringford, to be sure, but I found I didn't mind it. We folded ourselves in quickly, and Watson put a hand on that spot on my hip (*the fourth time in a car boot in Connecticut,* I thought), and when the car was stopped at the Sherringford entrance by the police, the driver said something muffled about being a teacher returning to use the copier, provided his fake ID, and we trundled slowly up to the sciences building parking lot.

The car stopped. Watson tensed but didn't move as the driver rounded to pop the trunk. He leaned over us, unseeing— the zipper on his jacket was close enough to swing into my hair—and took his briefcase from behind Watson's head. I had a moment to see where he'd parked: the corner of the lot that I'd directed him to, one I remembered having a cluster of thick bushes.

He put the bag over his shoulder. Then he shut the trunk, gently. It didn't latch.

Footsteps. "Evening, officer," I heard him say. "Just here to use the copier."

"I'll let you into the building," the cop said, her voice stern. "Do you know how long you'll be?"

"I'm doing class prep. Won't be more than an hour." As he kept talking—about the quiz he was writing—I heard them make their way to the entrance. His voice, then hers, began to fade.

This was our chance, while their backs were turned to the lot. Our driver hadn't said "midnight," our code word for policemen lingering in the area. We were in the clear.

By the time the officer returned, Watson and I were in the bushes; by the time she returned to her car, we'd made it to the Carter Hall tunnel entrance.

"Elizabeth texted me the key code earlier," he whispered,

pressed up against the door. "57482."

"You're much quieter than you used to be." I punched in the code.

"Thanks," he said. "I've been practicing," and when the door clicked open, we crept down the stairs.

We were a half hour early for Watson's rendezvous with Elizabeth. The way time had passed tonight reminded me of an accordion, of all things: as we went on, it expanded *here*, contracted *there*. Our time in the safe house had felt like mere minutes; our mad rush to Connecticut, hours. And now we would wait for Watson's ex-girlfriend to tell us information about Anna Morgan-Vilk I most likely knew, while Lucien Moriarty mobilized the police force to haul us in for assaulting him.

I hadn't been in the access tunnels in more than a year, but I remembered their layout. The Carter Hall entrance put us by the academic buildings and the chapel, far from Watson's dorm. Hopefully, any searchers would be stationed there and not down by us. Any detective worth their salt would know to search these tunnels for a missing Sherringford student, but then, only Shepard really seemed particularly salty, and I supposed we had him on our side. Besides, the tunnel access code hadn't been changed since Elizabeth had texted him. That could mean everything; that could mean nothing.

That left the obvious fact that the access tunnels, which were customarily lit day in, day out, were tonight in total darkness.

Watson's hand in mine. A murmur: "Should I turn on my phone's flashlight?"

I waited for my eyes to adjust, but the darkness was too complete. "No," I told him, running a hand against the wall. "Follow me, and stay silent." I heard him slip off his boots and tuck them under his arm.

We moved slowly. Three doors on the left, before the hall-way turned—a generator, a water heater, an empty room that had once been used by snowbound nuns for prayer. The latter would work for our purposes (all I wanted was a room to hide in while we finalized our plan), but the door was locked. My kit had been strapped to my leg below my dress, but when I'd changed, I'd thrown a few picks into my useless little purse and left the rest. I only had my snake and my variable tension wrench—quick and dirty tools. One-size-fits-all tools. I could break the lock if I made a mistake.

I hadn't picked a lock in the dark in some time. I hadn't attempted a lock I didn't have the specific picks for in years.

The night was looking up.

As I positioned my picks, Watson shifted behind me. He was always so impatient. Moving his weight around, crack-ing his knuckles, visibly counting ceiling tiles. The world was immensely interesting to him, but only the parts of it he wasn't supposed to be studying. He didn't have the sort of laser focus that a delicate art like this demanded, and yes, there it was, the lock giving under my fingers—

"Holmes," he was whispering. "Holmes." When I didn't reply, he reached out and physically removed my hands from the door. "Do you hear that?"

I had been too focused on my work, on listening to my

fingers, to hear the girls around the corner. They had to be girls, or slim boys wearing very smart shoes: the hard tap-tap-shuffle-tap gave it away. Two of them, moving slowly through the dark without speaking.

Watson and I put our backs to the cinder block wall. It was only luck that they didn't have on their phone flashlights, that we were wearing all black, that the Exit sign above the Carter Hall door had been turned out with the rest of the power. That we were for all intents and purposes invisible.

They stopped just feet from us.

"You're meeting them here," one whispered. "When?"

"Twenty minutes."

"Do you know what you'll say?"

"Anna, we've gone over this a million times," Elizabeth said. "Of course I know what to say."

twenty-seven

jamie

I COULDN'T SEE THEM. SEE HER. I COULDN'T SEE ANYTHING in that dark. All I knew was Holmes's arm flung across my chest, keeping me against the wall. Like I had any desire to move.

Like I'd be able to even if I wanted.

"You'll need to go," Elizabeth said. I knew that whisper. I'd heard it over the phone at night, her wishing me goodnight after her roommate was asleep; I'd heard it at the lunch table, when she was snarking about Tom's new sweater-vest under her breath.

Neither of them said anything for a moment.

"You don't trust me," Elizabeth said. She wasn't whispering now.

"I trust you," Anna said. "My dad says I shouldn't, you know. But I do."

Elizabeth sighed, a pitchy sound. "Well, if your dad says it, it must be true. And sane. Completely sane."

"He doesn't have to be sending me to Sherringford, okay? He could have just forgotten about me like everyone else. It's not a lot for him to ask for, that I help him out with this. Jamie and Charlotte *killed his brother*. Okay? The police aren't even looking at them!"

"I know." She didn't sound convinced.

"Maybe I should call *your* dad," Anna hissed. "Maybe I should remind him that Lucien Moriarty"—she said the name with such pride—"holds the deed to his apartment in New York. Or that one phone call can get him fired. My dad *owns* the Virtuoso School."

Beside me, Holmes's spine went stiff and straight.

"Because this is the way to make sure someone's loyal to you," Elizabeth said. "Make the same threats every chance you get. Gloat. This is total gloating. It's gross."

"Is the money gross too?"

"I'm not doing it for the money," Elizabeth said.

"Then give it back."

"You haven't even *given* it to me yet. So how can I give it back? We came down here to get it, not to have you question my loyalty again."

"I wasn't the one who cut the power!"

"No. You're just the one with the imaginary thousand dollars."

"Screw you. Seriously." Anna started off down the hall. "I'll get you your money. You can have your pathetic shopping spree."

As soon as Anna was safely down the hall, Elizabeth whipped out her phone and tapped out a message. The light from the screen illuminated her hair, her upturned nose. It cast shadows under her eyes. Had she looked up in that moment, she would have seen Holmes and I staring her down, a pair of vultures ready to pick her bones.

But she didn't. She turned as she texted, looking down after Anna's retreating form, and when she'd finished, she locked her phone. The screen went dark.

My ex-girlfriend might have been plotting against me, kissed me and lied to me and gaslit me in my own dorm room, but she hadn't gotten too far into my heart. Had I known, deep down, that something had been wrong from the start? Maybe. But maybe that gave me credit for intuition I didn't have.

Even if Elizabeth was being blackmailed, even if her actions weren't her fault, she could have told me what was going on.

I'd been too hurt to let Elizabeth all the way in. Too lonely not to be alone. I'd been missing Holmes with a ferocity I didn't understand I felt until she was back beside me, and maybe Elizabeth had known all that. Maybe she had been scared of how I would have reacted if she'd told me the truth about Anna. Maybe she'd thought I would have blamed her. That I would have run.

In a way, I was responsible for all of this.

"Come on," Anna called. "If you want your money so bad.

302

My dad will be here soon." With a snort, Elizabeth started down the hall.

There was so little to be relieved about right now, but I let out a silent breath anyway. Beside me, Holmes relaxed.

Then the phone in her back pocket buzzed with a text.

twenty-eight
charlotte

WHEN I WENT LOOKING FOR A SOURCE TO KEEP ME apprised of the goings-on at Sherringford School in my absence, I needed someone that I could rely on. My former roommate Lena would seem the obvious choice: we trusted one another; she was enterprising and resourceful; she responded to texts within seconds, even when in the shower. For a few weeks at the beginning of the school year, I had asked her for updates. But she wasn't close enough to Watson anymore to be able to give me workable data. *He's fine I guess?? Didn't eat much at lunch today but maybe he's cutting now for rugby he was bulking before lol gross right. How is London girl?* Heart emoji. Detective emoji. Two shopping bag emojis.

It wasn't quite what I was looking for.

I hadn't wanted information on his personal life, or I'd told myself I hadn't. I only wanted to know that he was safe. I was on the cusp of writing my awful older brother for help when I'd received a call on an October afternoon. I'd answered only because it came from a blocked number—I had hoped that my uncle Leander might be calling. I always hoped, with him.

"I don't know if you remember me. I'm Elizabeth? From last year. I got your number from his phone." She hadn't had to say who "he" was. "I get that this is weird, me calling. But I think he misses you a lot, and it would help him out if you got in touch. Even to tell him good-bye."

I didn't respond. I was sitting at a table in my favorite café by the Thames, and the water was quite loud, and I had nothing to say to this girl.

"Do you even care if he's okay?"

"Of course I do," I snapped.

"She speaks," Elizabeth said with a lonely sort of laugh, and that was when I knew that if she wasn't dating him, she would be soon.

But if she wouldn't tell me that, I'd pretend I didn't know. It was more convenient for my purposes, which were taking shape as we spoke. "I need time," I'd told her. "I want to come and see him in the new year, and I'll tell him good-bye then. But for now—could you text me every now and then and tell me how he's doing? Make sure that there aren't any more incidents like what happened with Bryony Downs?"

Useful for her: an end date for her boyfriend's psychic

misery. Useful for me: a regular word or two on Watson's well-being.

At first that was all it was. A line here, about where he was applying to college. A line there, about how the rugby team was doing. There was nothing useful about this information, really, and still I craved it. I reread her messages in transit, at my desk, in bed when I woke in the morning. *Jamie has a cold.* Two days later: *He's better.* Prosaic things. Things no one would care about.

I found I cared immensely.

What was she getting in return? I had always loathed psychology, but I began to think these messages gave her a sense of control. Her boyfriend was still upset about a girl in his past; ergo, by managing that girl's knowledge of him, Elizabeth could feel as though she had control over her relationship.

It was untrue, of course. You couldn't control how someone else felt. You could hardly control how *you* felt most of the time. And so the holidays came and went. New Year's came and went. Elizabeth pressed me for plans to visit, to finally have it out with Watson, and I provided her with none. This week, when I began getting messages that said *I'm worried about Jamie, I think bad things are happening to him and he's not telling me,* and *He's getting hauled in to see the dean, and I think he's suspended,* I thought I knew why. Her plan was to force my hand. If I wouldn't come to help ease Watson's mind, I would perhaps come if I thought he were in danger. If she had to manufacture the danger herself, so be it.

It seemed a petty reason to delete someone's school

presentation, but then, I was the girl desperately rereading text messages about Watson's new shoes.

But Elizabeth Hartwell (*Hartwell*, of course that was her name) was nothing if not a survivor. Watching her walk away now—watching the darkened hallway where I could hear her walk away—I realized I had given her too little credit. She had been put into a situation where her family was in danger; she had been blackmailed into going along with Anna Morgan-Vilk's plan; she was forced into hurting Watson, a boy she clearly cared for, and in response she had called in the one person she thought could help, knowing full well that person was me.

The text on my phone read, *I don't know if you're coming with Jamie tonight, but you need to be careful. Lucien Moriarty and his daughter are in the tunnels. The police are everywhere.*

I knew that was what it said, because Watson dragged me into the now-unlocked prayer room, shut the door, pulled the phone from my hands, and read it out to me in a voice shimmering with anger.

"'Jamie seems like he's forgiven Tom,'" he said, scrolling up with his thumbs. "'Jamie's dad keeps picking him up to go somewhere.' 'Jamie is rereading *His Last Bow*. He looks sad.' 'Jamie and I had a picnic today'—what the hell is this, Holmes? How long has this been going on?"

"Keep your voice down," I said. What else could I say?

"My voice. You're worried about my *voice*. Jesus Christ, this is—this goes back for months. This goes back to homecoming. To when she asked me out. Did you have some kind of *plan*, the two of you? God—" He spun around, and the light from my screen strobed up and down the cinder block wall. "I thought it was bad when you disappeared. I thought it was the worst thing. The worst thing. But this—this is worse."

"I told you I was keeping tabs on you. I needed to know you were safe." It came out small. "I needed to know Lucien wasn't coming after you."

"Yes, he does really love to ruin picnics, doesn't he. Rugby games. My shoes. He just loves to ruin my *shoes*. All of that was necessary information. It wasn't you washing your hands of me and then getting to keep being my friend by *proxy*."

"What you saw out there—she's being coerced. She's not working with Anna because she wants to."

"I got that," he snapped.

I went to him and put my hands on his shoulders. He shrugged them off, clutching his boots to his chest.

"Lucien's here," he said. "Somewhere. Anna is here. Call Detective Shepard. Call Leander. Do whatever you need to do."

"And what will you do?"

"I'm going to think about some of my life choices," he said.

This was not an unreasonable response to the situation. Still, I swallowed. The room was cold and dark and bare, and Watson was in sock feet on the concrete floor. If I were him, I'd be looking for a metaphor. Instead I said, "I'm sorry."

Watson turned to stare at me, my phone still in his hands. The light from the screen made me flinch.

"You're sorry for a lot of things, aren't you?" he said.

◗

WE ONLY HAD TEN MINUTES UNTIL WE WERE MEANT TO meet Elizabeth, and if we'd had a plan before, we didn't now. The worst was knowing that this betrayal of mine was fairly small, in the grand scheme of recent betrayals, and that given the proper amount of time (a few days, perhaps a week) Watson would no longer be mad at me. It made it difficult for me to take his anger seriously, as its timing was so inconvenient.

He was being a bit of a monster. He was doing that by being human.

In short: I did mean my apology; I would not have done anything different; I thought it very stupid for Watson to go thundering out into the darkened access tunnels, and yet he did.

And then I wondered if these were the thoughts a horrible person would have, if perhaps I hadn't changed in the slightest, that any development I'd made as a human being had been in a vacuum and not in the more demanding arena of my day-to-day life, or that perhaps it was Watson, my indispensible Watson, who brought out the very worst of me—the part of me that loved someone, and then I thought *aegres cere medendo*, I have come looking for my heart only to be broken by it, and, how pathetic, I am quoting proverbs in a grungy empty room while my idiot best friend is stomping off to get his idiot self killed, and there was no real way to rid oneself of oneself, there was no real way to imagine it, Watson dead, myself dead, or Watson gone, and his mother—his mother and her faith that she had found herself a partner. My veins burned. They burned horribly, and my head was a broken steam valve, and it was like I was under the porch at Watson's family home, dug into the snow to preserve my own body prematurely—it would be less work in the end—and really I had put my oxycodone in my bag as a challenge to myself, I carried it as a challenge, it would be the sane thing to have been rid of it months ago, and I threw the pills on the ground and crushed them under my heel.

There.

If Lucien Moriarty was in these tunnels, I would find him, and I would deal with him myself. I found that, right then, I had a need to break someone open.

I would see his blood spilled all over the floor.

twenty-nine
jamie

I'D DONE SOME STUPID THINGS IN MY LIFE. SELFISH THINGS.
The occasional well-intentioned thing that still nearly got me
killed.

That made this a hat trick, then.

The issue wasn't Holmes. Or the issue *was* Holmes, and the
issue was also Elizabeth. And fear. And sleep deprivation, and
being utterly in the dark and out of control while also knowing
that (a) she'd been keeping things from me, again, when not
two hours ago she was apologizing for that very thing while (b)
my now very firmly *ex*-girlfriend had the sort of bickering session with Lucien Moriarty's illicit daughter one would expect
from a pair of divorcees while (c) my kid sister was somewhere
held captive and who *knew* what was happening to her and (d)

Lucien Moriarty himself was probably stalking these corridors, looking to end me, while (e) I, the utter idiot, couldn't think clearly about any of this, couldn't make a plan, could only hear the heavy beating of my blood and (f) lash out at Holmes out of fear (because nothing had changed, nothing) and then I'd wanted to do the thing my old therapist had told me about walking away and calming down, and (g)—I was at (g) already, wasn't I, I had frittered away minutes in this hallway when I could have apologized and been done with it already, and still, even when I turned to put my hand on the doorknob, I knew it was already too late.

By now, I knew the sound a gun made as it was being cocked.

"Going somewhere?" Lucien Moriarty said behind me.

Some distant part of me thought, *He's been waiting years to say that to someone.* The rest of me was screaming.

"Hands up," he said. He'd lost the Welsh accent in favor of his own, and it was unnerving to hear a voice not unlike August's arranging my execution.

"Okay," I said, obeying. Like a fool. How could he even see me? The hallway was pitch black.

"Dad," Anna was saying, somewhere farther away. "Dad, what do you need me to do?"

"A flashlight, girl."

The cinder block wall in front of me went fluorescent.

"Turn. Slowly."

I did, flinching as my eyes adjusted. Lucien, in silhouette, and still I could see his cut lip, his two black eyes. His hands around a pistol. An explosion of light from behind him that had to come from his daughter's phone.

"On your knees," he said, and I lowered myself painfully to the floor.

"Dad?" Anna said, and this time, she sounded terrified.

That made two of us.

Lucien took a step forward. Another. He held the gun steady. "Now," he said, not three feet away, "we'll just wait. Where there's smoke, there's fire."

And, just like that, the door behind me opened.

"Lucien," Holmes said. She stepped forward, close enough that I could feel her looming over me.

He kept the gun trained on my face. "Do you want to skip the formalities, then, and go right to the conversation?"

"Which conversation?" she asked, levelly. "The one where I apologize for what I did to August? Again? You could have just called. Or blackmailed my parents. Again. As that worked so well the last time."

"Did it," he said.

I could hear the smirk in Holmes's voice. "It got your idiot brother killed, didn't it? A win in my book."

Anna's light wobbled wildly. I shut my eyes against it, against Holmes maligning August, even though I knew she didn't mean it.

"Girl," Lucien snapped at Anna, without turning around. "Keep your hands steady."

"You could turn back on the lights," Holmes said. "Though I imagine you want a certain amount of drama for this . . . confrontation."

"You always have this need to mouth off." He sucked on his cut lip. "He used to tell me about that, when he'd call on the train back from your house. He'd go back to that awful bedsit in Eastbourne, that was all he could afford on the pittance your father paid him, and he would call me, eating beans from a tin, and say, *It was like she was raised by wolves*." I kept myself from startling. Lucien was a wicked mimic. He had all of it: August's strangled sincerity, his doubt. "He'd say, *She doesn't understand authority. She thinks she's some ultimate power. She's so smart, but she's a hazard to herself.* And then he'd go back to working on his dissertation. That was it. That was his sad little apprenticeship. Him paying his dues. I should have just supported him, but he wanted the damn job. Thought your father could help him find a university lectureship, that maybe he could make some calls—" Lucien's eyes narrowed. "My brother. He'd always been like that. So determined to prove his mettle, be better than his *name*. In some ways, I have to think he had it coming."

"Did he," Holmes said, like an echo.

"Anyone that trusting? It's willful. It isn't instinct. They're overriding their animal sense. But then, mine has told me from the beginning that you're a dog that needs to be put down, and still here we are, aren't we? With you still alive."

"Are you done bloviating?" Holmes asked him, and Anna's phone wobbled again. "Do you need me to hold that for

314

you—what's he calling you? Girl?"

"Give me the phone, Anna," Lucien said, holding his hand out to her, "and go fetch our little surprise."

She stumbled forward, pressing it into his hand, and there was a second's reprieve from the light before Lucien held the phone up himself. I could hear her footsteps down the hall.

"Where were we?" Holmes was asking, her voice like tempered steel. "Was this the part where you were pretending that you hated your brother? That you think he deserved what was coming to him? It's rather funny, you know, it's been quite some time since I've been around someone who's so thoroughly erased their tells. Your face doesn't give anything away. I imagine that's all the political training? Good job, you. You might as well be reading me the phone book."

"I'm so happy you approve," he growled.

"Yes, very nice work. Your gaze never wavers, you never look to either side; even your eyelids are controlled. No blinking out of turn. Your hands, as well. Very steady, and of course you don't shuffle your feet, you aren't a *child*." Even now I could hear her satisfaction, in the pleasure she found—even now, even despite everything—in reading him. "It makes it all the more impressive that your feelings are still so transparent."

"Remind me why I'm listening to you," Lucien said. "Remind me why I haven't just shot you down."

Holmes sighed. "Because you've had years of opportunity, and made the decision to toy with me instead. This last year I was sending up *flares*, Lucien, you could have ended me at any moment. No. This is different. This is about justice, isn't it? This was about thinking you'd lost August only to discover that he was alive . . . and then you lost him a second time. Because of me."

The flashlight wavered. Very, very slightly.

My head was beginning to ache. I squinted against the light, shifted my weight slightly from knee to knee. Tried to focus on the pain to keep from thinking.

Holmes was just warming up. "All this? It's you making the kind of world you want. It's interesting, one would think from your actions that you were entirely amoral, and yet all along, you've been living by your own code. It was all fine, wasn't it, when we were playing our prescribed parts? Hadrian and Phillipa, your not-as-bright siblings, tedious but useful, in their way; you, young master of the universe, running Britain's government behind the curtain; and August, your brother, the innocent. August living a life of the mind. August obsessed with *maths*—can you think of a thing more pure? A thing further away from your dirty dealings?

"But it got muddy, didn't it. It got muddy when he came to work for my family. All this began there. Not with the drugs in the car, not with my stupid *crush*. It started when August walked through our front door. When he started playing politics. Because it was a political decision, wasn't it? He wanted a favor from my father. My father, whose last name made him nobler than you, no matter what terrible things he'd done. In the eyes of the world, you and your family would always be *less than*. Because you were a Moriarty."

"Brilliant," Lucien said, hoarsely. I wished I could see his face. "How much did you pay for that psychology course?"

"I've had quite a bit of time to think about it," Holmes was saying. "I've had some time to put it together. I know, for instance, why you've turned a corner since August has died. Oh, sure, fucking with me was your *hobby*, but before his death it was never your full-time job. Bryony Downs? You encouraged her with a few phone calls, then let her do the rest. Hadrian and Phillipa? You don't trust either of them enough to tie your shoes, much less *kill* me. And poisoning my mother—that you arranged on your own, I'm sure of it, but you didn't stir yourself to do it. But look at us now. All together, one happy family. Honestly, Lucien—marrying Watson's mother? Kidnapping his sister? That's grandstanding, and you know it."

"Grief does that to a man," Lucien said. I couldn't believe that he was still standing there, listening to her; I couldn't believe I was still alive.

"Of course you're grieving," Holmes snapped. "Grief doesn't make you chuck over your whole life to go hunt down a teenage girl at her *boarding school*. No, it's more than that.

"I think you were happy when you thought August was dead. I think you were *relieved*. You could put him back up on his pedestal—no more of his pesky little life choices, clouding up the narrative. You could make him a saint again.

"And when he died the second time, on the *Holmeses'* estate, by a *Holmes's* hand, you saw a way to rewrite the story. A girl like me? A *villain* like me? I was an opportunity. What if the Moriartys were the victims all along? What if—horror of horrors—they were the heroes?"

"Shut your mouth," Lucien snarled, and I knew, then, that she'd won.

And that her victory didn't matter, not at all.

Because he was going to kill me, quite literally, at her feet. To make a point. As though I were a bag of garbage he needed to spill out on the ground.

I guess I won't be going to prison, then, I thought. I wanted badly, then, to look up at Holmes, to see what she was thinking, but I was too afraid to move my head.

A SCUFFLING SOUND. A DOOR OPENING. "GIRL," LUCIEN was saying, and I could make out a small figure next to him, a bag over her head. "Come here." When she didn't move, he said, again, *"Come,"* and for a moment, his flashlight beam blinked off, and we were in darkness.

"Faster," Lucien was saying.

The world sharpened slightly around me. Something had changed. Something small. A click. Where had it come from? From behind me?

Was it just wishful thinking?

Maybe it was, because Lucien hadn't heard it. "Take the gun from the holster on my hip," he said to the girl, and he clicked his flashlight on, its light trained on the floor.

Why did Lucien need two guns?

In that small moment of distraction, Holmes dropped something small and hard onto my legs. The backs of my calves, specifically, which were out of Lucien's sight. She tapped her foot on the floor, once, in confirmation. She wanted me to know that she had done what she had done on purpose.

"Bring the gun to Charlotte," Lucien told the girl, and she did. Slowly, with dragging steps, and as she came closer, I could feel my vision start to go. I had assumed, dully, that he had dragged out Anna again—but this girl was smaller. Slighter. Was she? Was I just imagining things?

All I knew was that she had on a pair of gray Converses with mismatched laces—one pink, one green.

My sister, Shelby, had shoes like that.

"Holmes," I said, low, and she said, "Watson. I know."

"Shut *up*," Lucien said, and I saw then that he was shaking. "Don't talk! Neither of you says a word, or this ends the fast way. *Now*, Shelby." Lucien lifted his gun so that it was pointed at Holmes. His flashlight ran over my face, my shoulders.

The backs of my legs.

I caught my breath.

Shelby paused. She paused. And she handed Holmes the gun and backed away, backlit, that gunnysack over her head like a girl playing a game, like a demon from a story.

"Kneel," Lucien said. "Now, girl. At my feet."

I couldn't help it—I made a horrible, inarticulate sound.

"Charlotte. Keep the gun pointed to the ceiling. This is how we're going to do this," Lucien said. "You'll follow my directions, or I'll shoot the girl right here. Do you understand?"

"Yes," Holmes said, steadily.

"Take three steps to your left. Keep the gun pointed up. Good. Turn. Back toward the boy. That's it. And the gun should be—ah, I see you've guessed it already. Clever girl. The gun should be pointed at little Shelby's head."

I couldn't help it—I wrenched my head around to stare at Holmes. I needed the confirmation. Her pale face, the long line of her arms, the pistol at the end of them.

Lucien laughed, softly. "You've been so quiet, Jamie. You don't have any questions for me?"

"Holmes," I said. "Holmes—please. Lucien. You don't want this. You don't. You can just have her—you can have her shoot me."

"You?" he asked, idly.

I swallowed and plowed on. "Wouldn't that be worse? Her killing her best friend? Like, if you wanted to punish her—or me—"

"We are done," Lucien snarled, "guessing at my motives. We only have a minute, you know. But you know? I'll humor you. I *am* punishing you. How about, even if you get out of this, somehow, your life will still be utterly ruined? How about, you'll spend every night wondering what you could have done to save your sister's life?

"Try this—how about, how your mother is doing, back in the hotel room, crying over how her son is the kind of delinquent who beats up his new stepfather in a restaurant bathroom? No questions about what she'll say when they find your body here and haul away your ex-girlfriend in irons for this? She'll have no one to shelter her. No sympathetic parents, no brother, no Watsons to take her in. No money. No one but herself." He hummed a little. "I'm hoping to use my influence to get Charlotte committed, you know. I know this wonderful little hospital in D.C. that might be able to help her—I've been setting up a room for her there. Not a lot in it, truth be told, but then again, she won't need all that much—"

"No," I said, my skin crawling. "I don't have any questions for you." I wasn't going to go out listening to Lucien Moriarty monologue. And even if Holmes had come up with some kind of escape plan, if she had dropped a pistol or a knife or a bomb for me to use to get us out of this, I couldn't reach for it without Lucien gunning Shelby down first.

Maybe I wasn't brave enough to try.

That was that, then.

"Shelby," I said, desperately, "it's okay—"

"Don't *speak to her*," Lucien said, "or I will kill all three of you. You have a minute, Charlotte. James, you have permission to change your girlfriend's mind. It's Shelby's life, or hers."

I couldn't see well, it was true. The light from the phone flattened the world out, made it bright, took its detail away. Holmes looked like an illustration. A black-and-white sketch. Her long black sleeves, her shaking white hands, the gun. She had pointed it right between my eyes.

I was close enough to see that she had bitten her lip through completely.

"Hey," I said. "Hey. It's okay."

"It's not," she whispered. "Of course it's not."

"It will be. You're going to be okay."

Holmes shook her head tightly. "Me? We are not *talking* about me—"

"We are," I said. "We are. Holmes, I can't make this

decision. I'm not deciding between the two of you. I don't—I can't—whatever you choose—the hard part's almost over."

She was still shaking her head. "I knew this would happen. What's the point of knowing if you can't stop it?"

Shelby wavered back and forth on her knees.

"No. Hey. You couldn't have changed this. Don't worry—"

"I'm not worried about *me*, Jamie," she said. "I'm sorry—"

"It's better like this. You have control over it, this way. I'm sure—you know where to shoot, right? So that it's over quickly. For Shelby." I swallowed. "So that—that's better. It's better. See?"

"You think I'd let her die."

"I don't know what I think, I can't think—"

"I should have told you to run," she whispered.

I laughed a little at that. What else was I to do? "I think you did. But I'm kind of stubborn when it comes to you."

She nodded. She squeezed her eyes shut.

When she opened them again, I could see that she was furious.

"This is as bad as it gets," she said to me, and it was almost like she was giving me an order. "The hard part's almost over."

This is as bad as it gets.

Lucien snorted. "Adorable. Are you finished?"

The hard part's almost over.

"Just to be clear," Holmes said, her voice thick, "what exactly will happen when I refuse to shoot her?"

"I'll take care of you," he said, his gaze flickering over to her. "*Then* Shelby. Don't think I'd be so stupid to keep my eyes off you for a—"

He didn't have time to finish his sentence. In the second his eyes were off me, I'd grabbed the pistol Holmes had dropped onto my legs and fired off two shots into the darkness.

One went through the door, into the room with all the bicycles. It narrowly missed clipping Shelby's shoulder. In that final second, kneeling there in the hallway, my world had narrowed to be so small, so claustrophobic, that I'd forgotten she was kneeling there. But she wasn't hurt. Only startled enough to scream, to drop her phone, to pull the bag off her head.

Because it wasn't Shelby at all. It was Anna Morgan-Vilk, kneeling there in my sister's shoes, where her father had just offered her up as an honor killing.

My other bullet went into Lucien Moriarty's leg.

It was a lucky shot. I had never fired a gun before.

He was screaming. He had gone down, hard, and he was screaming, and God, I couldn't think. Did he still have his gun? *No*, I thought, *Holmes would have gotten it*, and I had gone down to my hands and knees on the linoleum, my stomach heaving, my vision gone. Or was that the lights? I wanted to pass out, and there was so much noise in my ears, maybe from the gunshot—I tried to reorient myself—

Fast footsteps, coming toward me.

I scrabbled back against the wall, put my hands up. Anna? Was it Anna? Was she coming to finish the job?

My eyes focused.

Elizabeth. Elizabeth, in her school blazer.

"Lena called the police," she said, crouching down beside me. She reached out to take my hand, but I jerked away from her. I couldn't be touched just then. I couldn't even look at her—I was staring up into the ceiling, Holmes's pistol in my hands. Elizabeth reached out and clicked the safety back on. "Jamie, it's okay. Look. Look, I have Lucien's gun too. I have them both. See? Do you hear me?"

I nodded.

She kept talking, trying to reassure me. "It's okay. Anna was supposed to keep an eye on me, that's why I was down here, but she flipped out when she saw her dad, and I managed to text Lena from my pocket and she said that Shepard's coming, he should be here any second, she had this plan with pulleys and like a feather duster and I think she's really mad that she didn't get to do it? But it's okay, it's okay, Shepard I guess said he was waiting to hear that—that—"

She had turned to look at Holmes, who had, for the last few minutes, been quietly bleeding on the ground.

thirty
charlotte

TIME HAD GONE FRAGMENTED, STRANGE. IT STAYED THAT
way for some time.

What I remembered:

1. Lucien Moriarty shooting me in the shoulder while Watson fumbled for the gun.
2. The look on Lucien Moriarty's face as he fired. Something
   like an angel seeing the gates of heaven, exaltation, et
   cetera. It was fascinating.
3. Thinking *Oh, I've been shot*, in the same manner one would
   think about ordering takeout.
4. Watson yelling. A gurney. More yelling, mostly Watson,
   though I thought I heard Shepard join into the fray. Black.

Roiling black, laced through with bits of bright pain, and me saying *No morphine, you can't, I'm an addict,* or I thought I did—could they hear me, through the *oxygen* mask? A monitor, beeping.

5. I remember, too, asking for my mother.

5b. I didn't get my mother. I got my brother instead.

6. Milo shouting Watson down in an elevator, saying *This is your fault, this is your fault, you idiot child—*

7. Morphine, which was something I could feel in my system even when that system was broken, blinking red. I could feel it even more then.

8. Leander, in a dark room that smelled like plastic. The hospital? He was saying something I couldn't hear. A national newspaper left on my dinner tray, open to the politics section. Someone had circled a headline: *Morgan-Vilk Assists in Manhunt; British National Captured.*

9. Shepard asking me questions. Shepard, asking me questions the next day, and the next, and I dreamed them even when he wasn't there: *How long did you know? Were in you touch with anyone at the Yard? What happened to Anna Morgan-Vilk? She's disappeared—*

10. And Watson. Watson there every day. On the hard plastic couch next to Leander. Watson speaking with the nurse. Watson asleep with his head in his hands. Always there when I was struggling in or out of sleep, when I was still wordless. When my dreams were all red weather. Watson there until he wasn't.

Thirty-one
charlotte

Two weeks later

I STILL COULDN'T MOVE MY ARM.

Or my shoulder. Or my neck. There was a physical therapist. We were practicing small motions together. It was straightforward and infinitely boring.

The withdrawal from the morphine was something else. Because it was all the same thing—oxycodone, morphine. Opioids, all of them, and my body rid itself of them the same way. Poorly.

This was boring in its own way, too. But the nausea had passed by then, and the runny nose, the teary eyes. The dreams where I woke up screaming. I had hoped, somehow, that withdrawal this time would be different. It wasn't. Not really. Only the incessant yawning was new. My body demanded sleep it then refused to allow me. I spent nights watching the television bolted to the wall, shows mostly about men rebuilding houses. *This has good bones,* they would say, or *This is a gut job.* The episodes about gut jobs brought back my awful stomach cramps, and so I moved on to hospital shows instead.

Those annoyed the nurses, at least, and I felt a pathetic sort of triumph about that. The worst thing about the hospital was how available I had to be. A kind of girl art exhibit, there for gawking at, to be examined at all angles and interpreted. There were so many comments on my accent that I adopted a Texan swagger just to be contrary. There were so many people in scrubs calling me *Miss Holmes.* The cheeky addiction specialist called me Charlie. That, I found, I didn't mind.

Leander hated it, I think. He spent almost every minute by my bedside. When I'd read about that kind of behavior in books—the doting relative in the hospital room—I'd always thought it to be unbearably gloomy, someone clutching the patient's hands, weeping, while a synthesizer groaned out a soundtrack. It wasn't much like that. Leander kept his blazer on, though he left his collar unbuttoned. He played quite a bit of Sudoku. He read to me from novels and poetry books and the newspaper. Mostly the newspaper; he liked to read out savage film reviews in a swashbuckling voice, and when he ran out of those, he moved on to the good ones. Together, we made a list of movies to see. He was appalled to find out I'd never seen *Alien.* After he demonstrated said alien ripping its way out of someone's chest, I found I was appalled too.

James Watson came by, with flowers but without his son. He didn't bring his wife, either, which I supposed was intentional, as he and Leander took the opportunity to go out to the hall and have a very loud fight. *There is no way that Shelby is going to that godforsaken school, it nearly ate your son* and *Of course he doesn't hate you, James* and *Don't be a martyr, I know it's your default setting, get over yourself.* Then they stole the Connect Four set from the nurses' station and made me watch them play each other. I began placing bets on Mr. Watson. It wasn't good strategy, but it made my uncle furious. Well, as furious as he could be with Jamie's father around.

Shelby came; I had always liked that girl, her enthusiasms, her happy voice. Her face so much like Watson's. How she let herself in and immediately said, "We aren't talking about it, it's too screwed up, can we just watch YouTube videos instead?" and then proceeded to French braid my hair into pigtails. She'd smuggled me in a whole dozen old-fashioned donuts and then ate ten of them in sock feet, talking so fast that I could hardly understand her, a lone sprinkle on her shirt.

She was so much like her brother it made me want to cry. I didn't. I braided her hair instead, much to her surprise and delight.

It hadn't ever been a decision, really, whether to choose her life or mine.

Lena came by, sans Tom; she'd given him up as a bad job, she said, but I knew there were still three more months left in school, and that Lena had a thing for a boy in a sweater-vest.

DI Green called, and Detective Shepard. He'd finished questioning me to his satisfaction, he'd said. I wasn't facing criminal charges. Yet. I rather wanted to get back to England before he changed his mind.

Hadrian Moriarty sent me a bouquet of lilies, most likely because he knew they were funereal. Bastard. My brother sat tragically by my bedside and pledged that he'd never leave me again. Save for prison, as he had made a full confession to the police. He would serve his time with dignity, he said.

Four years ago I would have severed a limb for such treatment from Milo Holmes, but today I just made him sit in the plastic-covered chair and watch *Ugly House Rescue* with me until he fell asleep. He was gone in the morning. His assistant said he'd gone to Taiwan. I doubted he would ever really take responsibility for what he'd done.

My mother called; we had a very civil discussion about my injuries, and she invited me to visit her in Switzerland. Her language made it clear: it was her home, not mine, and I wasn't welcome to think of it as a refuge anymore.

If I ever had to begin with.

That was all. My mother didn't want me, and my father never showed, and still the nurses called me *Miss Holmes, Miss Holmes,* like I belonged to that family, and it had been days since I'd seen him. Watson. He'd left, and not come back.

Until he did.

Leander was down at the vending machines. The nurses had just done their rotation. We were working on the paperwork for me to be transferred to a rehabilitation facility. They didn't want me to fly, but Leander was insisting on bringing me home. There wasn't much they could say to it—I was a British national, and I would wait until I wasn't in immediate danger any longer, and then I would be gone.

Seeing Watson in the door made me wonder at that. Danger. Why he and I found that we needed it. Why I felt it even now, him being there. He had on his leather jacket, and his ridiculous watch, and the boots that Morgan-Vilk had given him. He didn't say anything for a long time.

Until, like a fool, I said "Jamie," and he came to me like a man compelled, feet slow, eyes dark, almost against his will. Almost against his will he put a hand on my shoulder. Dropped down to his knees. Put his face in my hair. For a moment—just a moment—and then he straightened and stood.

"I did this," he said. "I should have—you should have just shot *me*."

"You realize how ridiculous that sounds."

He stared at me. "You'd kicked it, hadn't you."

"In a way." I met his eyes. "You don't ever really kick it, you know. Not completely. Though the current treatment plan certainly isn't the best."

"The current plan?"

"My getting shot, and needing morphine."

He smiled, despite himself. "That's not much of a joke."

"That's too bad," I said. "I'm usually quite funny."

We talked. He was finishing his college applications; his suspension had been hand-waved away, and he was installed back at Sherringford in his single room. I had the sense that he was counting the days until it was over.

I hadn't seen Shelby in days. She wasn't, as Mr. Watson had insisted, remaining in America. She was returning to her mother in London, for now.

Watson hadn't spoken much to his mother. "I don't know when I will again," he said.

"Give it time," I told him. It was advice I'd heard given before. I assumed it had some merit.

And really, only days had passed. I had begun to feel unstuck from time, somehow, in a way that was particular to hospitals, and as I was explaining it to Watson my uncle appeared in the door with an armload of crisps and chocolate. Then he saw the two of us, and slipped away.

Not before Watson saw him. "I should go," he said. "Leave you to it."

"Why have you been away?" I asked him, all at once. "You were here—and then you left."

I had always been good at reading people, and Watson was a bit of an open book. I don't know how to describe the expression that washed over him. Not then. There was something wary about him, and something devastated too. Something too like a boy left out in the cold.

"We aren't good for each other," he said. He took my hand. "There's actual evidence for it, Holmes. We're not. Not as we are."

"Does that matter?" I asked, quietly.

Watson nodded. "It does. It does when it ends with you like this."

"Me? Your sister were almost shot—"

"By you," he said. "That isn't even my point. Do you understand how messed up all this is, if the worst part isn't you getting shot or pumped full of drugs? We're like some kind of wildfire. We make terrible decisions. We make *each other* make terrible decisions. We're not—we're not good together, and I can't keep doing this to you."

All of this. All of this, and to hear him say it.

"I'm going back to London. It could be as soon as tomorrow," I told him. I hadn't meant to. It wouldn't change anything.

He nodded. Once. Twice. Three times, very quickly. "I guess—good-bye then."

A memory: the two of us on his father's couch, Watson the one recovering, me running his scarf through my hands. *It wouldn't be London without you.*

"Come see me there," I said now, imagining that younger Jamie. "Come see me. I'll be living with Leander."

"I don't know," he said. "Do you really want me to?"

"Is this about you doing penance? You don't have to do penance," I told him.

He sighed. "Neither do you."

The machines hooked up to my arm continued their steady beeping. Watson traced one long IV line down to my arm.

"Have I told you that I'm sorry?"

"We need new words for sorry," I said.

Fits and starts. Always as though we were warming up a car that had been left in the cold.

"I'd like that." He was still staring at my arm. There were

newer needle marks there, I supposed. At least they were from blood work. "I apologize. I am ashamed. Shamefaced. I feel guilty—"

"Stop," I said, because he was too far away, and soon he would be farther. "Do you see my bag? There, on the chair. There's a folder in there for you."

It was an account of the last few years. I had been working on it at night, in my hospital bed, when I couldn't sleep. It was ugly, and at times deeply pathetic, and full of the occasional Watson-style simile, and truth be told, I had no idea how to spell the word "necessary," and he would think far less of me after he had read it. Still I could feel the pages staring at me at night, almost as though the act of writing it down had given it flesh.

He knew it for what it was in moments, the pages flashing in his hands as he flipped through them. "Are you sure?" he asked, finally.

"It's our story," I said to him.

"No," he said, and he was smiling. "No, it's not. It's yours."

Epilogue

JANUARY

FROM: C. Holmes ‹ chholmes@dmail.com ›
TO: James Watson Jr. ‹ j.watson2@dmail.com ›
SUBJECT LINE: Leander

I thought you should know that I've been discharged from the rehabilitation center, and that I've been back in London a week now. Uncle Leander does not currently have an occupation, save for parenting me. The results have been varied. And awful. When he is not making me pancakes in the shape of mice or rabbits, he is dragging me to pubs to eavesdrop on perfectly innocent people. For fun, he says. Never mind the fact that I am still in three separate plaster casts and about as inconspicuous as an elephant. Neither is Leander, who spends these expeditions noisily eating crisps and grinning at me.

I told him he had to find a new hobby. This morning I awoke to a poster of Harry Styles he had affixed to my ceiling. In said poster, he is wearing very tight leather trousers, and glitter. So much glitter.

He badly needs a case. Leander, that is.

Please go murder someone or rob a nearby bank. Please. I beg you.

FROM: C. Holmes ‹ chholmes@dmail.com ›
TO: James Watson Jr. ‹ j.watson2@dmail.com ›
SUBJECT LINE: Perhaps

Is it in poor taste for me to be joking about murder?

FROM: C. Holmes ‹ chholmes@dmail.com ›
TO: James Watson Jr. ‹ j.watson2@dmail.com ›
SUBJECT LINE: Re: Perhaps

I assume that's why you haven't yet responded. Though it's unlike you to be offended. Or rather, it's like you to be offended while also enjoying feeling offended.

FROM: C. Holmes ‹ chholmes@dmail.com ›
TO: James Watson Jr. ‹ j.watson2@dmail.com ›
SUBJECT LINE: Re: re: Perhaps

Watson. I can't make any deductions from across the pond. Not good ones, anyway. If you're upset with me you're going to have to spell it out. Is this part of your needing "distance"? I assumed two thousand miles would do the trick.

FROM: James Watson Jr. ‹ j.watson2@dmail.com ›
TO: C. Holmes ‹ chholmes@dmail.com ›
SUBJECT LINE: Re: re: re: Perhaps

C,

You do know that you sent all four of those emails over the
course of like twenty minutes, right? I was in class. Some
of us still have classes to go to, if they want to do things
like graduate and not go crawling home to one of two Broken
Homes afterward. Which, by the way, I'm officially making
jokes about, because (a) my mother is still not speaking to me
and (b) my dad and Abigail are fighting so often that I can't
take more than ten minutes of being in their house, and it's all
so awful that it's almost funny. So college = important.

What are you doing for school, anyway? Have you thought
any more about whether you're going on to uni? Is the total
sum of your education right now Leander dragging you down
to the Dog's Arms or the East Sider or (God help us) the
Sherlock Holmes pub and ordering you fried food?

Also, if that's the case, can I come too?

I'm back in my room over lunch hour. By the way, Lena
says hi, and that you and I should switch to texting like
"normal people" because someone needs to teach you how
to use an emoji and anyway only "adults" send "emails." I'm
not sure if anyone's disputing whether or not an email's called
an email, but when I told her that, she called me a pedant
and stole my brownie, and Elizabeth laughed so hard that she

337

started coughing, and then Tom made a joke about her choking on a diamond, and Elizabeth choked but for real, I think you actually have some competition in the Offending People category.

I miss you, you nut. Tell Leander hi for me.

] xx

FEBRUARY

FROM: C. Holmes ‹ chholmes@dmail.com ›
TO: James Watson Jr. ‹ j.watson2@dmail.com ›
SUBJECT LINE: Re: re: re: re: re: re: re: re: re: re: re: re: re: re: re: re: re: re: re: re: re: re: re: re: re: re: re: re: re: re: re: re: re: re: re: re: re: re: re: Perhaps

All I am saying is that it is a completely acceptable act to eat alone in the cafeteria and I don't understand your fear of it. You don't need to have someone along with you every time (i.e., Elizabeth or similar) in order to eat your meal. They'll serve you either way, I guarantee it.

FROM: James Watson Jr. ‹ j.watson2@dmail.com ›
TO: C. Holmes ‹ chholmes@dmail.com ›
SUBJECT LINE: Look

You can just ask if I'm dating her again. (I'm not.) (Also I only eat with her with everybody else, so your "or similar" means "Lena Tom Randall Elizabeth and Elizabeth's boyfriend Kittredge.")

FROM: C. Holmes < chholmes@dmail.com >
TO: James Watson Jr. < j.watson2@dmail.com >
SUBJECT LINE: Re: Look

I suppose it is nice to have someone keep you company while you eat.

Which is, coincidentally, something I've been speaking to my therapist about. She is the thirteenth therapist I've seen, which is both shameful and slightly invigorating. She's also the first to speak any kind of language I understand. (Though she keeps referencing someone named the godfather when I talk about Moriartys and Moriarty-adjacent events.) Anyway, I like her quite a lot, which is surprising. Currently we are spending some time discussing my eating habits, and you, and outpatient programs, and the doctor that Leander keeps bringing in to see me, who is very handsome.

My uncle is still refusing to take cases, by the by, because I "need some proper looking-after." He has thrown himself headfirst into my "education," where we at first worked through the syllabi for several graduate-level humanities courses, reading a number of quite interesting nonfiction texts and novels and some poetry and of course the relevant associated cultural criticism, but after a week or so of this my uncle chucked the whole thing over to make me watch television with him at night. Bad television. According to Leander, my father entirely overlooked my "social and emotional education" in favor of his "uselessly specific curriculum," making me into some kind of "automaton who actually enjoys reading Heidegger—Good God, Charlotte, who enjoys that? Or Camus? Were you just reading Camus and laughing?"

Apparently the only way to rectify this is to watch loads of old *Doctor Who* while eating Thai peanut chicken crisps on the couch.

I am working through the Heidegger on my own.

FROM: C. Holmes ‹ chholmes@dmail.com ›
TO: James Watson Jr. ‹ j.watson2@dmail.com ›
SUBJECT LINE: Re: re: Look

C,
That's great about your therapist, that it's working out. Less great about the Heidegger. Medium great about the *Doctor Who*.

Is there a particular reason that you're talking about the doctor? The handsome one?
J xx

P.S. Please tell me I can make you a whole list of TV shows and films for you to try out . . . maybe you should start with Coppola. Like, *The Godfather*?

FROM: C. Holmes ‹ chholmes@dmail.com ›
TO: James Watson Jr. ‹ j.watson2@dmail.com ›
SUBJECT LINE: Re: re: re: re: re: Spring break

Really, why on earth would I invite you to stay at our flat unless I did in fact want you there? Leander does too. He told you to stop being a numpty (Scottish for "a stupid," I had to look it up and am now getting very strange ads on my phone) and to "get here already," although he knows as well as I do that your break doesn't begin until next week.

FROM: James Watson Jr. ‹ j.watson2@dmail.com ›
TO: C. Holmes ‹ chholmes@dmail.com ›
SUBJECT LINE: Re: re: re: re: re: re: Spring break

I just don't want to step on any toes. Like your toes. Honestly I guess I just don't know where we stand? Like, this feels healthy, us just talking like this and in a situation where nobody is dying or disappeared or actively trying to kill us. I sort of just feel like I'm holding my breath, a little, and things are going really well right now, and maybe we need more time before we see each other to let things keep being great. Which isn't to say that you specifically make them not-great.

341

But also I miss you so much that sometimes I feel like I
can't breathe.

I guess . . . what does your therapist think?

] xx

FROM: C. Holmes ‹ chholmes@dmail.com ›
TO: James Watson Jr. ‹ j.watson2@dmail.com ›
SUBJECT LINE: Re: re: re: re: re: re: re: Spring break

Dr. Kostas thinks that we need to allow ourselves time to get
to know one another in said new, healthier context, and that,
in the meantime, we should avoid "pledging ultimate loyalty" to
each other again, as that had suboptimal results the last time.

Ultimately, she says it's my decision. And yours.

Though I know you've already made up your mind.

I've already ordered in new bedding for the spare room and
have begun making a shopping list (Jaffa cakes, Tunnocks—the
bars not the tea cakes—and that Irish breakfast blend from
that obscenely expensive shop in Piccadilly. And the frozen
naan from Waitrose. And Milk Tray. Obscene amounts of Milk
Tray. Also the orange juice from Tesco that you had a year
and a half ago when we were wandering the city together. In
the plastic bottle? It had mangoes in, and carrot, and ginger,
and smells wretched. I put you down for four).

Of course, if I've misread you, please tell me. But you tend
to overuse the word "just" when you've made a decision and
are attempting to justify it to yourself or others.

FROM: James Watson Jr. ‹ j.watson2@dmail.com ›
TO: C. Holmes ‹ chholmes@dmail.com ›
SUBJECT LINE: Re: re: re: re: re: re: re: re: Spring break

Are you bribing me with Milk Tray? Because it's working.
   Yes, yes, of course I want to come. If you're okay with it,
and your uncle, and your therapist. And if we take it all kind
of slow.
   Also, you are like . . . sometimes you are just the best.
The actual best. I hope you know that. I don't know what I've
done to deserve you xxx

FROM: C. Holmes ‹ chholmes@dmail.com ›
TO: James Watson Jr. ‹ j.watson2@dmail.com ›
SUBJECT LINE: Re: re: re: re: re: re: re: re: re: Spring break

Something terrible, probably.
   Leander and I will meet you at Heathrow arrivals. He will
be holding a sign he's making with puff paint. Right now his
plan is to have it read WATSON WUZ HERE. I'd apologize but
also it's rather hilarious.

APRIL

FROM: James Watson Jr. ‹ j.watson2@dmail.com ›
TO: C. Holmes ‹ chholmes@dmail.com ›
SUBJECT LINE: King's College London!!!!!!!!!

I got in!! I got in!!!! This is worth all those rejections and the not sleeping and the dragging my GPA up to a 3.85 with my actual teeth and even if they only let me in because they feel sorry for me or that story in *the Daily Mail* about how we're both unhinged or something I am TOTALLY GOING TO TAKE IT I DON'T CARE I am going to take you out to dinner as soon as I get back to England!!!

FROM: James Watson Jr. ‹ j.watson2@dmail.com ›
TO: C. Holmes ‹ chholmes@dmail.com ›
SUBJECT LINE: Re: King's College London!!!!!!!!!

Which isn't a date or anything!

FROM: James Watson Jr. ‹ j.watson2@dmail.com ›
TO: C. Holmes ‹ chholmes@dmail.com ›
SUBJECT LINE: Re: re: King's College London!!!!!!!!!

Unless you want it to be? Do you want it to be? (Oh God.) And this isn't only because I got into school or anything—I didn't mean it that way at all. And it's okay if you don't want to! Date me, I mean. I know the last time we tried anything like that was a while ago and I know it wasn't like that over spring break—I did really like bumming around London with you and going to bookstores and drinking iced tea.

    Was that a date too?

    Please put me out of my misery.

All I want to do is explore London with you again. You know parts of the city I didn't even know existed. Sometimes I feel like it invents new parts of itself just for you. xxxx

FROM: James Watson Jr. ‹ j.watson2@dmail.com ›
TO: C. Holmes ‹ chholmes@dmail.com ›
SUBJECT LINE: Re: re: re: King's College London!!!!!!!!!

I know you're online. I can see that you're on chat. So are you letting me flounder around writing you awkward emails because it's funny or because you're horrified?

FROM: C. Holmes ‹ chholmes@dmail.com ›
TO: James Watson Jr. ‹ j.watson2@dmail.com ›
SUBJECT LINE: Re: re: re: re: King's College London!!!!!!!!!

Because I'm charmed, and a bit nervous.
    Congratulations, Watson. I know how badly you wanted this, and I'm so very happy for you.
    Will you call me? I'm awake. I mean, of course I'm awake, as I'm typing, and not a sleepwalker. But call. If you want.

MAY

FROM: James Watson Jr. ‹ j.watson2@dmail.com ›
TO: C. Holmes ‹ chholmes@dmail.com ›
SUBJECT LINE: Re: Uni

Right but you are the only human being on this earth who can decide they want to go to Oxford while having like one-third of a high school diploma AND a police record and then have them be like, oh sure, totally come, just take some summer courses first!

I'm jealous. Actually I'm not because Oxford is, like, really scary to me, and really I'm not actually jealous—mostly I'm just really proud and happy and I think it's going to be great for you to be able to focus on the kind of work you want to be doing: blowing things up. (Do they have a degree in that?)

Will you still be around in London when I get back from Sherringford? I'm trying to figure out where to stay—things are a little better with my mother but I don't know if I want to move back in just yet.

FROM: C. Holmes ‹ chholmes@dmail.com ›
TO: James Watson Jr. ‹ j.watson2@dmail.com ›
SUBJECT LINE: Re: re: Uni

It's called chemistry, Watson.

And I'm enrolled in seven summer courses, in point of fact. I suppose they only required me to take four, but they had classes in biochemistry and music theory and statistics and poetry that sounded interesting, and so we're currently configuring my schedule. I may or may not be meeting my Poe tutor at midnight on Tuesdays.

The summer program also offers a fiction writing workshop which confers one semester of university credit. It begins two days after Sherringford's graduation and runs for six weeks.
They offer scholarships.

FROM: James Watson Jr. ‹ j.watson2@dmail.com ›
TO: C. Holmes ‹ chholmes@dmail.com ›
SUBJECT LINE: Re: re: re: Uni

1: Please tell me that you aren't meeting said Poe tutor in a catacomb, at midnight, on Tuesdays.

2: Are these, like, Leander Holmes rugby scholarships?

3: Also, wait—poetry?

4: Also, is this your weirdly formal way of asking me if I want to do this summer program thing with you?

FROM: C. Holmes ‹ chholmes@dmail.com ›
TO: James Watson Jr. ‹ j.watson2@dmail.com ›
SUBJECT LINE: Re: re: Uni

1: Possibly. Would it make a difference?

2: Possibly. Would it make a difference? (A joke, Watson. Of course they are.)

3: I've been writing quite a bit of poetry recently. It's very bad. I think in fact it might be the first time I've been terrible at something and still enjoyed it. Other than being your best friend, of course.

4: Please come. If it sounds at all appealing to you, or if you're still casting around for something to do. I miss you.

5: I miss you enough to say: please don't let me bully you into doing anything you wouldn't want to do.

FROM: James Watson Jr. ‹ j.watson2@dmail.com ›
TO: C. Holmes ‹ chholmes@dmail.com ›
SUBJECT LINE: How long until I see you?

Stop. You're the best friend I've ever had, and you'll always be. Unless you decide to Reichenbach on me again, in which case, we need to talk.

Someday your uncle is going to get tired of paying to send me to school. But I'll never stop being grateful. I'll give him a call tomorrow to say thank you; it's late there.

I just checked with my dad, and he's surprisingly gung-ho about me going. (Well, not surprisingly.) So yeah, I'm in! Twist my arm. Honestly it sounds kind of amazing and I've always wanted to spend time in Oxford and it'll be nice to try out a college writing workshop if I really want to make a run on this whole novelist thing. Did you tell Lena about this? Today at lunch she was talking about it too. Tom went a little pale and was looking at flights on his phone.

I miss you too. I miss you like breathing. Have I already said that? I do, though. I miss you like naan pizza and builder's tea. Like you're the home I never knew I had.

FROM: C. Holmes ‹ chholmes@dmail.com ›
TO: James Watson Jr. ‹ j.watson2@dmail.com ›
SUBJECT LINE: Four weeks, two days, three hours, seventeen minutes and forty-two seconds

Also, please don't use Reichenbach as a verb. xxxx

ACKNOWLEDGMENTS

THANK YOU SO MUCH TO THE WONDERFUL KATHERINE Tegen and everyone at Katherine Tegen Books for all your support. You really are my dream publisher. I especially want to thank my incredible editor, Alex Arnold, whose kindness and care is only matched by her intelligence and insight. Thank you to Rosanne Romanello—I am so grateful for your fierce championing of Jamie and Charlotte!—and to Sabrina Abballe and to everyone at Epic Reads. I am so lucky to have your support.

Endless thank-yous to Lana Popovic, dream agent and dear friend. None of this is possible without you. Thank you to Terra Chalberg (and everyone at Chalberg & Sussman) and to Sandy Hodgman and Jason Richman for your work on this series.

Love and thanks to Kit Williamson and Emily Temple, my found family.

Emily Henry: critique partner, coconspirator, angel sister. I love you. Jeff Zentner: you are a dear friend, a bastion of sanity, and pretty much the only person I want with me in a candle store. Thank you for being a rock. Evelyn Skye, Charker

Peevyhouse, and Mackenzi Lee: my incredible friends and adventuresses. Some books are written alone, but mine feel firmly seated in the community you've all made.

Thank you to all my readers. Hearing from you is the best part of any day! Thanks especially to Ashleigh, Katie, Anthony, Abby, Eline, Kathleen, Kristen, Sarah, Melissa, and Suzanne for their early support of this series.